More praise for *In Dark Water*

"Mermer Blakeslee writes with the intensity and mesmerizing voice of a Dorothy Allison or Mary Karr, but her story is wholly original. In her heartbreaking novel, there is a great deal of pain, but there are no villains. Indeed, the gift of the novel is the idea of deliverance: a young girl and her mother given back to one another through the unceasing devotion of the father and the stubborn intervention of unlikely (and fascinating) friends who know how to love. This book is at once familiar and utterly exotic, a foray into the strangeness of a child's breakdown and the power of her intelligence and spirit. It is also one of the most generous novels I have ever read."

> —Sandra Scofield
> Author of the National Book Award–
> nominated novel *Beyond Deserving*

"Stupendous—and humble. I have never read anything at all like this book. It is so down in the earth, so sweet in its heart, so incredibly accurate in detailed perceptions. Mermer Blakeslee has found the language of the instinctual psyche."

> —James Hillman
> Bestselling author of *The Soul's Code*

"Dorrie's delicately drawn journey to despair and back is riveting, and the re-creation of time and place, upstate New York in the 1950s, is true. A fine novel."

> —*Library Journal*

"Written with a fine ear for the voice of a child, Blakeslee builds a lovely portrait and a memorable character in Eudora Buell."

> —*Kirkus Reviews*

"The novel deftly shuttles between narrative voices, touches all the bases and nicely traces the uneven topography of sorrow and struggle."

> —*Publishers Weekly*

IN DARK WATER

A NOVEL

MERMER BLAKESLEE

BALLANTINE BOOKS • NEW YORK

A Ballantine Book
Published by The Ballantine Publishing Group

http://www.randomhouse.com/BB/

Library of Congress Catalog Card Number: 99-90232

ISBN: 0-345-41778-X

Cover design by Heather Kern
Cover photo by Gary Isaacs
Text design by Debbie Glasserman

Manufactured in the United States of America

First Hardcover Edition: August 1998
First Trade Paperback Edition: May 1999

10 9 8 7 6 5 4 3 2

FOR ERIC

AND EEO

MY ANCHOR AND SAIL

IN MEMORY OF

DAVIS HAMERSTROM

AND SALLIE CALDWELL

I am grateful to:

my son, Hansen Bergamini; my teacher, Dick Humphreys; Ginny Lawrence; Annette Schultz; Ani Helmick; Jean Naggar; my editor, Peter Borland; and my first and last reader, Eeo Stubblefield.

I used to say her name. Florence Benham Buell. I used to write F.B.B. after my name like doctors write M.D. and dentists write whatever, I wrote Eudora Buell, F.B.B., Langdon, N.Y.

PART I

APRIL 1958

I ONLY TOUCHED his toe, his big toe, 'cause it was hidden under the sheet and *she* couldn't see me squeeze it as hard as I could. I didn't care that it was cold, but I wanted it to hurt. I wanted David to yell or hit me 'cause it hurt. I squeezed it as hard as I could without making a face she could see. My hand started to ache but his toe still didn't flinch or pull away. It just stayed there, hard. He did nothing. But he did, he did do something. He got more dead. He was getting more and more dead the more I squeezed. I squeezed even harder then, even with my hand aching, I squeezed till I knew he was all the way dead, till his toe had won, it had beaten my hand.

She was lifting my other wrist. "It's time," she said. She walked me away from him. David was theirs now—the two men lined up outside the door. They were dressed in black suits and red ties and white shirts. "I'm very sorry for your troubles, ma'am," the first one said to her, and then to Dad, too, behind me, "I'm very sorry for your troubles, sir." The second guy repeated after him, "Sorry for your troubles, sorry for your troubles." *Like a song,* I thought, and then David added, *Yeah, the lead and the backup,* and I smiled 'cause both of the men leaned forward in exactly the same way shaking Dad's hand and nodding their heads one after the other. I smiled but it was really David smiling.

"Will they put different clothes on him?" I asked when we got in the car. She nodded. "Even his underpants? Even new underpants?" I asked and she nodded again. "But he didn't even know them," I said. Dad gave me a look that meant STOP but I knew to anyway. Her jaw was already up and stiff as if it was holding something very important she couldn't drop. They had argued last night about me seeing him. She said yes. Dad said no, 'cause of the bandages covering his head and most of his face. "She should remember him the way he was," he kept saying. Their voices got quieter and quieter. I lifted my head off the pillow but I still couldn't hear. I knew though, not to *push*, not to ask if they would put shoes on him. And even without her nodding, I saw in my brain the lead singer leaning over David's feet and jamming a shoe over his toe. He covered his toe.

Her jaw hardened more when she saw the smile. She didn't know that David had given it to me, that it was a different smile than the bad smile.

The bad smile first came when Dad told me he was dead. Dad was standing but she was sitting down and I heard her spit out toward the table, "That damn motorcycle!" and Dad leaned down to her and her fist circled his back but it was weak, it was opening into just her hand again. I was standing alone by the door where we always stood whenever we got called in by Dad. I heard him say it once more in my head, *David was killed*, and then it came, the smile. I put my head down but it was too late. Her eyes saw me from under Dad's arm. I saw them see me and I ran. I ran to my patch, the grass. I just stood there looking at it. The smile was gone. As soon as I got out, it was gone. But still I didn't sit down. I just stood there and watched the grass bend.

PEOPLE ALWAYS SAID she was beautiful, but that was before David died. She had dirty hands then 'cause she spent so much time in the garden. She'd wash them afterwards but some dirt would stay in the cracks of her skin, and around her bitten finger-nails. She'd go out to cut flowers for the house and end up weeding. But she'd still come in with a whole armful of flowers. "Lots of flowers, that's the key," she'd always say as she'd begin arranging them. That was her rule, lots of flowers. Arranging them was her favorite thing, but only when no one was around. Well, us kids, okay, but not Dad. 'Cause of the time, she said. She didn't want to feel rushed. So Dad just saw the arrangements after she put them on the buffet. He never saw her lean back and stare for the whole time it took for her to smoke a cigarette. She'd lay it on the ashtray and lean toward the flowers, just like they were Dad she was about to kiss. Sometimes, she'd say their names. Daisies, bachelor's buttons, petunias, zinnias. She'd move just one flower and then she'd pull back again and smoke and stare. I always thought the flowers were beautiful way before she did. Each time she would lean toward them again, I would try to guess which one was not yet right, which one she was going to move. I knew when she was finished 'cause she wouldn't step back to stare. She'd stay close to them and lean only her head back. She would smile and sometimes she'd turn the vase toward me so I could see, too, the flowers that were just now beautiful.

It was after finishing the flowers once that she told me what dying really was. She told me not to tell anyone. Not *anyone*, she said again, and I knew she meant at school. She said it's different than what they say. And I knew that, too—"they" meant "the church." "It's not really dying all the way. It's like getting rid of old clothes," she said, "and then forgetting all about them." "But could I still ride a horse?" I asked and she smiled and leaned down and kissed me like I was the flowers. She said, "Oh, honey." Then later she said, "Each time, you have a completely different body."

I knew right then. "I was an animal," I said. "Before." She put her coffee down and looked at me. "Which one?" she asked. "A cat." She frowned her pout frown. She hated cats. David had one once and it peed in her plants and killed them, so we could never have another one. She picked her coffee up with both hands. She would move her face back and forth over it, like it was a fire. "Not a horse?" she asked.

I shook my head hard, but I didn't tell her why not, that I didn't think a horse could ever feel little and I was little, way little for my age. A cat's little but sure—sure-footed, Mrs. Peterson would say, and she's where I go to ride. I'm very sure-footed, too, but only when I'm outside, and even more when I'm out and alone.

I'm different outside. Inside, Dad says, I'm just klutzy, I try to move too fast. But outside, I forget everything, even that I'm little, everything except what's right in front of me. And even though I'm not thinking, I know things, like where my feet are going to land when I jump a log. I never miss. That's one thing about me, I don't miss.

I asked David if she told him, too, about what dying was, but he said, "Are you kidding?" He was holding a record the way he taught me to so fingerprints never ever get on the grooves. He lived in the attic. It was a big room but low and he had to duck down to put a record on. He was eight years older than me, so we weren't like regular brother and sister. We didn't fight and he taught me things.

"See, Mom thinks you're like her. And that I'm like Dad. So she doesn't tell me things that are strange." He had to spin the record to get it up to speed before he put the needle down. It was Chuck Berry, his all-time favorite.

I liked being up there on his bed more than anything 'cause the ceiling comes right down almost to the floor so you always feel close to both. *"There,* hear it? There!" He was trying to get me to hear the bass. I nodded each time but I didn't really hear it. He must have known, too, 'cause he kept on trying. He'd point with his finger like the bass was something to see. "There! Got it?" and then he'd make a rumbling noise in his throat. "Like that," he'd say. "Hear it? Like that." I would always nod.

"Why do you think she hates cats so much?"

"They're creepy," he said. "And you know, killing her plants is like killing her."

I didn't ever tell David about my patch, the grass up behind Mr. Rone's where I would go almost every day so I could take off my clothes and stalk like a cat. I'd stretch my neck back and pretend I was hunting a mouse or a chipmunk. I didn't kill it though, not even after she told me what dying was. But since David, since that time after they told me, I never went back there, not once.

THEY LOWERED HIM in the ground with a thud, two thuds. It happened all at once after Father Bob stopped speaking. One end of the casket dropped in, the end away from us, and then the near end dropped in and it was gone. You had to move forward to see it, but all you'd see was the top covered with roses. Then all these women started to line up around her. They took turns hugging her and saying her name, Florence, before they'd start crying, and Dad was shaking hands, but he held each hand for a long time close against his tie. Some of the men I never saw before, but each one looked right into his eyes and Dad looked right back and most times he just nodded and didn't speak at all.

I wanted to get away before anyone came up to me, and I saw it, the place to go. Back by the trees at the bottom of the hill where there was still some dirty snow left that hadn't melted yet, there was a blue pickup truck with men, four of them, leaning against it and smoking.

David would lean against the back of the garage to smoke. He'd let me sit there by his feet 'cause I snuck cigarettes for him from her pocketbook if he was all out, even though she smoked L&M's and he smoked Lucky Strikes. He'd let me take a puff if I wanted but it made me cough, so mostly I'd just hold one. He'd laugh when I held it boy-style like him, between my thumb and forefinger, and then I'd stretch my lips back and suck in hard. Mostly though, if he was talking, I'd hold it like she did, between her two long fingers, and then I'd feel just like her, old and very fine.

As soon as I got away from all the people, walking down the hill, I could see the men had shovels in the back of the truck. One guy was hunched over laughing and two others had big smirks on their faces. And I thought, just quick I thought, *This must be where David is.*

Even though I was dressed up in my stupid navy blue coat

with the big stupid collar that she had bought in Albany, a whole hour away, I walked right up to the man that wasn't laughing, the one that stopped talking as I came near.

"Do you have a cigarette to spare?" That's how David always asked.

"What? A cigarette? Little girl, you ain't 'sposed to be smokin' at yer age. How old are you, eight?"

But I told him, "I'm ten. And I don't wanna smoke, I just wanna hold it."

"Ain't no harm her holdin' it, Jim."

And then the guy farthest away said, "Come on, Jim, hand one over. Closest you'll ever get to a purdy girl's mouth."

"Yut. Just gotta let her suck on it awhile."

They all laughed except the guy named Jim, who held out his pack with a cigarette sticking out for me to take. Then he leaned back against the truck with his one foot up behind him. I held the cigarette boy-style like them and like David.

"Someone you know up there died?" Jim asked.

I nodded and took a deep pretend-puff.

"Yer purdy good at that, yut, look real good," the guy said who was leaning on his knee, his foot propped up on the bumper.

"My brother taught me," I said and took another puff. I looked back at all the people up the hill, but they didn't look like people anymore, just one big blob of black that was moving, but inside itself—it never changed shape.

"You know why we're here?" the guy farthest away said.

I nodded. "You're gonna cover him up."

"Yut. That's it. That's why we're here."

"Otherwise, we wouldn't be crashing *this* party," Jim said.

"Nope!" and they all laughed again, and Jim spat.

"Tell him some jokes," I said. "He likes jokes."

"Oh, we'll do that. Won't we, boys?" Jim said. "Yut, we'll do that." They were all smiling.

"Thanks for the cigarette," I said 'cause I saw the black moving, changing shape as if water had been poured over all of it so the black was thinning, seeping away toward the road. I turned around halfway up the hill. One of the guys was already getting in the cab.

I'm good at sneaking 'cause I'm little and outside I can be so quiet that even she never knows I've come up behind her till I've already scared her. That's how come no one saw me do it, no one, not even when she was coming toward me from the big car to get me. I watched for her to look away and then I threw the cigarette in to him. It dropped down beneath all the flowers, down the side of his casket to the bottom of the hole so no one except David, not even the men, would ever see it.

AFTER DAVID DIED, her fingers stayed very clean. She stopped going out to the garden even to pick flowers for the house. Walking in from school, I would hear her from the porch laugh out loud. She'd be stretched out on the couch in front of the TV still in her bathrobe. Sometimes I would watch *The Honeymooners* with her before she got dinner, or *The Life of Riley*, but *I Love Lucy* was her favorite. She started telling Dad at dinner every Wednesday night what Lucy did that show. And once she called her best friend—Mrs. Gallagher—she called her "my Ethel."

Dad brought home a new dishwasher from work. It was "sand beige" just like the refrigerator. I had to put the dishes away. It was an indoor job on purpose. All my jobs used to be outdoors with my dad but then I heard them talking about me one night, through the wall. She wanted me to stay inside with her. After that, my dad burned all the garbage himself and dumped the nonburnable, too, in the big gray cans for the dump. It wasn't that bad being indoors except when it was after dinner and just getting dark. Then I could barely stand not being out. Like it was my last chance.

I started sneaking out after they went to bed. I never ever wore pajamas so I'd put on my bathrobe that used to be David's when he was little and I'd sneak just into the pasture where the people who were here before us used to keep horses. That's why we call it "the pasture" even though it's just a field my dad has Mr. Miller mow twice a year. We're right in the middle of Langdon but it's only got one street, so there's nothing behind us but the pasture and behind that the creek and behind that Cave Mountain.

There were lots of groundhog holes now 'cause Dad didn't shoot groundhogs anymore. They were the only animals he ever shot. On either Saturday or Sunday, David and him would go out there and Dad would carry the .222 and David would carry the .22. David never hit one. He didn't really try, he told me. He liked holding the gun up on his shoulder and he liked aiming, but that was it, he said. He didn't like the rest. After, Dad never went out again. And there were more and more groundhog holes to watch out for. Mrs. Peterson hates them 'cause a horse can fall in one and break his leg and then you have to kill the horse, or, like she says, put him down.

One night, it was raining so hard it sounded like bullets hitting the roof, but still I moved only an inch at a time so they wouldn't hear the bed squeak. It took probably half an hour to put on my sneakers and my bathrobe. I tried to put my weight down on each foot slow so the floor wouldn't creak, and I did good, too, until I reached the screen, which slammed shut with the wind.

After I could see in the dark, I still couldn't run all out 'cause of the ruts where the water runs through the pasture every spring. I took off my robe so the rain hit my back and the back of my

neck like little stones but wet and real real cold. Then I started to
lift up to it and it hit my face and my chest and I started running
faster and faster, and I never, not once, hit wrong on the ruts.

I ran almost as fast as on Field Day with David watching. The
first time I beat Peggy Weaver, who was always the fastest and the
biggest, too, David lifted me up and held me over his head so I
was flying. When we got home, he kept waving the ribbon in *her*
face and yelling, "Can you believe it? Can you believe it? She's a
whole foot shorter 'n that Weaver kid."

I started running in circles. David was gone. I wasn't a girl running. I was a horse being ridden. The dark turned lighter. I could
see everything, every hole and every rut and the bunches of burdock that had grown up faster than the grass. I slowed myself to a
stop, shaking my head, like it took a lot, a strong rider to bring me
in from a canter. Then I walked straight, in a perfect straight line
like you want a horse to do, otherwise they're fighting you. I was
dripping wet, a horse sweating from ring work and being hosed
off hard before I walked myself out.

I heard it but I didn't get it, I heard the big dinner bell that's
outside the kitchen door so my dad can hear from the garage anytime she needs him or there's a phone call or dinner. I heard it
like a face you see in the wrong place and you don't get who it is.

I dropped to all fours. I wasn't a horse anymore being ridden.
No one could ride me. I was a cat again. It had been over a
month since I'd gone to my patch to stalk. I had to stretch my
neck all around to each side before I held my head up and
opened my eyes way open. The timothy tickled my face and I set
my mouth against it. I know it's called timothy 'cause I helped
the Petersons hay and that kind of grass they called timothy.

The rain stopped but the rainwater stayed in beads lit up along
the blades of grass and on the heavy bunches of burdock leaves. A
pile of dirt rose up in my path like an anthill but I knew it was

from the hole just beyond it. It was the biggest one I had seen. I stopped, perfectly still, in front of it. I stretched and waited. Nothing came out. *The groundhogs can smell me*, I thought. I backed up one step and then waited again. My body was ready to spring, but then it came to me, a groundhog is too big for a cat. I turned away, stopped hunting. I pointed my nose into the wind and smelled the air coming in the way Mrs. Peterson had said all animals do. There was no danger. I curled onto a circle of short, soft, darker green grass that didn't scratch my skin. There was water everywhere to drink. If I moved my lips along the fat blades, I could catch the beads that were shining before they fell.

Her hand grabbed my wrist tight. Pulled me up. I couldn't see her face, just the outline of her hair and her robe. I wasn't a cat anymore, or only a cat, I was a girl, too, standing, only my sneakers on, my one hand holding my privates. I lifted it away. She grabbed both my arms. I felt her thumbs go into the skin above my elbows as she lifted me up and set me down hard facing the house. I saw that it wasn't my eyes at all but the spotlight on the porch that had lit up the dark and the beads of rain.

She started pushing me from behind. The points of her fingers hit my shoulders every few steps. "Stop lagging!" It was her hard voice that was worse than a yell, madder than a yell. I heard her once say to Dad how every time I'm indoors I hold my elbows. It was like that, I was just drinking from the ground and holding my privates. But then I swallowed. I tasted the water I had been drinking and it wasn't water. It was different. It was sweet, or lemony, too, or just different. It was my fingers down there. I had been tasting my fingers and then going back there like it was rain. But it wasn't, it wasn't even water. I kept swallowing. I wanted what I had tasted to disappear but it didn't. We were getting close to the house. I swallowed faster and faster but it wouldn't go away.

Her hand stayed constant now, her fingers squeezing my neck

as she pushed me toward the porch light. I hated the light. It was taking away the dark, making me more and more naked. David's robe was still back there in the grass. We reached the porch. I hunched in away from the light but her hand stayed fast on my neck, holding my neck so it hit me. The light hit me. It lit up my chest and my privates, too.

She let go to open the door and I ran. I reached my room, yanked my shoes off and hid quick under the blankets. I didn't care my skin got the sheets all wet. "Eudora." Her voice was the same hard, even from the hall. The door opened. I could see the light flick on through the blanket. But then it turned dark again. The door was closing. She was going back down the hall. She was going toward my dad. I wanted her back, but different. I wanted her soft voice back and all around me, her body covering me from the light. The bathrobe was still out there in the rain. I didn't want it anymore. I didn't want to go outside. It was wet in here, too. My hand crept in toward my privates. I found the bone right there in the front. I pulled up against it, hard, like I was pulling myself up out of water, out of a pool. But then I let my hand sink back down and stay there, I let it curl in under the bone.

I HAD TO cut onions and they made me cry but I couldn't stop chopping till she had two cups. Each time I would scrape all the little pieces into the measurer, I'd look and they still wouldn't have reached the mark. My eyes kept burning more and more and the crying didn't help at all. I could taste the salt from my tears 'cause they were running down into my mouth but I didn't wipe them away. I was trying to hurry. At first she just said loudly that I was taking too long, but then when I was only up to a cup and a quarter, she started yelling. "What are you doing over there? Are you playing? Are you just playing?" I started crying then from the inside, too, and my crying was falling into the onions and I wondered if she would taste the extra salt in the food after it was all cooked.

I was crying about her yelling but I was also crying about David. It was the first time. I didn't cry when everyone else did at the service. I didn't miss him yet 'cause I didn't know really he wasn't going to come back. He just wasn't here for now, but then the now got bigger and bigger and longer.

I wanted him to finish the puzzle. It's a world map and it just fit on the dining room table, so visitors had to eat in the kitchen but they would always admire the map anyway and say things like "What a wonderful idea to do that together"—though we never did it together. Only my brother worked on it when he was waiting around the half hour before dinner or between dinner and ice cream, and to get out of her way I would watch him and a few times I gave him the piece he needed. Most of the countries in Africa and Asia weren't finished yet but all of Europe was. Every day I checked when I came home from school to see if she had taken it away or changed it but she hadn't touched it.

She was cooking for Father Bob. He was the first visitor since David. She always cooked a big meal when he came, not 'cause he was a priest, either. "He knows good food," she'd say. She used to be Catholic until she had the Argument. "With the priest?" I heard a friend ask her once and she said, "No, with God." And then she added, "With their God." She smiled. "You know the one. The one who sits up on high." When she smiled she could get away saying anything. Dad would sort of brag about it to friends. "She could tell someone to go to hell," he'd say, "and they'd enjoy the trip." And he'd throw his hand up.

David didn't have a funeral. "They're barbaric," she said to Dad. "Just standing there in front of all those people watching you"—and then she added, lower—"and having to listen to all that Christian claptrap."

Christian claptrap Christian claptrap Christian claptrap . . . It went on in my head for days. It was like a horse trotting.

David had a *service*, they called it, and the whole Mountain Top came, which meant not only Langdon but Kaaterskill, too, and everyplace before you go down off the mountain toward the Hudson. Father Bob did it, but he was different from a priest because she loved him. They would talk long talks in the afternoon about books and writing poems, and recipes. I think Dad liked Father Bob as much as she did, but they talked about different things. Roads mostly. They both knew route numbers. But some-times when she was talking about a restaurant, she'd ask Dad the name and he'd always know it and then Father Bob and Dad would talk about which road it was on before they went back to talking about the food. Dad would even remember the name of what she had to eat and the wine they had. She never remem-bered names but she would talk about what she thought was in the sauce. Father Bob had the same face she did when he tasted something new. His forehead wrinkled up so it didn't look like he was tasting at all but like he was in school trying to answer a ques-tion. She would watch him, and everybody, even David, would wait for Father Bob to put his head to one side and say the an-swer, which he always said like another question. I remember the time he got it all right. "Tarragon?" he said and she nodded quick. And then he added, not as a question either, "And celery salt!" And her smile broke even wider than before.

I heard a car drive in the driveway but I didn't say anything. Her voice was still hard. "You're just *trying* to be slow," she kept saying.

But when she answered the door, she smiled and her voice be-came soft. "You always bring a good wine," she said when she looked into the bag Father Bob handed her. "Michael, look, one of our favorites." But Father Bob just shrugged his shoulders. I thought, *Maybe some adults feel like kids do sometimes, like they don't know what to do either.* He said hello to me. He was very tall but he looked down and waited. I knew he was waiting. I had to look up and he looked right back at me. "Hello," he said again, smiling. I wondered if he saw the burning still in my eyes. It was almost gone.

She stopped holding her mouth tight. Even when she turned to me to ask if I would get out the good butter dish, her mouth was loose. And she said, holding the cheese-and-cracker plate, she said, "Come on into the living room, dear." But I couldn't look at her or nod. I stayed back in the corner of the kitchen by the stove so I wouldn't hear their voices mixing in with laughing, but I could anyway. I could hear her laughing and laughing. I put my face over the onions in the pan on the stove. I brought my eyes as close as I could but the onions didn't work. She had cooked them, they didn't burn now or make me cry.

I ran outside. I ran to where David smoked cigarettes behind the garage. And to where I peed once when I didn't know he was there. I was looking under my legs to see the edges of the pee spread out in the dirt and he kind of coughed so I would see him and I felt stupid staring at my pee like that in front of him, but he said as I stood and quick pulled up my pants, he said, "What country is it?" I looked back at the pee which had stopped spreading and I said, "Spain?" "Close," he said. "France."

But even out there, where I couldn't hear her laugh, I could see her face loose and happy and smiling. "Come on in, dear, to the living room." I said it out loud. "Come on in, dear." *Crackers.* I heard it in David's voice. He would talk when he was blowing out smoke. "Come on in, dear, and have some crackers." It sounded so funny in his voice, but I didn't laugh 'cause I saw right then by the wall of the garage a cigarette butt, one he never covered up with gravel. I saw it and I ran.

I ran toward the porch light. I could sneak in through the playroom door and they'd never know I was out. I got back into the kitchen but I didn't stop. I went through the dining room door and still they didn't hear me. I walked only when I heard their voices. I was up to the puzzle when it suddenly turned very very quiet in there. "Eudora?" I held my breath. "Eudora?" she said again. I grabbed France and turned for the kitchen. The lights were so bright. "Eudora, what are you doing?" she said, loud, but

I had already made it to the hall, which David had always called "neutral territory." "What. Are. You. Doing?" she said again, but louder. My room was dark, a good dark. I sat in my spot, on the floor between my bed and the wall so no one could see me from the door. I was never afraid in my spot.

I heard voices, Dad's and Father Bob's. They were coming from the dining room. I couldn't hear the words. Then I heard her but not her voice. She was sobbing. It got louder and louder until it was like the first night and Dad was saying her name. "Florence, Florence . . ." He was saying it over and over.

"Red and white, but mostly red." She had said it to the flower man about the roses covering the casket. "But make sure they smell," she said, and then again she said it when we left. "They've got to smell." When we got back to the car, she looked down at her list and crossed it off, *roses*.

When I knelt on the kneeler in front of him, I couldn't breathe all the way in. The roses smelled so strong. Just like after she got in the car and closed the door when we were going someplace she dressed up for, just like that, I had to hold my breath.

Something was happening. Father Bob was leaving. He hadn't eaten and he was leaving. She was still sobbing but I could hear Dad at the back door. "It'll all be okay with time. It'll all be okay with time." And Father Bob was saying, "I'm sorry. I'm sorry." And I thought, *For what?* And then for a second I thought, *He did it, he killed David*, but then I shook my head hard for such a dumb thought.

Her best friend, Mrs. Gallagher, came in before the service started. She went straight across the room to her and held her for a long time, but when she pulled away she saw the casket and she went, "Oh!" And then, "Oh, Florence, it's beautiful." I was looking up at her. She didn't speak but she nodded. *Red and white, but mostly red.* Mrs. Gallagher held a tissue in her hand and it had black all over it from her eyes, the stuff she wore on her eyes. But *she* didn't wear anything on her eyes. They looked beautiful, more beautiful than I had ever seen because they were shining. I was looking at them but I was waiting, too, for Mrs. Gallagher to hug me. But she turned to sign the guest book, she didn't know I was waiting, I was too small.

The light turned on. It was her, I saw her shoes. "Give it to me." I saw the bottom of her pants just barely touching her shoes.

"Give it to me," she said again. I shook my head slowly. I was holding France under my shirt and under my undershirt against my skin. "Eudora. Give it to me," like she had sandpaper in her throat. It wasn't her voice but I didn't look up. "Give it to me, Eudora." And then Dad was there, too, saying, "Florence. Florence, please."

"Get out of here, Michael." That *was* her voice, her hard voice. There was no sandpaper. "This is between Eudora and me."

I kept shaking my head. I hadn't stopped shaking my head. I could feel France pushing into my skin. I was holding it as hard as I could, as hard as I held David's toe, but it wasn't hard enough. She grabbed my arm. She was pulling it straight. She was opening my fingers, each one of them, and then keeping them open. I didn't scream, even when she got my last finger opened and took France from my hand, I didn't scream.

She walked out of the room into the hall and into the kitchen and into the dining room. She had turned my light on. I had to get out. I followed her. I followed her right into the dining room. It was dark but I could still see. She was standing across the table just staring at the map and holding the piece to her throat. I looked down at Europe. France was there! I saw the color. I looked for Spain. It was gone. I had gotten Spain instead! She was holding Spain. I reached for France. "Don't you dare touch it," she said slowly. But I did, I grabbed France. It was light green, a yellowy green. "Eudora!" she yelled but I didn't run. I turned to her and I watched her because it didn't look like her or sound like her either. "Eudora!" she yelled again but not as loud. Her hand was over her mouth, and Spain, too, Spain was over her mouth. She was backing up, moving away from me. I watched, holding France to my chest.

IT WAS HIS teeth why I couldn't look at him. I stared at the sign at the edge of his desk. It didn't say *Mr. Owen*, just GUIDANCE COUNSELOR in white letters surrounded in black. Like teeth, too, in a huge open mouth—but only if you exaggerate inside your brain. That was one of my problems, exaggerating, Mrs. Klepp said. And the smile. It came back. I tried to close my lips to hide it but it wouldn't go away. "Ornery, just plain ornery," Mrs. Klepp muttered when she sent me down the hall, "and *that smile*."

Mr. Owen didn't really smile, but he showed all his teeth every time he said anything, even a question. It made it hard to think of an answer. He would lean across his desk and look right at me. I couldn't look back more than a second.

I wondered what he was in his last lifetime. I couldn't see him an animal. What would *she* say? She never said animals. She would always look up to the side first, then say something like "A milkman." Or once, "The first pilot." We hadn't played that though, not since David.

Mr. Owen wouldn't stop looking at me. Maybe he was waiting for me to say something. I glanced quick at him. He leaned back onto his chair. "Well, Miss Buell"—I knew right then he was going to say it—"I'm going to have to call your father." I didn't look up. I nodded quick so he would reach forward and sign the pass slip.

SHE WAS UP and even dressed when I walked in after school. She was carrying a pillowcase full of wash into the laundry room.

"Hi, honey," she said, shaking the last of the dirty clothes out onto the floor. "Hungry?"

"Yeah, real hungry." It was like before. She used to feed us as soon as we got home. She would never eat with us, though, not between meals. It was one of her rules. "Three square meals a day," she would say, and her friends around her would nod 'cause she was so thin.

"Okay, just a sec." She was bent over, sorting the clothes, throwing only the whites into the washer filling up behind her. It was a brand-new Automatic. When Dad brought it home, she even came out of her room to see it, and she kept shaking her head and saying, "To think, an Automatic."

"Just a sec," she said again. It seemed so much like before, I was waiting for what David used to call "the standard question." He would say it like he was Ed Sullivan, holding the saltshaker for a microphone. "Here comes, ladies and gentlemen, the *standard question*." And it did come. She closed the top and turned. "How was school today?"

I should have told her everything that went wrong right then but I didn't. I said instead, "Mrs. Klepp dyed her hair." And I had practiced, too, all day in my brain. I had told her about Mr. Owen and how *creepy* he was even though that was one of David's words. "It's dark dark brown now."

She smiled. "Oh gosh, I can't imagine." I looked at her hair. It was brown, too, but with red highlights that she would "keep up." You could see them outside. Like mine. My hair turned red outside.

"She looks," I squinched up my face, "even uglier."

Mrs. Klepp was an army lieutenant before she was a school-teacher so she always said "about FACE!" and "ha-ALT!" in the hall when we were lined up in twos going to lunch or music. David had her, too, and ever since he would boom out "ha-ALT!" and his friends would crack up. She explained it when I came home the first day of fifth grade. "It's her signature," she said, and every time Mrs. Klepp yelled it out now, I saw her writing her name.

I didn't mind Mrs. Klepp was ugly but I hated she was mean, and tricky mean. On Parents' Day, she acted like the kids were all her best friends. She'd even said, "We have a good time," over and over. "What a show," Mary Beth had said and rolled her eyes, and everybody said, "Yeah," mostly 'cause she was right but also 'cause she was the most popular kid in the class.

I followed her into the kitchen. She put her hand into the bag of bread. "I don't want toast," I said quick. She was thinking of David. The shaker with cinnamon and sugar was still there on the counter, full.

"Oh," she said, "right." She shook her head. "Rice Krispies?"

I nodded. I really wanted Cheerios but I still nodded.

She was shaking when she put down the bowl of cereal. And when she let go the milk carton, her hand was shaking in the air as she turned away.

Last night after work, Dad asked her first thing walking into the playroom, "Did you eat?" She started to tell him a few things that she almost ate but then Carol had called and then . . . He didn't let her finish. "Did you eat?" he said, and she started up again saying all why she hadn't and he just kept saying, "But did you eat? Did you eat anything today?" And finally she stopped talking and shook her head. "No," she said. "No."

"You've got to get something in your stomach," he said. "You're shaking again." He walked straight to the refrigerator and poured her a glass of milk.

I wanted to say now, "Maybe you should eat," but I didn't. I started to tell her a joke instead, the one Peggy told Mary Beth and me at lunch.

"Three Chinese men go to America and they don't know any English." I stopped to see if I should go on or if she wanted to go back to the laundry but she stood there with her half smile and her hand on her hip so I knew she would wait for me to finish the joke.

"So the first one stops in front of a music store and all he hears is "Me me me me me. . . ." I sung it with my arm swinging out like Peggy did and it made her smile. She was nodding me on.

"Then the second guy stops in front of a restaurant and all he hears is "Knives and forks, knives and forks. . . ."

She turned to the counter and started to get out some bread, white bread, which only Dad ate now, since David. She was putting it in the toaster, but still, I kept going.

"Then the third guy stops in front of a candy store and all he hears is "Goody goody gumdrops, goody goody gumdrops. . . ."

She was watching the toaster, waiting. I couldn't picture her eating. Especially toast, and *white* toast, not rye.

"So they were walking along and there was this dead man on the street with a policeman and the policeman says, 'Who did it?' And the first guy sings out, 'Me me me me me. . . .' "

The toaster popped. She was buttering the toast very fast. I hurried up my voice. "And then the policeman yelled out, 'With what?' And the second man yelled, 'Knives and forks, knives and forks. . . .' "

She was shaking the cinnamon and sugar over her toast, David's cinnamon and sugar. I didn't finish. I stared at her. She looked back at me. "We can't let it go to waste. Can we?" And then she started to laugh.

Her laughing made me quick finish the joke. "And then the policeman says, 'You're all going to jail,' and the third man goes, 'Goody goody gumdrops.' "

But she didn't know the joke was over, she was laughing too hard. She had sat down in her chair with the cinnamon toast in front of her but she was just laughing, and holding her belly, shaking up and down. She had stopped making noise except at the end of each laugh when she'd say, "Oh, oh," before she started up again. I hadn't seen her laugh like that for so long, when Dad and her used to have friends over for cocktails.

"Did you think it was funny?" I asked, but she couldn't talk yet, she was just starting to stop.

"Oh, oh." She wiped the edges of her eyes. "Oh God."

"I mean the joke, did you think it was funny?" She looked at me. She had almost completely stopped. She let out a big breath. "Oh," she said, "the joke. The joke. Well, it was a bit long."

She was staring at the cinnamon toast. She picked it up but she was shaking too much. It was dancing around in front of her mouth like it was playing a game with her. But she grabbed it quick with her teeth and got it. She started to chew it but very slowly like I do when I have to eat something I hate. She didn't look beautiful. It was the first time I thought that. Her face looked all swollen up. She stopped chewing. Something was happening. She was getting sick. She rushed into the bathroom.

I watched her from the doorway throwing up into the toilet. She was throwing up but nothing came out. Nothing. But it wasn't stopping. She held her belly like she had when she was laughing and her body was shaking, too, but in big, slow shakes that made a horrible sound and threw her whole body forward.

I stood there until it stopped and she stood up. She was breathing hard. "Oh dear," she said. She was blowing her nose. Her face was all blotchy red. "I need some rest." She put her hand on my head as she passed me in the doorway. "Don't worry. Mommy will be okay."

Mommy will be okay. Mommy will be okay. It kept going through my brain after she walked into her room and closed the door and after I heard her flop down on her bed.

I WAITED IN the hall for her to come out. I waited where the edge of the wallpaper had started to curl near the baseboard. I could fit two fingers in under the bulge the paper made. I remember when she picked it out of the huge book. "That one," she said, and I looked and it was just leaves and stems. At one edge there was part of a pink rose cut off and at the other edge a small bit of red. She was smiling. There would be pink and red roses you couldn't see yet, she explained, it was just a sample. The paper had pulled away from the wall just where one of the stems would have reached a rose. My finger kept pushing along the edge of the bulge, making it bigger. *There would be pink and red roses, lots of them and big.* It was cold in there, and gritty, too, little chips of plaster.

Mommy will be okay. I wouldn't ever knock on her door anymore, not since David. I just kept waiting. *Mommy will be okay.*

The hall rug was dark, and dark was spreading out from the corners of the wall. It reached almost to where my fingers hid. I got up and went into my room. I took my Mary off the dresser and sat down in my spot. I didn't mind dark in my spot.

I loved my Mary 'cause of her colors. I could barely see them now but I knew them exactly. She wore a blue robe over a plain white gown and on her head a white scarf that folded at her face like long hair. Her arms were spread out to the sides so you could see the inside of her robe. It was pink, but not sick pink, a browny pink.

Maybe she was holding her Mary, too. Her mom had given it to her before she died. It wasn't any color, but still she would kiss it every single night before she went to bed, even after the Argument. I knew that 'cause I peeked into her room one night and then I still kept peeking in 'cause I loved to see her pick it up from her bedside table and bend over to it. They'd meet halfway. Her lips completely covered Mary's face.

I tried to kiss my Mary but she felt cold. Under the colors, she was just plaster. There were blotches of bright white all over where she was chipped and you could see under the paint.

I put my thumb over her face so it would turn warm. I wanted her face warm. The last time Grandma came here, she told me about the wooden Mary in France. She was in a town that only had five houses and they all burned and the church burned but the wooden Mary was left unhurt and even her veil—which was made of "tulle," Grandma said—that wasn't even scorched. It was declared a miracle and now *that* Mary is in a museum but people go and kneel down in front of her anyway like she was in a church.

I put my lips to her face again but she still wasn't warm. I put my thumb back. I wanted her completely warm. *Then kissing her might work*, I thought.

But her face never got warm enough 'cause Dad came home. He was calling from the kitchen, "Florence? Florence? I thought you were up. Florence?" Then he said to himself, "Damn!" before he called again. "Florence! I'm home! Florence!" He kept calling all the way to the bedroom. When he opened the door, I could hear her crying but the door shut again and I couldn't hear anything. Maybe his voice, but no words, I couldn't hear any words.

I don't know how long he was in there, but as soon as he came out and shut the door, he let out a long breath. He didn't know I was in my room 'cause I could hear him say again as he walked down the hall, "Damn!" I never heard him say that before. No one did. She used to say to people, "Michael *never* swears," and then she would smile. "He says it's just poor vocabulary."

He opened the kitchen door outside. "Eudora! Eudora!" he kept yelling into the yard. "Eudora?" He shut the door. "Dammit! Where is she?"

I should have jumped up right then and run into the kitchen. It wasn't I was hiding. Or listening in. I was just hearing, and all of a sudden I didn't want him to know that I was right here hearing him breathe out hard and swear. So I kept sitting and then I *was* hiding.

I heard the pots. Noodles again. That's the only thing he could make. Sometimes we got pizza at Eva's. Noodles and the sauce that she canned last summer from Mr. Thomas's tomatoes. Every few minutes, he'd call out into the yard again for me. The longer it got, the worse it got, the more I couldn't come out.

I didn't hear him, but all of a sudden the light was on and his steps were loud and his feet were right in front of me. "What? What are you doing here?" I didn't look up. "Didn't you hear me? Huh? Didn't you hear me? What are you doing?"

Me? I thought, but my brain went, *Me me me me me*, and it came back, the smile, it came before I could hide it.

He didn't yell. He said each word slowly: "Wipe that smile off your face." I looked away but he could still see it, 'cause he grabbed my arm again and lowered down onto his knee. His face was so close. "Right now!" He had never yelled at me before. *Please,* I thought, *please go,* but it was there now to stay. It always stayed unless I got outside. I squeezed my Mary as hard as I could.

"Right now," he said even slower. He tightened his grip. I was about to say, "I can't, I can't," but he yelled, "Goddammit! Right now!" I started to squeeze out of his hand. I almost got away. I was half turned and it must have made him even madder 'cause he got me on the ear. He hit me across the ear. I was free but I didn't run.

He didn't get up. He dropped his head onto the bed. "Oh God, what am I doing?" He just stayed like that, with his head down on the bed.

"Honey, where are you? I'm sorry. I'm sorry. It's just, it's just . . ." He couldn't finish. He was crying.

I wanted to hug him. I wanted to jump up on his lap like before. I wanted dinner. I wanted to smell dinner. I put my lips to Mary's face but I didn't kiss her. I bit her. I bit her nose off and part of her cheek. The plaster was like flour in my mouth and there were little gritty chips of paint. I tried to spit it all out but I couldn't. I could still feel the grit.

I HAD TO see Mr. Owen now every Friday. That was the agreement everybody made. "On account of the family tragedy," Mr. Owen said. He talked mostly about Jesus, about how He saves people in times of crisis and distress. He'd talk louder and louder till he'd jump up from his chair and stand facing the window. His body would start rocking back and forth and sometimes his head would even knock into the blind. With him covering the only window, the room seemed like a closet with no air. He'd go on about what was moral and immoral and whenever he said the word "moral," he'd close his one hand into a fist and hold it with his other hand. "It's not what you do," he'd bellow out, "it's whether you believe." *I could believe in Jesus,* I thought. But then he would always say, looking back over his shoulder at me, "Not just in Jesus as Man but in Jesus as Lord." I didn't know what that meant. But if you did believe, you'd go to heaven, and if you didn't, you'd go forever to hell. That seemed funny 'cause he sometimes called Jesus "the All-Merciful," and I thought, if He was all-merciful, why would there be hell you end up in forever? I didn't ask though. I just kept nodding whenever he looked back at me till the bell rang. Luckily, gym was right after.

Sometimes at night I'd think about David and I worried if there really was a hell, maybe he'd be there, his soul. I knew *she* didn't think so. "Sure I believe in heaven and hell," I heard her say once, "sure I do"—and then she smiled—"right here on Earth. Right here." And she pointed down to the ground. She would always smile when she said things like that, and people would say, "You know Florence! She speaks her mind."

I wanted her to come into my room now and say good night even though it had been a long long time since she did. Before David, she'd come in even if it was too late and I should've been asleep. "Do you know what time it is?" she'd say. "You *have* to get to sleep." But still, she'd sit down on the bed and most nights, we'd play the thing game. First, it was the color game. We'd see people as colors, and towns, too. Langdon was brown, David was green but green like the ocean, Mrs. Gallagher was red. We'd take turns. First, she'd say a name and then I'd answer back a color. Then we'd switch. But then one night she said, "Father Bob," and I said, "A big book." She laughed and said, "Yes, exactly, yes, yes." And ever since, we named everybody a thing instead of a color. Dad was an umbrella for a while and David was a swimming pool. We did vegetables, too. Mr. Thompson, my fourth-grade teacher, he was broccoli. David was Swiss chard after that and Dad was corn. The funny thing was we'd *always* agree—not once was either of us wrong. We never did each other though, we never spoke each other's name.

She was coming down the hall. I closed my eyes. Tonight was different 'cause she wasn't already in bed. She was up when I got home from school and she stayed up even after I got my homework done. She read the paper on the couch and Dad was in his chair. He was asleep but still, it was like they were together 'cause he never talks anyway unless people are over.

Her steps stopped right by my door. I curled up tighter in my

blankets I was so happy. She turned on the light. I poked my face
out so she'd know I was awake. She sat down on the bed. She
seemed like before, like she used to be. She folded the sheet over
the very top of the blanket and smoothed it down by my cheek.
She would always pull the blanket up before she left. It made it
even cozier inside.

"You're gettin' older, my baby's gettin' older."

"No," I said, shaking my head. And she laughed and then I
laughed. I squinched up even tighter, happy tight.

"What vegetable do you think Mr. Owen is?" I asked.

"A mushroom," she answered almost immediately and
squinched her nose up funny.

"Yeah, he is. A squishy old mushroom."

"You gotta go to sleep, Eudora." I looked at her face. I hadn't
seen her this close in a long time. I closed my eyes and tried
to see her perfectly in my mind. Then I opened them to see if I
missed anything. Her eyebrows. I didn't make her eyebrows right.
I made them too skinny so I closed my eyes again to do it right.

"Good night, sleep tight." She stood up and leaned over to
kiss me.

"Mr. Owen always talks about heaven and hell," I blurted out.

"Really?" She sat back on the bed again.

I nodded. "On Fridays, when I go in."

"But he's . . . he's trained as a counselor," she said, shaking
her head.

"He talks on and on about Jesus, about believing in Him."

"He does?" She breathed out hard. "Damn," she said quietly. I
think it was supposed to be farther under her breath. Then her
mouth became like a straight line. David called it her "mad
face."

"What I hate most about believing in Him," I said, "is that it
means whether you go to heaven or hell."

"That's illegal," she said. "He's not supposed to say those things." She was shaking her head.

"Yeah. It makes me scared."

But she was looking away, up to the side. Maybe she was talking to Mr. Owen in her head. I liked she was mad. She was mad for me. But she was looking away.

"Not Jesus, he doesn't scare me," I said. "Just heaven and hell. They scare me."

"Heaven scares you, too?"

"Yeah, 'cause you'd always, every second, be right with God. Every second." I shuddered. "But hell scares me more."

She was looking off to the side again, shaking her head. I wanted her to say something back, but by now, she was probably yelling at Mr. Owen in her mind. "I've got to go in and talk to that man," she finally said. "This is illegal!"

"What if David is in hell?" I asked.

"David!" Her head flew back. She looked at me for a moment like I was Mr. Owen. "David!" But then she put her arm back on the blanket. "Oh, honey, there is no such thing as hell! There is no such thing!" I nodded as fast and hard as I could each time she said it. "There is no such thing!" I kept nodding but she kept saying it like I didn't believe her. And then she was crying again, and shaking, her whole body started to shake. She stood up. "I'm sorry, honey," she mouthed to me and then she was gone.

I waited. The light was on. I knew it meant Dad would come in. He never sat down. He'd say, "Good night, Eudora," and lean over and kiss me on the forehead. I could smell him after. As he turned off the light and turned back around at the door to say "Sleep tight," I could still smell him. He smelled always the same.

WEEKENDS WERE THE worst 'cause I had to stay home, I couldn't ride, and home usually meant staying indoors to help her. She never went outside anymore. She'd wear her blue robe and her blue slippers till just before dinner. I had to put away the dishwasher and set the table and wipe it off after she cleared the plates. Those were my jobs but they weren't what I hated. It was bringing her things to eat, oranges mainly. Eating was now her new *job* 'cause Dad and the doctor said it was the most important thing she could do, she *had* to eat. She'd be in front of the TV but she wouldn't actually watch it, not anymore, she'd just stare at it, and sometimes she didn't even bother to pretend, she'd stare off to the side, or lie back down on the couch. But even Dad couldn't turn it off. She'd yell out, "Keep it on! I'm listening to it," even when the sound was off.

She'd call me and no matter where I was, I'd have to run and still I wouldn't get there fast enough. That's why I hated it so much, it didn't matter even if I was doing my homework. "Didn't you hear me?" she'd always say. "Do I always have to yell before you hear me?" She'd wait for me to look at her before she'd say what to get. "An orange, will you?" and then after, I'd have to go back to the kitchen and bring her a saucer, too, so the peels wouldn't leave any juice on the coffee table.

If I went outside, she'd get really mad. "Do I always have to ring the bell? Do I? Do I?" She'd say it till I answered her, but when I started to answer no, 'cause I thought that's what I was supposed to say, she bit down on her lip and took in a big breath so I quick said, "I guess so," and she let the breath out. It was having to get up that got her furious. "You're hiding from me," she'd say after she laid down again. "I know. I know what you're up to." But that didn't bother me as much as her calling me "sister." "Okay, sister!" she'd say. "If you're gonna be that way!" And it was always 'cause I wasn't fast enough or if the smile came.

One time, right after I got her a bowl of cottage cheese, her kind with pepper and onions—and she said, "Thank you," even—I ran back to my room. I felt good 'cause I had time, lots of time 'cause she wouldn't call again till probably the middle of the next show. Then it would be coffee she'd ask for, *with* milk. She couldn't have it unless she had it with milk. That's what the doctor said. *She's down for a while,* I thought and it was funny to me to think "down" 'cause that's what Mrs. Peterson calls a sick horse or one that can't be ridden. Even if he's standing up, she'll say, "No, we can't use him. He's down." Not down for good, though, killed—that's "put down."

I got back to my room but I didn't turn in to it, I kept on going past it and up the attic stairs. I tiptoed as soft as I could up each step. I opened his door. The back of it still had a poster of a man on a Harley-Davidson and the "David" part of "Davidson" was colored-in red even though he didn't have a Harley, he had a Norton. I held the doorknob back from turning quick so it wouldn't click as the door shut.

As soon as I let go, it happened. I spread out. It was like letting out a big big breath but it didn't stop with air, I was letting me out, too. I got really big, not my body, but me, I was thinner than air and I filled all the way out to the walls and up to the ceiling. I didn't know if my body could move but it could. I waved my arms in the air. I started to giggle. I was waving me inside of me, a thick, heavy me inside a lighter me. I stepped farther into the room, into the middle where it was dark, where the light didn't reach from the windows on each end. I walked around and around inside of me. I kept giggling. It was funny and not at all scary. In fact, it was the opposite of scary, it made everything else that was normal seem scary, everything not this.

It was dark even though it was afternoon. I didn't turn on a light. *Then I'd definitely be caught,* I thought. 'Cause you can see light under the door from the bottom of the attic steps. David always had the light on, even in the day, and she asked him every single morning when he came down to breakfast, "Did you turn off your light?"

I walked really careful so the floor wouldn't squeak. All his shoes were lined up in front of his dresser. I picked one up, one of his black dress shoes he hated. The inside was smooth and cold. It didn't smell like feet, not even a tiny bit. He hated it but I didn't, not now, but it was far away, like a foot is farther away than a hand and this was even farther, much much farther, this was on the very edge of me. I put it down.

His globe. That was closer to the middle, somewhere in the middle of me. But his radio. That. The gray plastic seemed almost bright compared to everything else. I touched the first knob. It felt almost eerie, it was so close, like my ear or my cheek, that close. And it seemed, too, no one else had touched it, not even her. I turned it on, but with no sound, I turned it just to the hum of on. She hadn't been here. I knew. Not to this knob. I was touching *his* fingerprints. I turned it off. The hum stayed for a second before it died out.

There was a 45 on the floor against the hi-fi. "The Stroll" by the Diamonds. And an empty jacket, too. "The Ten Commandments of Love." He had just gotten that. Harvey and the Moonglows. The hi-fi was open and I could just see, in the half dark, a circle of white, gray-white. I stepped closer. It was dust. Dust on his record. *David would die*, I thought. I smiled. I didn't care if it was the bad smile or a good smile or David smiling, I just smiled. *David would die.* He'd laugh at that.

The dust was so thick you couldn't see any black of the record. It was funny because it was me, the dust was me, and I wasn't even dead. "From dust to dust," Father Bob had said so many times that day but it sounded like just a name.

Dust to dust. A perfect round circle of dust. I touched it with the tip of my finger. He hated if I ever got fingerprints on even his old records he didn't play anymore. *On the Moonglows, he'd kill me*, I thought. I smiled again. Dust to dust. We'd be dust together then. I touched it in a new place. There were two black spots now. And they were floating, floating in the gray-white circle. The dust was so soft, like the hair on a horse's belly between its back legs, or like a horse's nose.

There were steps! I heard steps below in my room. Then she was calling, "Eudora? Eudora?" Her voice wasn't mad yet, but she was looking for me. I crunched up even though I knew it was dumb, extra dumb 'cause I was everywhere, I was all through the room, but still I crunched up my body as small as I could.

"Eudora? Where are you?" She was right underneath now. I didn't move even to breathe. "Eudora? Are you playing tricks again? Where ARE you?" She was moving back down the hall again. "I'm gonna get mad, Eudora." She was going back to the kitchen. I stretched my neck. I heard, I thought, the screen door. Maybe she was going outside to ring the bell.

I tiptoed quick to the door. As soon as I got out, on the first step down, I closed in small again. What was me stopped right at my skin. I seemed even smaller than before. I was tiny.

I had to get into my room before she came back inside, and I did, I got to my spot. On my spot I could always think. And I had to, I had to make up where I had been, but I couldn't. I didn't have time. She was coming. Both of them were! Dad, too! Was it that late? They were walking toward here. I squirmed in under the bed. *Pretend I was asleep under the bed.* It was dumb but it was the only thing left to do.

I didn't feel small under the bed. It was even darker than in David's room. It was like night, permanent night. And it smelled. Dusty. She was always complaining about dust. Beds and radiators especially, they were the worst, she'd say, they both *create* dust. My finger was still covered with it. But it was *that* dust, his dust. I touched it on my cheek. *Like silk,* I thought, like her orange silk blouse. I touched my tongue to it. Ick! It was bitter. Powdery bitter. I tried to swallow it but it was too fine, it wouldn't go away. And it was no longer me. *Dust to dust. Dirt. He's turning into dirt. He's rotting.* I pressed my eyes together. I kept swallowing. *He's rotting.*

"There she is! See? See her foot?" He was shaking my foot. "Come on out, Eudora, come on out."

Dad's hands were on my ankles. I let myself go limp, let him drag me out from under the bed. The taste of the dust wouldn't go away. I put my hands over my eyes. They had turned the light on. Why, when it was day? "Shut it off," I said. "Shut it off."

"She's been asleep, Florence."

"I just got worried. I got so worried."

When I heard her voice, I forgot. I ran to her voice and I forgot, I hugged her. It wasn't until I reached around her back that I remembered, it was different now. But it was too late, her hands were already on my hair.

"You were just asleep, honey, just asleep."

"Shut it off," I said, crying. "Shut the light off." And she did with her one hand and the other ran through my hair the way it used to when she would sit by me in bed. She'd start at my forehead, go up and then down again to my neck. "Crescent moon," she used to say, "little fingernail moon." And then when she was about to go, she'd say, "Good night, moon," and I'd answer, "Good night, Mom," but still for a while longer her hands would stay, and they did now, too, they stayed, making over and over on my head its exact shape.

I WAS THE youngest person and the littlest by a lot that ever got to work at the Petersons' farm. I had to do four stalls a day and that meant I could ride for a whole hour. But usually I did Twinkle's stall, too, and sometimes even Nighty's, so I was Mrs. Peterson's favorite. I didn't even have to call her Mrs. Peterson after a while 'cause no other students did, and even though they were all adults, it didn't matter I was a kid, I could call her Mary. And even her husband, I called him Buddy.

I went every day after school. I rode on Mr. Holcomb's bus and most days I could get all my homework done by the time he left me off at the farm. Then Dad would pick me up after he finished work, which was getting later and later, so I started to eat supper more and more at the farm 'cause they always ate early, around five, and then Mary would teach her evening lessons now that it was staying light longer. "To make ends meet," she said. At first they pulled up an extra chair for me but then they stopped putting it back against the wall, it was my seat and even if I wasn't there a few days, when I came back, the chair was still at the table. Mary's mother did all the cooking and she always cooked too much. "Finish it," she'd say. "Finish it, I wanna get rid of it." But still she'd make more the next day and too much again.

Mary would be teaching already when I got off the bus but she'd leave the horse I was supposed to ride in the barn for me to lead out and join the lesson in the big ring. Then, after supper, I'd stand by the gate and watch and sometimes she'd yell for me to pick up a crop or fix a cavalletti. I liked most the days no one was scheduled. Then I'd help her groom the horses. "There!" she'd say whenever we finished one and she was unclipping the cross-tie. "Now I just have to throw a quick brush on him in the morning." That made it a lot easier for her 'cause she had to get them all ready and tacked up before eight. Some days it was raining hard and I wouldn't get to ride but it didn't matter, it was better than going home. And it got better and better the more work I knew how to do. "You are such a help to me," Mary would say about two or three times a day and she meant it, too, 'cause even though I was little, I could carry a five-gallon bucket full of water from the pump to the farthest stall where Nicky was. Even Buddy, who didn't ever say much, said, "Would you believe that?"

I never told Mary that I didn't want to go home but I think she guessed. And one time she even said, "If you ever need to stay here for any reason, you know you can," but then the truck from Five Oak Farm pulled up so she didn't say anything more.

Dad would pick me up most nights around seven or seven-thirty but sometimes he'd call and wouldn't come till nine and then I'd be there to help her hay in the horses and water them for the night. I loved that the best. And when Mary came in from the barn and Buddy came in, too, from the garage, which was full of people's furniture he was fixing, whenever they got back in, they'd sit down and eat a bowl of ice cream. And sometimes Dad was late enough so I got one, too.

It was one of the nights my dad came late that I found out about Bogey. He got cut to only three quarters instead of a whole can of feed. When I asked why, Mary said, "Well . . ." and kept on scooping the grain up so I knew not to ask again. But still I couldn't help myself. "Why doesn't he get a full can anymore?"

"Well, Eudora . . ." She paused a long time but I waited, even after she handed me the full can and said, "Nicky," even then I waited and she said, "There's a hard side to this business."

I nodded and kept waiting.

"Well, you see, Eudora, he's not going to ever be sold." I took the feed to Nicky's stall, and came back to trade her the empty can for the two full ones she had ready for me. "Proud. Thaddeus."

When I came back to trade cans, she asked, "Understand? Here. Baron. Showtime. Understand, Eudora?" I almost nodded. I knew this was one of those times I was just supposed to nod, not push. "She pushes," is what *she* had just said to Dad about me. And Mrs. Klepp, too, had said to the principal, "That girl never knows when to stop." But I didn't nod, it was too fast, I took the cans and I shook my head, no, I didn't understand, and then I turned away quick to continue the feeding.

"I can't afford to keep him going," she said but her voice was deep into the feed bin. It was Monday night and Dean's Mills delivered a new load every Tuesday so only her legs showed each time she scraped a can of feed up. Her voice sounded eerie from in there. When she came back out, she handed me the last two cans. "Twinkle. Son. And that's it for tonight, I'll get Nighty's and Chesty's." They got a tablespoon of vegetable oil and a scoop of vitamins in theirs.

But I didn't turn away 'cause Mary was looking at me. "We're going to put Bogey down." She watched me hear it.

"But—" I started.

She shook her head. "He's too old to sell. Except to the glue factory. And I'd *never* do that."

I knew not to ask any more questions. I watched her feed her two horses that only she rode. She wouldn't use them for lessons.

She was looking at me again as she walked back with the empty cans to throw into the feed bin before she put a clip on it so no raccoons could get in. "It's the hard part, Eudora. I can't afford it and I can't afford to let him go fat into the grave."

Fat into the grave. I couldn't get it out of my head. Every day after that, when I ran into the barn, I looked first to see if he was still there. And even before I looked to see who was saddled for me to ride, I'd go into his stall and check if I could feel his ribs. His coat was still shiny even though it was heavier now than the others. I rubbed my hands back and forth over his side. I couldn't feel any bone, and I'd think, *Fat into the grave. Going fat into the grave.*

In school, it went around and around in my brain on its own, *fat into the grave.* Every time I wasn't thinking or doing work, if I was just writing down our homework, I could hear it going on in the background, *fat into the grave.*

Each day on the bus I thought, *Maybe today, maybe I'll walk into the barn and he'll be gone. Disappeared.* I wanted to see it. But I never thought, Ask, jusk ask. Till it popped into my brain out in the hall.

I ended up in the hall 'cause I hated Mrs. Klepp. So when she asked me why I didn't finish my homework, nothing came into my brain except what I said. " 'Cause the bus ride wasn't long enough." And when she asked, "What?" to give me a second chance, I didn't make up something else, I said the same thing over again and it came onto my face, I felt it come, the smile.

That was it. She knew I hated her then and that was better, I thought, than just being bad. She stood up from her desk and said, "Okay, Miss Buell." She called me Miss Buell when she was really mad. "Okay. Okay." She kept saying, "Okay. Okay," as she walked straight to my desk. "Get up! Come on! Up! Out of your chair." I took my notebook and pencil with me. And then she picked the whole desk with the chair hooked to it off the floor. I could hear all the books slide down inside. I thought she was going to take it to the back corner where I sat for a week at the beginning of the year, but instead, she wheeled around with it and walked to the front of the room. Some of my pencils fell out. Mary Beth leaned over to grab one and then she got up to get the rest from the floor. She gave them to Peggy, who sat right in front of me. I knew Peggy was waiting for me to look at her. Mary Beth and Peggy were both looking, waiting in case I needed to look back at them, but I didn't, I watched Mrs. Klepp instead. I watched her walk out the door. And then I stood there a moment, even after Peggy handed me my pencils and whispered, "Witch," I stood there in the empty spot where my desk used to be.

I heard my desk and chair slam down in the hall just outside the door. "There!" Mrs. Klepp said, just like Mary finishing a horse. Mrs. Klepp walked back in the room so I looked down. I didn't want her to catch my eyes. I made it out the door without her catching my eyes. "Till the end of the year," she said but that was only a little over a month.

It was darker out in the hall. I started the copying. She always makes anyone who's bad copy a hundred times the quote she writes on the board each day. I always write all the numbers down the side of the page first. Today's was " 'It is better to know some of the questions than all of the answers.' James Thurber." You had to write the man's name each time.

I was right next to the wall. The yellow tiles ended above my head, and I felt where they curved into the regular wall, which was always shiny white. Walking to music or gym, I'd always be next to the wall so I could walk with my hand cupped over that curve. But what I wanted now was the cold. I pressed my whole side flat against the tiles so I could feel the cold seep into my arm.

It didn't last long. I only got to number 36 and my arm had already turned the tiles warm. I wanted more cold. I pressed my cheek against another tile farther up. I waited till the cold spread completely over my face. I liked it out here. I could think. The cold helped me think. I knew 'cause it was right then it came to me to *ask* Mary, Mrs. Peterson, what I had been wanting but never thought to ask for. I could just ask. It seemed so simple. Cold always made things simple.

I was afraid of one thing, though. What if Mary asked back, "Why?" I didn't know. I only knew I had to see him fall, go into the hole. Anything, I'd watch anything, even if there was blood, as long as he didn't just disappear.

I waited till after five when all the other riding students had driven away and we were about to go in to eat supper. There were no lessons scheduled for the night.

"Mary?" I had practiced so many times the exact question but still my mouth felt dry. I closed my eyes.

"What is it?" she asked. "What?"

"Can I see you put Bogey down?" *There!* I thought. *I did it, it's over.*

She was quiet for so long I thought maybe she hadn't heard, except she stopped walking. She was standing at the gate that separates the barnyard from the lawn. I just waited. I looked at the ground and waited.

"I don't know," she finally said. "I don't know. Why?" I shook my head. I couldn't look up. "Why, dear? Why do you want to?" but I kept shaking my head. I could feel tears behind my eyes so now I definitely couldn't look up. If she saw me cry just asking, she'd never let me watch a horse get killed. I kept shaking my head. She knelt down and held my arms. "Eudora?"

"I don't know," I said, and all my hope left that she'd say yes. "I just don't want to see him gone, have him gone without . . . without seeing it."

She stood back up but she was still touching the top of my shoulder. "Okay," she said. I couldn't really believe it but then she said, "Next Saturday he's coming, pretty early. You should be here by nine."

I let out a big breath. I had only thought about asking. I had practiced in my brain only the asking part. I never thought about after, about right now, about her actually saying yes, that I could see it. I thought for a second I was going to get sick but I swallowed it back. It was only for a second.

Saturday, I knew the date, May 26, 'cause it was my birthday. But I didn't tell Mary that. I didn't want her to know. Dad had already explained to me out in the garage why I couldn't have a party. The doctor had said no, it would be too much for her. But I knew it anyway, I knew it as soon as he said, "Your birthday is coming up. How old are you gonna be?" I knew right then they had talked to the doctor. He hugged me when he said, "I'm sorry about it, Eudora, I'm sorry. Really, I am, I'm sorry." He always repeated everything but I didn't mind. It made the hug last longer.

On the way home in the car that night, I felt lucky. It was all perfect. I could ask Dad to drive me to the Petersons' on my birthday, that Mrs. Peterson had said it was okay even though it was Saturday. And he'd say, "Yes, of course." He'd never think to ask if I was riding or not.

SHE CAME INTO my room that morning and kissed my forehead, counting each kiss, "One year, two years, three years . . ."

all the way up to eleven. "Eleven years old!" And then she sat down beside me. "Happy birthday." I curled up and smiled under the blankets, but not for what she thought. I was sneaking my birthday. I felt almost bad but not, not really. It was like a real birthday that was going to happen inside the regular birthday.

When Dad left me off, Buddy had already dug the hole. It was in the field with the old apple trees back of the barn. There was a big pile of dirt beside his backhoe and beside that, the hole. I looked in. It was so much bigger than a horse.

When Hogan's truck came, Mary told me to stand back with Buddy. Mary led Bogey out beside the hole and fed him a scoop of grain in the black bucket Buddy had brought out before. He still didn't have any ribs showing. Bogey was eating with his head down when Mary said, "Okay," and the man came out from behind the truck and laid the gun right between his eyes and shot. Bogey fell sideways. I saw a little grain drop from his lips and then he was gone, he was in the hole. I heard him land. "There!" Mary said, but then she turned away. She brushed her hair back over her head and let out a big sigh. "Done."

Buddy and I walked up. The hole seemed smaller now. Bogey's neck was bent to its shape and his face was turned up toward us. His mouth was open, so I could see what was left of his teeth, worn down to almost nothing. There were little clumps of grain all over them and over his lips, too. "Died eating," Buddy said. "You could go worse." I didn't know what I felt, if I felt anything, but I moved my shoulders and arms around like something big had just happened. I moved them to find out: Were they different now? Was everything different? But there was no blood on his face, not even a drop. I couldn't even see the hole in his head. Everything had happened inside.

Buddy said, later, it's the kind of bullet they use, it's small and it explodes in their brain and kills them instantly. "More humane than a needle," he said. "T.D., he needed three shots before he fell." That was the last time they used the vet. "Costs more, too," he said, "by the time you get him out here."

Mary asked if I wanted to go inside the house. She was going to make some tea but I didn't go in with her. Instead, I watched Buddy on the backhoe scoop up all the dirt and dump it into the hole. I watched until the pile was gone and Buddy was using the loader to scrape the ground flat.

Graveyards are never flat. The ground sinks in wherever the graves are. In front of every stone, you see a hollow almost the shape of the coffin. I didn't want to ever go back to David's grave 'cause I didn't want to see the hollow. I didn't know how long that would take but I didn't care, I never wanted to see it, ever. They went every Sunday but I stayed in the car. I wouldn't get out. I looked away from them, out the window on the opposite side. I didn't mind seeing the ripples in the ground on that side and if I squinted they even seemed like a sea of water, green water like where Uncle Peter lives in Maine, with lots of white sails sticking up.

When Buddy turned off the motor, I walked into the house. "Well, now you've seen it," Mary said. I nodded. "Still want horses?" I nodded again. "They all go, one way or another."

"Yeah," I said. I felt eleven, and eleven seemed so much older than ten, much more than a year, just the sound of it, *eleven*.

"Have a cup of tea with me," she said. I had never had one before. She showed me how to press out the tea bag with the spoon. "So you get more tea," she explained. I put lots of milk and two teaspoons of sugar in it. I cupped my hands around it while I sipped at it. It was just the right hot and just the right sweet. I didn't want Dad to come ever.

I KNEW DAD had a cake in the back 'cause he was throwing his jacket over a box on the seat when I walked out of Mary's house even though it was too chilly for just his shirt, and then he said, "Here. Sit in the front," even though no one else was in the car so of course I'd sit in the front. *She* always said, "You're so OB-vious, Michael," and now I knew what she meant. At first I thought it might be a present but then I thought of the cake. She probably wouldn't bake a cake 'cause she was usually lying down now in bed or staring at the TV with the sound off or on a good day she might be on the couch reading *Look*. She never read real books anymore. Then I saw the box on top of the washer in the laundry room so I knew for sure.

She brought it out after dinner. And her and Dad sang "Happy Birthday." It didn't look anything like her cakes. Her white icing was never really white. This had bright white icing, as white as a sheet, and a pink braid along the outside edge. Inside the circle of pink, it said *Happy Birthday Eudora* like hers always said but it wasn't in her handwriting and then there was the number 11 beneath it in pink, too. I hated pink.

I blew out all the candles on the first breath and Dad clapped. I started to take them out so I could lick the bottoms off. That was always my favorite part. But I hated the icing. It wasn't like hers at all. It was slippery, like pure grease. I wanted to spit it out. The fat was lining every inch of my mouth. *Fat into the grave.* The words came back. I thought they were gone, gone 'cause I had watched Bogey fall, but they were still there. *Fat into the grave.* I hated that the words were still there. I lined up all the other candles on the side without licking them off.

She cut me a piece first and then Dad a piece. And then she put the knife down. She wasn't going to eat any.

I stood up and reached over and dragged the cake toward me across the table.

"What're you doing, honey? What do you want?" she said. But I didn't answer, I picked up the knife and cut into the cake. It was the first time I ever cut into a cake.

"Come on," I said, "you have to eat a piece. Come on." I got up to get her a plate.

"No, no, I can't. I'm too full."

I put the plate down and flipped the piece of cake onto it like I had watched her do maybe a hundred times. I had always watched carefully with all my attention, waiting for cake. *Now, I'm it*, I thought. *Now I'm the one to be watched.* I even got her a fork out from the drawer. I didn't care she kept saying, "Dear, dear, I can't, I really, I just can't. I'm too full."

She was trying to laugh. "Eudora, really." I was almost laughing, too, or just smiling. Dad was smiling.

I handed her her plate. She took a very small bite and then put her fork down. I sat back in my chair. I took a bite. I hated it even though it was white. I took another, and each bite I hated it more. "Come on," I said. "Come on, eat it." I was no longer smiling. I took another bite. It was like a job I had to finish. It was my cake and I had to eat it, but she didn't. I hated her. "Come on," I said again.

She started shaking her head, "Please," she said.

"What's wrong?" I said. "You don't like it? You don't like my cake?"

She looked up at me quickly. "Oh no. I like it okay."

Dad was almost finished. "I'll have another one," he said. "I'll eat hers. Here, give me yours, honey."

She gave him her plate.

"What is it about eating, huh?" I said, but inside, I knew it wasn't a question. It was coming out of me fast and hard, it was all hate. There was a tiny tiny part in me that was sad for her but it didn't have a chance, not then. I kept on. "I know what it is. You think I don't know but I do. I know."

She kept looking at Dad but he was looking down. He was busy finishing her cake.

"You don't want to go fat into the grave. That's what it is. You'd hate going fat into the grave."

"Michael!" But there was nothing Dad could do. It was over for her.

I said it again, "FAT into the grave." I loved it. It was like a song, like a song with a drum. "FAT into the grave."

She couldn't look up. I was staring at her. The smile might have even been there, too, but it didn't matter. I don't know how many times I said it. "FAT into the grave. FAT into the grave." Even when Dad yelled, "Stop! Stop!" it was still making me stronger. "FAT into the grave." I sang it again and again and he grabbed me, both my arms, yelling, "Stop!" But singing, I could hold on to the hate. I held on to it like on to David's toe. I held on to it tight tight. I squeezed it.

IT WAS SUNDAY. She stayed in bed all day. Dad brought her rye toast with coffee or milk every couple of hours and each time, he waited in the room so she had to eat it, she couldn't put it down and then say later that it was too cold.

In the afternoon when he came back out to the kitchen with her dishes to put in the dishwasher, he said, "Well, it's almost full. What do ya think? Should we run it?"

"Yeah. It's close enough." I opened the cabinet for the soap. I loved that now he asked me questions like that. Dad and I had been doing the dishes for a couple of weeks and now he even let me screw the hose onto the kitchen faucet and turn it on. But he usually never ran it till it was all the way full and that sometimes took two days since she never cooked big meals with lots of pans anymore.

It was when I was shaking the soap into the dishwasher that the phone rang. At first his voice seemed surprised, but then he started to say, "I'm sorry, I'm very sorry," over and over. I thought right away someone died. I didn't start the dishwasher 'cause I knew it would be too loud. "Thanks for letting us know," he said.

"Thanks so much for letting us know." And then, at the very end, he said, "I'll tell her. Yeah. I will. Yeah, I'll tell her. Don't worry."

I thought for sure *she* was the her he had to tell, until he hung up and turned to me and even though I was right there by the sink, he said, "Eudora." And I said back, "Yeah?" but I had already dropped inside. Just in that tiny time, Dad saying my name, I dropped, or a big part inside me dropped till it hit a bottom and turned into rock.

"They have to sell the farm," he said. "There's no more money. They have to be out in two weeks, and with all the horses sold, too."

I stood there. "Money?" I think I said 'cause he nodded and said, "Yeah, it's a hard world out there." And then he looked at me and said, "It's awful. I know, honey. It's awful." He put out his arm for me to come into. He was going to hug me. I just stood there looking at his arm. "Awful, I know, honey. I'm sorry," he said again but I didn't stop looking at his arm. I wanted to go into it, inside its circle, I meant to, but I turned instead toward the door. "Eudora, come on, honey." But I walked out anyway. I didn't want to, I wanted to stay with him, or no, I wanted him to follow me and he did, he came to the door and said, "Eudora, come on. How 'bout we go down to the Dairy Bar, it's open now—" But I ran off away from him, I ran around the corner and behind the garage so I could cry. But I couldn't, not there. I was still rock.

I ran to the dead orchard at the back edge of the pasture. It was just broken trunks, branches, and twigs that stuck up into the sky all twisted and not even with any bark. But then I saw leaves. Just one branch on one tree had leaves. The rest had broken off and the trunk that was left was completely hollow. The side facing the creek had split open so there was a narrow slit that went almost to the ground.

I turned sideways so I could squeeze myself in. The floor inside was squishy. Dead bark dropped in all around me onto my hair and face and down onto the back of my neck and inside my shirt. I couldn't squirm or more bark would fall. My shoulders just fit. It smelled like dirt but wetter, and sour, too. I squinched my one arm up and picked off a little piece of bark from the opening so I could see out better. The opening made the pasture look like a thin road of grass that ended in the blackberry bushes that covered the creek bank. But after a while, I stopped seeing even a road. I just stared. I was waiting to cry, for the rock inside to go away or melt. I waited and waited but the rock didn't change even a little.

I heard Dad calling from the house and I heard the bell. But I didn't come out or yell back, not even when he walked through the pasture calling out my name. I could hear his steps hit the stiff brown stalks from last year sticking up through the new grass. He kept calling. But it got easier and easier to *not* move. I stopped even thinking about moving till the opening was all dark and then it seemed the tree swallowed me up.

IT WAS LIKE waking but it was dark. I thought, *I'm finished standing here. It's dumb standing here anymore.* It was all of a sudden like that. I thought I could just leave like I had been in a regular room with a regular door. I stepped over the bottom of the opening and turned my shoulders to squeeze out of the tree, out, I was out but the dark was all sky and I exploded, I was falling. I hated it, I hated being in the sky. I hated falling. I grabbed my elbows and hunched down as low as I could. I knew there was nowhere to fall, I couldn't fall, the ground was here, right here below me. But still I kept hunching down as low as I could. Cold wet circles spread into my knees but I didn't care, I wanted to stay close to the ground. I held my elbows glued to my sides. I held them for a long time till I knew if I let them go I wouldn't explode. I stood up slowly. I waved my hand around. "It's just air," I said out loud. "The sky's just air." And I breathed deep into my nose to prove it to myself, before I started to walk, just plain walk.

I looked in through the living room window like it wasn't my house at all. There were no people inside, just a long, light green couch facing the fireplace with two end tables piled with magazines and with matching lamps that were both on. There was a coffee table, too, with a tall, swirly pink vase, and a big leather chair on the far end. Back by a wall full of bookshelves were two fancy chairs, the same light green, facing each other.

I moved to the kitchen window. Still no one. The light over the table was on but it didn't look cozy. The bright white cabinets made the light look cold, like looking at a ghost house. Once Dad started selling kitchen cabinets, too, it would all match, the refrigerator, the dishwasher, everything would be "sand beige." There wasn't one thing not "in its place," which meant exactly where it was when she went into her room. It was important not to move anything so that when she came out, everything looked just the same. After school, I took my books straight into my own room, I never set them down on the ledge like we used to. Even Dad didn't throw the mail on the baking center anymore and he never left his shoes on the floor by his chair when he sat down to read the paper. He barely did that now anyway 'cause he'd go to her as soon as we finished eating. Either pizza at Eva's or noodles or, lately, baked beans. I'd open the can and Dad would heat them up as I got out our plates and forks. We didn't bother with napkins and sometimes we took our plates out to the playroom and ate in front of the news. Then he'd be in the room with her it seemed for hours. *They must be in there now,* I thought.

I opened the door as quietly as I could and tiptoed into the kitchen. I found the cabinet where her potato bin is, where she keeps onions, too. I didn't pull it out 'cause it would've made noise. I just reached my hand into it and felt around for the onions. The skins felt shiny and not dirty at all like the potatoes. I got a little one. I tiptoed to the knife drawer, opened it just enough so I could get a knife out, and closed it again without making any noise.

I closed the door behind me very very softly and even though no one would hear me outside I still tiptoed to David's spot behind the garage. I sat down but I had to wait till I could see enough in the dark to peel the onion skin back and pull it off. The onion looked bright white, as white as paper and perfectly round. I held it up close to my eyes. It didn't work. I put it down on the gravel and cut it in half and put both halves up close to each eye. My eyes started to sting but I still held them as wide open as I could till they burned and burned and I felt them coming, the tears were coming, and my nose started to run, too. It was working. But the rock still didn't go away. No matter how much my eyes burned and cried, the rock wouldn't go away.

After I had already washed the knife and put it back in the drawer, I opened the kitchen door again and banged it shut. Then I walked loud enough so I was sure Dad could hear me. Still, I was almost to my room when he came out.

"Where were you?" he whispered. "I was just about to call Jimmy Esker. I was getting worried, I thought maybe you started walking to the Petersons'."

I shook my head. "I walked down to the creek." Then I thought, *That was stupid to lie, he's not even mad.* But it came out too quick.

"You know you shouldn't stray off like that. You didn't even have a flashlight." But then he leaned his head closer. "I didn't tell," and he pointed to her room even though we were back in the kitchen. "You must be starving." He was still talking low.

"Yeah, kinda."

"I haven't eaten either. How 'bout a bowl of cereal? And I'll just have some toast."

"Yeah, that's all I want." I liked not having to eat real dinners. He seemed like David then. He wasn't like a dad all mad that I was gone for so long and he wasn't at all like a mother. She would die thinking we ate cereal and toast for dinner, that dinner wasn't fixed or at least hot, even though it was after nine.

He got a bowl for me. I could've gotten it but I sat down instead. I liked him getting it for me and the box of Cheerios and the milk. I liked to watch him move in the kitchen. He seemed almost in slow motion and a little lost, not like her. *Like a kid*, I thought, *but slow*. It was better this way, her being in her room all the time, not coming out. When it's just Dad alone, he doesn't ever yell at me. He just takes care of me. He never talks or asks me things like she used to, but he takes care of me.

I heard her once say to her best friend, Mrs. Gallagher, "You know that Michael. Talking isn't his specialty." Like it was obvious, but *I* never knew it. I thought, *Really?* 'Cause before, before David, when we still had dinners and lots of nights people came over, he talked plenty, he'd talk about work and what customers said and which models of washers and dryers and dishwashers were selling and which weren't and then sometimes he'd go on about why not, too. And there was always some customer who came in that he had a story about.

But I liked it now, not talking. I felt alone even though I knew he was there and I liked it a lot better than being yelled at.

He got up to make himself two more pieces of toast. Her voice came into my head: *He takes an extra large. 'Cause of his shoulders.* Mrs. Gallagher was surprised when she said it, maybe 'cause he's not fat, but *she* kept saying, "Really, he does. An extra large." I tried to see him like that, see whether he was big or just medium. But all men seemed just big, plain big. *It must be like looking at a horse for the first time*, I thought. *They must all seem the same big.* I looked at his shoulders while he was waiting for his toast, and his "wings" — that's what she calls them — stretching his shirt tight. I tried to see him like she did, like I knew all the different sizes of men and their shirts and I could say to myself, *Yes, he's an extra large*, or I could even be surprised that he was.

I finished my second bowl and I got up to put it in the sink and run a little water in it so the milk wouldn't dry and stick. He said, "You can still go tomorrow, after school. I mean to the farm. Mary said. For at least tomorrow."

He looked like he was going to say something else so I waited. "I'm sure there's another place you can go to ride. Really. We'll find a place. I'm sure there's someplace." I looked at him quick. I wanted to get to my room quick, but I still waited. "We'll talk about it tomorrow, okay, honey?"

"Okay! Good night," I said fast. I didn't want him to have to say any more.

WHEN I WALKED through the barn, I saw two horses saddled, Nighty and Wink. *Wink!* I still didn't know if I should change into my riding pants and boots that I kept in the tack room. Mary yelled in from outside by the ring, "Hi, Eudora! Change. I'll be right in."

I was pulling my boots on when she came into the tack room. She looked straight at me.

"Did your dad talk to you?"

I nodded.

"Well," she looked out the window. "I kept trying to make a go of it, but . . ." She looked back at me. "But anyway, YOU! You gotta keep riding." I looked down but I could tell she was looking right at me. She was waiting for me to look back at her, but I couldn't. "You're very talented, very very talented. You know that, don't you?"

I nodded. I still couldn't say anything.

"You just gotta keep riding. You've got everything it takes. I'll help you find someplace. Problem is that, well, around here, there's nothing. Only . . . you know, a bunch of trail horses they auction off every fall. Even Bill's place." She kept looking back out the window. "Wouldn't be so bad if you barrel raced. Can you see yourself, Eudora, hootin' and hollerin' and wavin' your hat around, huh? Down there in Cairo? Huh?" She was trying to get me to smile but I couldn't. "But anyway, I'll help you. Even if your dad has to drive you once a month up to Altamont . . ." I should've said "Yeah" or something 'cause she was quiet a long time. "Well, come on. I got Wink saddled up for you. We're just going out by ourselves today."

"No one else is here?" I barely got it out, my mouth was so dry.

"No, I told Enid and Mary Bradford and Liz yesterday, and now tomorrow, Maplecrest Farm is coming. They're interested in Wink, Twinkle, and Baron. Maybe Proud, too, but he might not have enough jumping in him for them. They pretty much want straight hunters and jumpers they can show, not a well-trained school horse that can jump. You know, that's a rich place down there. Lotta rich kids."

"Yeah," I said but she didn't hear 'cause she was already in Nighty's stall and I was in Wink's. Wink was only four and still narrow and lean, "like a teenager," Mary said, but he was almost seventeen hands. She always said he'd be her best, especially jumping. I led him out. I think I could've vaulted on 'cause she taught me to, even though it was just onto Twinkle who's only fifteen-three, but she said, "Here, I'll give you a leg up."

Then she got on Nighty, her horse. She was offered a blank check for him once at a show, and she refused. I didn't ask if she was keeping him. Or where they were going to live either.

When we reached the big ring with the course in it, she said, "Warm him up a little and then you can take him over a few. Do circles, especially going left, that's his stiff side."

I had been riding Twinkle and she was so stocky and wide, riding Wink was like being on stilts. And his stride sent you up so high, at first I felt off, out of balance, but then I started to like it. "He's a floater," Mary always said about him, 'cause watching him, he always looked like he was floating, only barely hitting the ground.

He wasn't steady at all. I had to keep a lot of leg on him to keep him bending. You gotta get a horse to bend his neck but mostly his body to the exact circle you're making, otherwise they just skid out stiff.

Mary stopped Nighty at the edge of my circles so I could hear her. "He's a little jerky, huh? Typical youngster, but just keep on him, strong leg, soft hand.

"Now, try taking him in just a bit. Have him come back to you just a bit, there, but don't stop him moving forward. You always want him to love going forward but get him ju-ust a little softer, yea-ah, like that, that's it, that's it, good, oops, bring him in again, he won't just stay there like Twinkle or Proud, you gotta keep with it, there, yeah, like your hand's a rubber band. Okay, a few more half halts . . ."

After about fifteen minutes she said, "Okay." I breathed out hard. Circles were a lot more difficult for me than jumping. "Just take him around the outside of the course first. He'll dart around a bit, but don't worry, he's just having fun, don't worry. But you won't, I know." I knew that she had said about me, "She's glued to the saddle, that girl." And when Enid asked why I seem to calm down every horse I got on, she said it again as the reason: " 'Cause she's on there to stay."

He was bolting straight up about every fifth stride, but it made me laugh 'cause even if she hadn't said anything, you could feel he was just playing. I didn't take him back at all and then he started to steady a bit especially near the outside wall. And his canter was so rolly, like a rockin' horse, but with the wind in my face and the ground going by in big chunks, I loved him. He ran so happy and we hadn't even started jumping yet. I started to circle him in between some of the jumps. Uneven. *Typical youngster*, Mary said in my brain.

"Okay," she yelled as I went by her. "Just start in here, with the cross-rails."

I came toward the first jump square, pulled him in for a few strides, but when he came up underneath me, he curled up like it was a five-footer. I couldn't believe it, he was like a field rolling up into a mountain. "Whoo," I heard her yell. "Have fun. . . ."

On the second jump, I checked him a few strides but he took off a little too soon and ticked it with his fronts.

The next one was a small jump, and it had two ground rails on the approach so a young horse doesn't chip or run it. I checked him, I checked him, and then *whoa!* he sailed, we went at least four feet high. There were two more and we took both just as high, but even without the ground rails, I had checked him in right.

When I circled him around her to get more instructions, she yelled, "See why I don't want anybody else on him? Except maybe Liz on a good day." I brought him down to a trot and then to a walk, and she went back to talking. "The others get too nervous and rile him up. He just loves to jump and he hasn't learned to conserve himself yet." She was smiling. "How do ya like him?" I broke into a smile. "I love him," I said. "He sure jumps high."

" 'Course he can't feel you on his back." She laughed. "Do a few more and then we'll take them both out. Nighty needs a workout, he's gettin' fat."

Later, after we got back in from the road, she said while she helped me rub his legs down, he was already pretty cool, she said, "Eudora, why don't you come tomorrow, too? Charlie Teague, he's the Maplecrest Farm man, their trainer, he'll be coming around three. Maybe you could ride Wink for him." She turned to me and smiled. "Show him off for me."

"Okay!" I was happy, 'cause I was only thinking about riding Wink again. I didn't think what I was saying, and that it wouldn't just be riding, like today, it would be riding to sell Wink.

I COULD SEE, walking from the bus, Mary lungeing Wink in the small ring. I changed before I walked out to them. A man in blue jeans leaned against the fence, watching. She yelled in from the middle of the ring after she brought Wink down. "This is Mr. Teague, Eudora. And of course, that's Eudora." He looked down at me with this smirky smile, I think 'cause of my size. So as soon as Mary unhooked the lunge line from Wink's bridle, I vaulted onto him. She didn't even have a chance to give me a leg up. She turned around and I was on and I couldn't hide my smile. "Yep, this is Eudora," she said, turning to the man. I think he was smiling, too, but I didn't look. I hated he was there.

Mary looked straight up at me when she was tightening the girth. She said, low enough so only I could hear, "Ride him loosely, but don't be afraid to pull him in when you need to." Then she backed up. "Okay," she said louder. "Just do a few circles and then start in on the course. Same order as yesterday."

But I hated that man and I even hated her standing there by him. I didn't want to ride Wink or ride him well. But I couldn't not. Wink didn't know. He didn't know the difference between yesterday and today. We were approaching the first jump and he was all there willing, he was ready to go, ready to roll into a mountain again, he didn't know, he curled up under me and we rose way way high. I couldn't not ride, I couldn't not love it, or not love Wink that he went as high as he could no matter what, not even to clear the silly rail but just to jump. He was a jumper, he couldn't help himself, he couldn't hold back, or "conserve," as she said, he didn't care the man was watching, or that he was selling himself away, or that I was, too, I was selling him away and he didn't even hate me for it, he was too simple, and I rode him, I didn't stop him, I let him go, I turned simple as him. I *was* him from the moment we took off and while we were in the air, I was him and we were warm, almost hot and moving through air, through nothing but air, and it seemed like a fact that should be in some book, that it was perfect to be warm and moving through air, but then we landed. We landed again and again, and each time, the rock broke. It broke eight times and I had to quick wipe my eyes so I could steer him toward the next jump that I knew would make the man say again, "Yes."

WINK CHANGED ME. I took my boots and pants home and I couldn't go back to the farm but I knew the day the truck came, and then another truck and another till they were all gone, the horses were gone, but it didn't matter, I had already changed. I was two of me. I was the me that rode, that sold Wink away to the man watching and hated the man for watching. But I was also Wink, or like Wink, simple and all open inside, and not able to turn back, or hold back or "conserve" or even hate the other me who was always watching, too. That me was too simple to hate.

Even her, that me couldn't hate her. She was out of her room again and everyone said that that was an improvement, Mrs. Gallagher and Dad and the doctor, everyone but me.

At first, things seemed almost okay but then Dad bought me a record player. Maybe he thought it would keep me busy after the horses were sold and I couldn't ride. Grandma had always said, "Keep a child busy and you keep it out of trouble." David loved more than anything to stay up in his room and listen to music and Dad knew I'd go up there, too, whenever David would let me, so he probably thought I'd be good then, staying in my room, and not always wanting to go outside, which made her even more mad than when she asked me to help in the kitchen and I was too slow or when I would drop something.

The night he brought the record player home, Dad called from the playroom, "Eudora! Florence! Come here! I have a surprise. Come on!" I ran in from my room and he was waiting there in front of where his coat was spread open over something big on the coffee table. I didn't think for a minute it was for me, I thought it was "for the house," like she said when the cuckoo clock came in a box from Germany. I could tell that Dad was still waiting for her, so I said, "She's in her room."

"Oh," he said, "okay, well . . ." He let out a big breath and for just a moment he looked like he was shrinking. But then he turned to face the box. "Well," he said loud, "here it is"—and he grabbed the coat and yanked it away—"la-da-da-daaaaa!" swinging his arm up high. But it was in front of just me so he let his arm drop back to his side right away 'cause it seemed so silly with just me in the room and I looked but all I could see was a box so he said, but in his regular voice, he said, "It's for you. It's a record player."

"Me? Really? It's for me?" I was so surprised and the whole room seemed empty without her there laughing at him, or David, who'd be trying to open the box by now. I was silent, I didn't say "Thank you," I forgot.

"I thought you would *like* a record player to play music on since you used to listen to it so much before, well, before . . ."

And I finished it for him, I was staring at the box but I finished it, I said, "Before David was killed."

"Yeah. I'll get the knife."

I didn't look at him when he came back. The words were still too loud in the air. *Before David was killed.* They wouldn't go away.

He started to slit the tape holding the box closed when I realized it was David who had all the records, I didn't have any records, and I couldn't ask to get any of his, I had already said too much. *Before David was killed.*

Dad set the record player up in my room so it was "all ready to go," he said. But since she was in her room already, he didn't get one of their records out from the living room. Or the next day either, and then it got too late to ask. David had gone all the way to Albany to get most of his records. Even in Cartsdale, you'd be real lucky to find anything good, he said, like the Coasters, you'd never find *them* there.

I waited a whole week without a record. It was getting worse and worse with her. She called me "my little witch" or sometimes just "*the* little witch." Mostly, I didn't even know it was going to happen. All of a sudden, I'd see her mouth turn and her voice would harden but then she'd stop after only two or three words and take a deep breath in and then you could see by the way she held her mouth and her cheek that she was biting her tongue, she'd stand there and bite her tongue.

But there were times, too, that she wouldn't catch herself and she'd start screaming and screaming and then the screaming would turn into crying and then I knew it was almost over and that she wouldn't be getting dinner that night at all, it didn't matter if the food was already started on the stove. Instead, crying, she would back up away from me, she'd never ever turn her back to me, she'd face me the whole time, backing all the way into her bedroom. The picture of the man and the woman walking with all their stuff on the donkey between them, they're walking down a dirt road, that picture is in the hall right by their bedroom door and it would always be cockeyed from her running into it before she'd feel behind her for the opening, back in, and shut the door.

Dad's face would set as soon as he walked into the kitchen from work and saw she wasn't there. He never said he was mad at

me but I heard him say once as he went into her bedroom before
he closed the door, he said, "What'd she do *today*?" And he said
once to Mrs. Gallagher out in the driveway—she had just
brought over a chicken pot pie but she ended up staying for over
an hour in the kitchen trying to calm her down till Dad came
home—just as Mrs. Gallagher was getting back in her car, I
heard him say to her in a low voice, "She just drives her to it."
And Mrs. Gallagher said, "I know."

It was mainly 'cause I was too slow all the time when she
called me to do something. But then when I tried to hurry I'd do
something really stupid like put the potato peels in the wrong
sink. And once she had already started biting her tongue, she
could explode at any moment. Like waiting for the cold water to
turn hot. If she spilled something or there was something dirty in
the icebox when she opened it, she'd say, "Get me a dishrag, a
HOT one," but she didn't have to say "hot" extra loud 'cause I
knew how hot it had to be—so I could barely touch it. But it always took so long for the water to turn and she'd say, "What are
you doing over there, playing?" Even though she'd be moving
things around in the icebox, she was really just waiting and she
hated waiting more than anything, and when I couldn't stand her
waiting anymore I'd hand it to her but it would never be hot
enough and her face would turn. "I mean HOT," she'd scream,
"HOT!" and she'd throw it back but sometimes not even toward
me so I could catch it. And I had to try to hide my face in case
the smile came.

If the smile came, it was over, she'd end up in her room. I always made sure the stove was off before I went back into my
room to sit down in front of the record player. I'd spin the
turntable with my hands so I could watch it turn round and
round, first fast and then it would start to slow down and I'd keep
watching till it slowed all the way to a complete stop. And then

I'd do it again. I didn't want to think about Dad, that he would walk into the kitchen soon.

But then, it was exactly a week after I got the record player, she wasn't home when I came in from school 'cause she had gone to the doctor's and even though her appointment was always at two, the hour from two to three, she wasn't home yet.

I ran up David's stairs as fast as I could. I didn't spread out into the air like before, but still I walked in slowly, very slowly. Without a light on it was dark, but a beam of light from the window shot down onto the floor all filled with dust so it looked holy.

No one *ever* came in here. The Moonglows was still on the record player, covered with the same dust. I started to flip through his 45s, but he had two long rows of them. I quick took two from the back, I didn't try to see in the dark what they were. I knew she'd be home any minute.

I had just gotten back to my room when I heard the door and then right away, "Eudora! Eudora! I'm home." When I walked into the kitchen she said, "I'm sorry, honey, I'm sorry. I'm so sorry I'm late."

"It's okay. I'm fine." I was surprised 'cause before David, she wouldn't be here a lot of days when we came home and we'd just sit down and have cereal and toast. I never ate now after school 'cause I was worried about leaving the dish in the sink. And if she was up, I didn't go outside. I usually went right away to my room till she called.

"Are you hungry?" she said. "Want some Cheerios?"

"Yeah, okay." I couldn't figure it out, what happened. She seemed happy.

"Kenny gave me some records," I said as I sat down in front of the bowl. "In school." Even though Kenny was Roger's brother, and Roger was David's best friend, I thought it would be okay to say his name.

"That's nice," she said, getting out the milk. If Dad was getting the Cheerios out for me, I could've gotten the milk myself but I was afraid to with her 'cause I never had before and it might ruin everything, her face might turn.

"What are they?"

" 'Great Pretender.' And 'Ooby Dooby.' "

"Maybe we can all hear them," she said. "Break in your new record player. A sort of baptism," and she flipped up her arm and laughed. "We can have a drink. Make a toast to it. I'll fix you up some of your lemonade."

I couldn't imagine them listening to David's music. When he played "Ooby Dooby" for me the first time, he turned it really low so they couldn't hear it and we put our ears right up to the speaker.

When Dad came home, she made drinks. Just like before. She liked vodka and Dad liked Scotch and I always brought it out to him. I loved doing that 'cause I loved smelling how bad it was—it felt like it had really really cold air in it that you couldn't breathe in. I'd always shake my head after and Dad would smile, looking up from the paper, and he'd say, "Oh, thank you, Eudora," every time like he was surprised.

Everything was almost like before, almost, except she was a little too laughy, everything made her laugh even before she had her second drink, and it scared me.

I don't think I ever had both of them in my room before *visiting*, but they were both there now and she sat right down on the bed and Dad stood. He looked too big in there, and uncomfortable. He was never in there for more than a short time and maybe he didn't think he could actually sit down.

I sat in front of the record player with my back to them so she couldn't see the two records. The top edge of the jacket was so dusty, and I thought she'd recognize the dust, that somehow she'd know it was *his* dust. I took out "The Great Pretender" first. Just like David taught me to, so no fingerprints got on the record. I put in the spacer, made sure the record player was on 45, and then even more carefully, I picked the arm up, it didn't have a nickel taped on top like David's did, but I let the needle down perfect, it didn't scratch at all. If David saw, he would've let me do it from then on and he didn't even let Roger do it.

"To the new hi-fi!" she yelled out, but in a low voice like a man's voice, like a big fat man's voice, and she raised her drink. "To the best record player in"—she paused—"in Langdon." And then she laughed and laughed so I think even Dad was uncomfortable 'cause he said quietly, "To Eudora's record player," before he took a sip of his Scotch.

I was barely listening. It was hard to hear the music without David. But I watched the record turn, staying the same speed around and around, never slowing down to a stop. I wasn't thinking about her getting up and walking toward the music, toward me. She was standing right behind me, right over me but I wasn't thinking about her till she said in the same fat man's voice, "To the Father, Son, and Holy Ghost," and then I saw it, a stream of what looked like water, like a waterfall pouring down onto the record, bouncing onto the record as she laughed and laughed and even when Dad yelled out "Florence!" she kept laughing and she said, "I was just baptizing it. Just *cleaning* its soul," and that made her laugh even harder.

Dad was helping me clean the record off with a towel. I don't know if I was more worried about the needle or the record, that it was David's and the Platters, too, he'd be so mad, and even though I couldn't say it out loud, maybe Dad knew 'cause he kept saying, "The record will be all right. The record will be all right." And then David said in my head, *Like a broken record*, 'cause Dad kept repeating it over and over so many times, "The record will be all right," and I smiled at David but it was okay, Dad didn't see 'cause he was turning to her now, saying, "We have to eat, let's eat. You need some food."

"I don't *need* food," she said in her hard voice. I couldn't believe she was mad at *him*, she was never mad at *him*.

"The doctor said, 'Food,' that it's the main thing, remember?"

"Just like a cow. Feed me just like a cow." Her voice didn't change.

"Come on, Florence, let's just eat."

I peeked into the kitchen from behind the hall door. There was no food cooking. She sat down at the table as if she was going to be served. "Well? . . ." She looked up at Dad.

I guess Dad realized it then, that he hadn't been smelling anything. Always if she was up, out of her room, she had cooked dinner or had at least started to.

"Well?" she said again and clapped her hands. "Let's eat."

"I'll drive down to Eva's," he said.

She clapped her hands again. "What a great idea," she said. "Pizza."

"Oh, you hate pizza."

"Well, let's *all* go there." She started to get up. "I'll have chicken Parmesan. Eva always has a Parmesan. Come on, let's go." Dad didn't say anything or move either. "What's the matter?" She threw her hands up and apart. "Why can't we go?" Still, Dad didn't move.

She looked at the hall door I was standing behind. "You can come out of hiding, Eudora." It was her hard voice again. She started to walk toward the playroom and the door. "Come on. The man says eat, I eat. Just like any good cow."

Dad still didn't say anything, but he followed her to the door.

I was in the backseat. Dad and I had gotten pizza at Eva's a lot together but we had never stayed there to eat since David and she had never come with us. Sometimes Eva would put a lollipop on top of the pizza box and say, winking at me, "For the little one." She had a heavy accent, Italian, but I could still understand her. She was always in a sleeveless dress even in the winter and her arms were huge. *Like pudding,* I always thought. *They shake like pudding whenever she moves.*

We were the only people there. Eva was the waitress, too. Except on Fridays and Saturdays, Dad said, then she brought in help. She didn't have a pad to write on and I asked her why not. She didn't hear me at first. She leaned down close to my ear and I asked her again. And she smiled. "Of course I remember," she said. "You are my guests." And she raised her arms up and they seemed to float like the pudding was made of air.

She ordered chicken Parmesan, and Eva smiled and turned to Dad. "Your wife, she knows what is good, huh?"

"Two. I want two of them."

Dad stiffened. But Eva kept smiling. "Hungry, too."

"Famished," she said.

"Hunger is the best sauce," Eva said.

She looked up at Eva and smiled at her.

"We can always take it home in a doggie bag," Dad said.

She turned to him with her hard voice. "The man said eat, didn't he?"

Dad looked down. Eva turned to me. "How's my little one? Hungry, too?" I nodded.

Dad said real quick, "We'll share a pizza," but then he looked at me. "Huh? Okay? Share one?" I nodded again. "We can always take the leftover slices home, can't we?" I nodded.

"Cat got your tongue?" Eva said, smiling. I smiled back. "Ah, what a sweet little thing," she said. And I thought, *Only one of me. Only Wink.* When she left, I watched her arms. I loved seeing the pudding shake.

She drank all her water up and then she asked Dad for his 'cause he never drinks water, and her voice turned back normal again. And then after a little while Dad, too, he started talking a bit, about work. "White goods," he'd always call all the appliances. TVs, they were "brown goods" and he didn't sell them. She started laughing again and even though that made me a little nervous 'cause he wasn't saying anything that was funny, still it was better than her hard voice.

Eva brought the pizza and then she put both plates of chicken Parmesan right in front of her. "So you can compare. The cook can compare. Maybe one is better than the other, huh?" And Eva looked at her with a smile and she was smiling, too. She looked almost like before, beautiful.

But then after only a few bites, she got up out of her chair and I thought she was going to the ladies' room and maybe she meant to but she didn't go, she stood there beside the table facing us. She stayed facing us and she peed and she kept peeing, she peed a whole pee, it was running down her pants and onto her shoes and onto the floor beside the table.

Dad just sat there. And I just sat there, too. Maybe I was still chewing.

And then he got up but he didn't look at her or the pee either. He walked around her and around the pee without once looking at her and he walked up to the bar where Eva was and I watched him give her money, he was giving her money and she was nodding, like me, she kept nodding, till he was about to walk away and then she waved her hand like a shrug, like "no matter," like "it doesn't matter." And I thought then that that wave was Italian or that it had an Italian accent. Mary Peterson's mother, too, she'd do that same wave if something spilled and I thought, *I love Italian.*

She was still standing there. She wasn't smiling, she was just standing, blank, like she wasn't seeing or hearing anything. Dad came back and he took her by the elbow and said softly, "We're going now, Florence." And he walked her out. And she leaned close to him, she leaned onto his arm as he walked her slowly out. *Like a cow*, the other me said in my brain, the me that could hate. *He's leading her out and she's following like a cow.* I left my slice of pizza and got up to follow. Eva walked toward me from around the bar and she leaned down beside me, down on one knee, and she put her arms full of pudding around me. It was like having pillows full of pudding on either side of me. She said into my ear, "God will take care of His children," and then she kissed me on the cheek and squeezed me softly. And I nodded, the me that was Wink nodded.

ALL I COULD think about was when I could steal the next record. If she just stayed late at the doctor's again, I could do it. I started to practice walking without ever making the floor creak. I knew almost every place in the whole house that you either had to step down on very very slowly or you couldn't step down on at all. The hall was the worst, but whenever she called me I tried to make it out to the kitchen without making any noise, not any, and I did, too, eight times. Or if she was in her room, I'd walk the whole house over and over and time myself on the kitchen clock. My record was seventeen minutes, but I didn't mind messing up 'cause I knew I wouldn't know all the places till I messed up at least once on each of them.

The problem was I couldn't practice in David's room. And I only knew the first three steps up. I didn't dare go any higher with her in the house. The stairs were even harder than the hall but if I stayed close to the edges, they didn't creak.

She hated I didn't make noise but I didn't know it till I got in trouble for not putting away the dishwasher after I came home from school even though I didn't know I was supposed to. I *used* to do it then, but all the time she was staying in her room I waited till Dad came home from work, and I did it while he read his mail. Sometimes it was even fun 'cause I'd pretend I was in the Olympics for Dishwasher Putting Away and I'd be the announcer talking in my head about either me or my hardest competitor but I was always the winner even if I was the underdog and had to come from behind. But now that she was up again most of the time, and cooking a lot, too, she thought everything should be the same as before and she hated anything that wasn't.

I heard her open the dishwasher and I felt the knot come in my stomach even before she started screaming, "Eudora Buell! Where are you?" I always ran but then I stopped short just before I turned the corner into the kitchen and faced her. "Get this dishwasher done NOW! And I mean NOW." She wasn't only screaming, she also had the face on which meant anything I did, *any*thing would be wrong and she'd tell Dad when he got home. But what really mattered now was to hurry, do it as fast as I could and get out of there. 'Cause she'd hate me more every second I was there without the dishwasher ready for her. At least it wasn't hot, like when it was first finished and it would steam into your face when you opened the door, which actually felt good but the dishes would be so hot I had to pick them up with a towel and whenever I tried to do that fast, I'd drop one. And that could be a "final straw," that's what she always called it when she'd start backing away into her room and screaming, "You little witch," or sometimes "You little red witch" 'cause of the way my hair shines red under a light or in the sun.

I never looked at her eyes *ever* when she had the face on. I looked at the dishes in the bottom rack *hoping* I knew where everything went, that there was nothing I had to ask her about. If I just put it away and it was wrong, she'd start yelling when she was cooking, she'd yell, "People just put things wherever they want!" But the people was only me.

"*At least* get these out of here!" and she'd throw her finger into a point. "So I can *at least* get the bottom loaded." I reached for the dinner plates first, it was important to always get the dinner plates first. I could still see her finger pointing, it looked just like bone, like the skin was only a thin glove over just bone. I hated her.

And I hated having to reach in my hand to get the top dishes out while she was loading the bottom. I couldn't pull out the rack. And I had to get each dish *in between* her loading dishes into the bottom 'cause if she ever dripped rinse water from the dirty dishes onto the clean ones, it could be a last straw. Or if she was ready to load a dirty dish, and had to wait, hold it in her hand for even a second longer while I was still getting a dish out of the very back, she'd say in that same hard yelling, "Will you hurry and stop your playing!" Or, "You're CROWDING me!"

I didn't know why she was in such a hurry. No one came for dinners anymore. No one was coming except Dad. I did it though, I got it all out without making a last straw. There were only two problems. A big pan lid I didn't know where to put 'cause it wasn't round like the others, and a jar I couldn't put on the basement shelf yet 'cause it didn't have a top to match. I knew not to ask, so I put them both on the kitchen table till I finished the silverware basket which I had just put on the counter to get it out of there. *After the silverware, then I can ask*, I thought.

But I didn't see the pan top leaking out the water it had in its lid, leaking onto the table and just a little dripped to the floor. I didn't see it, and she did, but I did see, for just a second, I saw her eyes before the screaming came. "What do you think you're do-ing, helping? You think you're helping? Get a rag! Now! A Turk-ish towel. Now!" She threw her point, her witch finger to the utility closet where the rag box was but I had already started to run in there, even though running didn't help 'cause I didn't know what a Turkish towel was, I knew it wasn't a sheet rag she uses for windows, but I still guessed wrong, I got the wrong rag and there was just a tiny bit of water but it was running toward the cabinets 'cause the floor sloped that way. She was still loading the dishwasher, she didn't stop. I knew when she turned, the rag was wrong. "Turkish towel! I said Turkish towel! Not flannel!" I ran back in even though it was dumb, I still didn't know what it was. *I hate you I hate you I hate you.* I didn't stop for a second saying it in my brain or there'd be a little space I could cry through. But she could tell, 'cause she said when I came back in, "There you go again, setting your jaw," which was how she knew I was mean, she said. She knew that under my jaw I wanted her back in her room, I wanted *her* to be the one that was dead.

I was holding the rag a little behind me, I didn't want her to see it, I knew it was wrong. The little bit of water had already reached the cabinets and if she had to stop loading to get herself the rag, that was definitely a last straw. She was looking down, I had to show it to her. I kept myself from her eyes, I didn't look even near her eyes. "Agh!" She threw up her arms. She wasn't loud then. "You are despicable, just despicable!" It was her disgusted voice. "I'm disgusted with you" was the next thing she'd say. I had made a last straw. Her words came slow then, like she had just given up. "Get out of here. Just get out." And I did.

It was better than when she hit me 'cause if I ducked, she'd hit me twice so I had to hold my head straight up and close my eyes so I didn't duck when I saw her hand come for my face. It meant, though, that when Dad got home, she'd tell him and he was supposed to hit me for her. He never did though. "Later," he'd always say. And she'd say back, "I know you, Michael. You'll just chicken out." But no matter what she said, he never hit me. And if he went out to the garage for something, I'd run out there and try to say what really happened and that I didn't mean it. But as soon as I started, he'd say "*shh shh*" and he'd start nodding, "I know I know," and then even if she was already in bed, he'd whisper like she could hear, "Let it go right over. Let it go right over." His hand would shoot back over his head each time. "Just let it go right over." But he'd never ever say that in front of her.

In my room I could cry but I didn't, I sat in front of the record player and turned it, it was even better than my spot, it was my new spot. I could hear her, I strained to hear her, in her tired, disgusted voice. "Mean. Just plain mean. You're just a little witch, that's what you are, a little witch." And that's when I heard it: "Sneaking around here. Never making any noise, just sneaking around. A sneak. That's all you are, a sneak. And if there's anything I hate, it's a sneak!"

From then on, I started walking loud. In between my practice, when I wouldn't make even the slightest noise, I'd step regular or louder than regular. After being so quiet, it seemed like I was stomping on the floor but I wanted to make sure she could hear me and know I wasn't sneaking.

But on Tuesday, something happened when I was in school. Dad wouldn't tell me what it was but he was there when I got home just to tell me he was going back to the doctor's to talk and that's where she was, and that she was okay, he kept saying, she was okay, but she was still at the doctor's even though it was Tuesday and her appointments were always Monday, Wednesday, and Friday. I hid my face from Dad 'cause I knew the smile would come. "Do you want me to get you some Cheerios?" he asked. "Before I go?" and I shook my head, hiding my face. I was happy 'cause I could go up to David's room and for a while, too, I could find the records he had taught me to hear. Chuck Berry. "School Day" and "Maybellene" and the Dells and Jerry Lee Lewis.

I didn't hear the door with the music on. The first thing I heard was Dad in the hall coming toward my room. I quickly turned the sound as low as it went even before he leaned in through the doorway and turned a volume knob off in the air. "Everything has to be extremely quiet," he whispered and put his finger to his lips. I nodded and turned the record player completely off. I was slipping the record into the jacket when I heard her say from the kitchen, in a voice that wasn't like hers at all, it was so low and so deep and tired, very very tired, she said, "I can't live with that noise." I heard her moving. She was walking slowly. She walked down the hall and passed my door like it wasn't there. I watched her through the doorway, I watched her back move away from me, move toward her room. I saw it drop, like she let out a breath, her shoulders and her back dropped when she moved into her room. *It was her spot,* I thought, *her home, and us, even Dad, both of us were still outside.*

SHE DIDN'T COME out for three days and it seemed like Dad lived in there with her when he came home from work. And then the first night she was out, she scared me. Just standing by the icebox talking to Dad about the mail, she was talking so quietly, like it was almost too hard to make herself heard, and then right in the middle, she didn't even finish, she stared off and as her face turned, I saw, from the corner of the kitchen, I saw her eyes. They looked fake, like they were made of glass. She wasn't coming out of them anymore, not even to see.

I went into the bathroom and looked into my eyes. I wanted to see what eyes were. It was the water in them, that's what it was. Her eyes looked dry. Her eyes were always so full of water before and now they didn't have any, they were dry. I squeezed my eyes over and over to pump up as much water as they could hold. I wanted them as full as they could be. I wanted them to look like they could overflow any moment.

The next day her eyes had a little more water. She started talking louder and she didn't yell at all either. She even started cooking dinners again. I started playing the records after school, but first real real quietly. Each day, I turned it up just a little and then I'd wait to see if it was okay. I thought of maybe asking Peggy over again like before, when I used to have Peggy or Mary Beth sleep over.

I'd only play one record a day. I had gotten twelve. And I had an answer ready in case she asked me where I got them but she never asked and she never asked me to help anymore before dinner either. I still did the dishwasher and right after school, too, but she got dinner by herself so I didn't do anything wrong.

I loved it. I didn't even care anymore that I didn't go outside. As soon as the music started, I didn't want to be anywhere else, not even on Wink. I'd close my eyes and then I could hear David listening and telling me out loud what he heard and then I heard it, too, I could hear him hearing the music as long as my eyes were closed.

That's when she came in. Dinner was over and it was after dark but before I had to go to bed. I was lying there and listening so hard and so good, it was "Suzie Q" on, I didn't hear her come in. I didn't even hear her walk over to the record player and lift the needle up. I heard only the music stop. I sat up. She clicked off the record player and stood back up, looking at me.

"I know they're David's," she said and she raised her arm to stop me from speaking. "I know. You don't have to lie. I know they're David's." I tried to speak again but she put her arm up. "It's okay. It's okay. He'd want them used. It's okay." She was shaking her head. "Especially by you. *Especially* you." She wasn't smiling but her eyes were full of water again. I loved her again. "It's okay. Really. It *is*." But then she walked out of my room. I stared where she had just stood, near the record player, where she had just left. It was so empty right there and so quiet. And then it spread, the quiet spread into my whole room, it started to come in on me, it was creeping into me.

I wanted to run, run outdoors where it's never quiet. Or watch TV, I wanted to have a TV in my head, a permanent TV I could turn on, I hated it, the quiet. I hated it. It was like him, like David on the metal table when I was squeezing, when I was hurting his toe, trying to hurt his toe, I couldn't hurt his toe, he wouldn't even hurt! He wouldn't do anything! I was killing him as hard as I could and he wouldn't do anything!

I got to the record player. I turned it back on but the quiet wouldn't go away. I turned it louder and louder but the quiet still stayed in my brain, it was all over everywhere in my brain and everywhere in my room. I closed my eyes, I tried to hear again what David would hear, the bass, I tried to hear the bass, it had become easy for me to hear the bass, but I couldn't, all I could hear was the quiet. I turned the music up louder and louder, as loud as it would go but it didn't help. I started screaming, I was screaming for David, he would get the quiet away, get it out of there, but he didn't come and it stayed, it stayed there even after she ran in to the room. I saw her run in. I was in front of the turning record, and I saw her eyes, they were beautiful, they were full of water, and I saw her one hand grab the cord and then the other hand flashed, bright like silver. They were scissors, her hand had scissors and they moved quick like swords, like little magic swords but then they stopped. They stopped against the cord and her hand closed down hard and it went dark, everything went dark except the music that wound down like someone sick dying before it was over, it went dark, too. I heard myself say his name, I said "David" one more time, I tried once more, but he didn't come. Even in the dark. The quiet crushed in on me, it was about to reach me, press me flat into nothing. But it didn't, her hands pulled me, they pulled me toward her next to me on the floor, toward her breathing, and they started to squeeze me. Her hands and her arms, too, squeezed every bit of quiet out of me and the dark that was left everywhere, inside me and outside me, all of the dark filled up with her breathing.

THE NEXT MORNING, Dad woke me up late, at quarter of, but he was all dressed. "Mommy's sick," he said. It was his serious tone, his David tone. He had driven her to the hospital that night, to Burtrum General, and he'd just gotten back. He said the word "stay" then. "She'll have a short stay." But it was over a month, four and a half weeks. She was gone when I beat Peggy again by just an inch on Field Day and still gone two days later when school let out for the summer.

Mrs. Gallagher came every day to make sure I was all right and that I ate a good lunch and when she said "good" she made a fist. She usually brought a casserole for us for dinner, too, and sometimes she vacuumed and dusted.

But then one day, almost a month into summer vacation, Mrs. Gallagher came in with crayons and some paper plates. "Today's the day!" she said, but I already knew 'cause Dad had just called. He still wasn't sure at breakfast. "Keep your fingers crossed," he said when he left for work. Mrs. Gallagher sat down at the kitchen table and wrote out WELCOME on one plate and HOME on another in big curly letters. She used blue first, then went over all the letters in green and then she added purple, too, so they were all fat and touching each other. She wanted me to draw faces on the plates but I told her I couldn't draw well, which was the truth, too, David was the one who could draw. "That doesn't matter," she said. "It's the thought that counts." But I just kept shaking my head till she said "Okay" and drew red hearts instead all around the outside. After Mrs. Gallagher Scotch-taped the two plates onto the playroom door, I knew *she* wouldn't like them. The hearts looked like they were floating in a white sea, like they were trying to get nearer the land where all the curly colors were.

When she came home, it looked like she was just visiting us 'cause she was carrying a little suitcase and Dad was behind her carrying a bigger one. I was glad Mrs. Gallagher was there 'cause she walked right up to the car and kissed and hugged her as soon as they got out. I followed behind Mrs. Gallagher and *she* leaned down to hug me.

"How's my Eudora? My little Eudora?" she whispered into my ear, her cheek was right up against mine.

"Good," I said, but it sounded funny, like she was just another adult. "It's *her*," I said in my brain as she stood back up again. But I didn't dare look at her eyes, I didn't want to look at her eyes, just in case.

I didn't look at them for three days. I waited till her voice got louder, up to normal, and till her hands stopped shaking. It was just after Dad left and I was finished breakfast and just about to walk by her to go outside. She was standing by the phone in her bathrobe, just standing there. I looked up at her eyes, quick, real quick, to see if they had the water in them. I didn't even know she saw me.

"What are you looking at, Miss?" she snapped toward me. She hadn't ever called me "Miss" before.

"Your eyes," I said, looking down. I wanted to lie, but I couldn't, there wasn't enough time to think.

"What? Speak up!"

"Your eyes," I said, louder, still looking down.

"Why? Why? Huh?" She had the face on. I didn't know she was going to snap 'cause she hadn't shown any signs, not any. She seemed happy all through breakfast. "You want to see what they've done to me! Huh? Huh? You want to see what they've done!"

I shook my head. "No," I said. "No." I didn't look back up.

"Huh? You want to see? You want to see?"

I tried to turn away but she grabbed my shoulders and squatted down so her face was right in front of mine. Then both her hands locked onto my head and held my face hard, pointed my face right at hers, right at her eyes. "You want to see?"

"No," I said again, "I don't. I don't wanna see." I squeezed my eyes shut.

"Look!" she said. "You asked for it. Now look. Open your eyes." Her voice was so hard. "Look!"

I did. She was staring right into me, her eyes were wide wide open, staring right into me.

"Are you happy now? See them? See them? Are you happy now?"

I tried to turn away again but she held my face, she wouldn't let my face turn. "You asked for it," she said, more hoarsely now, "so look. Take a good lo-ong look." And then almost under her breath, she said, "Look what they've done to me."

There was no water in them. I swallowed. And then she fell toward me, onto me. "Oh God!" She started to cry, she was on her knees crying and hugging me, holding on to me. "What's left?" she said. "What's left of me?"

"I don't know," I said. I couldn't lie. I couldn't say her eyes were just the same. I couldn't. "I don't know," I said again. I put my hands on her back. It was shaking.

"Oh dear, my dear, of course you don't. Of course you don't. How could you?" And she stroked my hair. "How could you possibly know?" Her back kept shaking under my hands. *That's where the water is,* I thought. *It's stuck down in her back.*

"I'm sorry," I said, "I won't look again."

"Oh, sweetie." Then she whispered very very softly, "I can't explain it. I just can't." And she backed her face up from me and looked at me but I didn't look at her eyes. There were no tears running down her cheeks. She was crying without tears. I looked at her lips, her plain lips that had no lipstick.

"Someday I'll be able to tell you everything. Okay?" I watched her mouth open and close. I watched the words come out one after the other. They seemed like little birds taking off from her mouth and flying across the air so they could land on me.

"Someday," she said again. "When you're grown."

I just kept nodding, looking at her lips. I wanted them to open again so I could see her white teeth.

IT WAS ABOUT a week after. She had gotten worse again, she didn't come out for breakfast, and one morning Dad called Mrs. Gallagher to see if he could drop me at her house for dinner in case she had to go back to the hospital. But I guess they decided she didn't have to go 'cause she stayed in her room.

I put the TV on low enough so I knew she couldn't hear it and I sat up close to it so when they showed the cowboy—I didn't know his name, I missed the title, but he was all dressed in black, an outlaw probably, but he was who the show was about 'cause they were showing just his head on the screen with the wind blowing his hair and I was close enough to put my hand right over his face—I covered his whole face and it looked like his hair was blowing out of my hand.

Then he turned and walked away, over dirt, everything was so bare you could hardly tell it was a road, and he kept walking away toward a tiny house way far away against the sky. Just his boots walking filled the whole screen.

But then a pioneer woman came out the door of the tiny house and the man in black held out some coins that she just stared down at and then he said the words, "This'll pay for my food the first week, ma'am. Then I'm mighty willin' to do chores for my keep."

I heard her slippers on the kitchen floor, *she* had come out. I went to turn the sound off quick, but just before I did, he said his name, "Shane."

I liked watching him work without the sound. He chopped wood and then he carried water and the woman was always smiling and she dished up food that steamed when it hit the plate and I could tell he said, "Thank you, ma'am," as he tucked the napkin into his shirt. Then he was swinging a sledgehammer over his head onto a fence post and a small boy peeked out at him from behind a rock. But then the boy ran back to his mom where she was hanging out the wash and they both stood very still, her hand on his shoulder, facing out at what was coming. First, all you could see was dust but it turned into the sheriff and his posse riding up on horses. None of them could ride at all, their elbows were flapping away like they were a bunch of chickens and their hands were way too high.

A commercial came on and I heard them again, the words. I didn't know till then but the whole time the sound was off, the words were going over and over in my brain. *This'll pay for my food the first week, ma'am. Then I'm mighty willin' to do chores for my keep.*

I wrote them down on a little piece of paper and each night I said them over and over to myself. I put the words in my pocket when I put my pants on every morning but I didn't need to, I remembered them. I practiced walking in the pasture to some point I'd pick out, the apple tree or just the edge of the creek bank, or the wild patch of dame's rocket she used to pick for arrangements, and when I'd reach it, I'd stop, hold out my hand, and say the words out loud. I had to hold my breath in while I was saying them to get my voice as deep as I could, like Shane's.

David had given me a pair of cowboy boots and they still fit me. I hadn't worn them, I just threw them in the back of the closet 'cause they made me think of the Western riders barrel racing down at Cairo. Mrs. Peterson and me hated them 'cause of how they rode their horses, jerking on their mouths, hootin' and hollerin', and waving their hats over their horses' rumps. But Shane would never hoot and holler. And he was actually really good even though he was an outlaw and had to keep leaving wherever he was, even the woman's and boy's place he had to leave 'cause he was wanted. It was probably not even his fault he was wanted.

I started wearing the boots instead of my sneakers and I kept both arms down and a little out from my sides when I walked and I kept my head up so I could look off to where I was heading. I'd squint as if I were going a long way off, some place I could barely see.

It felt like only a silly game but I'd still do it to make the days pass quicker, especially in the morning after Dad left for work and she was still in her room and it seemed like the day was gonna last a year. But then my tooth came loose, it was my last one and after that it didn't feel dumb at all 'cause when I pushed on it hard with my tongue, I could feel just like Shane as soon as I started walking out in the pasture. My jaw was set how she says it is when I'm mean but like his is all the time 'cause nothing could stop him from walking. And it wasn't 'cause I was mean anyway, I was pushing against my tooth with my tongue hard. Once I started pushing I couldn't stop 'cause of the way it hurt, it's like a ripping and it seems like it's going to take over but the hurt stays right in its place, in its little place, and there's just enough hurt so you can't think anything else.

Then I couldn't walk as far as the creek bank anymore or the apple tree, I had to be near 'cause when she came out of her room when Dad wasn't home, she wanted me to be in the house and if I didn't come right away, instantly appear just in front of her as soon as she rang the bell, she'd have the face on and start yelling about me hiding from her.

One day I picked the edge of the garage where David smoked to walk to, but as soon as I reached it and held out my hand, before I got to say the words, the quiet came back. It creeped in and I hated it, I pushed against my tooth harder and harder, it was holding on by one last string. I pushed the hurt farther than I ever had just to get the quiet out of me, and I did, but then it snapped, the tooth broke loose and I needed it back to push against. I rolled it around in my mouth as if it could still hurt but it didn't and the quiet came over me again.

I heard the bell. I knew it was about the dishwasher. I didn't do the dishwasher, I forgot. I went outside as soon as Dad left and then I forgot again after lunch, which was just anytime I got hungry, I'd make a peanut butter and jelly sandwich and I'd clean up all the crumbs perfect and rinse out the dishrag and put my plate in the sink and it would be okay, she wouldn't mind that Dad left the jars and bread out on the counter for me. I didn't even think about it, I went right outside again. It must have been three o'clock or four 'cause that's when she'd usually come out unless she waited till Dad came home. I held the tooth under my tongue like I was saving it there. I didn't want to take it out of my mouth yet.

I ran in. She wasn't in the kitchen. I started putting away the dishes as fast as I could, maybe I could get it all done before she walked in. But then I heard her, her slippers on the hall rug, maybe it was her bathrobe, too, swishing as she walked. *Like that skirt*, I thought. The woman's skirt that blew in the wind against the red sun. But then she walked into the kitchen from the hall and the air around her was so still, so windless, I smiled even with the tooth in my mouth 'cause how silly it was, seeing the wind and the sky and the posse, and it was just her in her blue bathrobe and her slippers coming into the kitchen.

I put my head down quick, she might think it was the bad smile, but she saw it and it didn't matter, her voice was completely normal. "We're having ham for dinner. You want peas or corn with it?"

"Ummmmmm, corn," I said and it didn't sound like I was holding a tooth in my mouth. Her voice made the quiet disappear.

She walked over to the sink and put on the cold and felt it with her finger. She was always drinking water now, sometimes two glasses, one right after the other, and she'd stand there with the water running over her finger, she'd wait for as long as it took, which was a long time, for the water to get really cold, as cold as it could get.

We were going to have a real dinner. We hadn't for a long time, since way before she went into the hospital and not at all since she'd been home. Maybe she was getting better. I hated what Mrs. Gallagher cooked 'cause they were always casseroles with everything all mixed up. "Muddy," *she* said once to Father Bob. "People make food all muddy, just throwing things in." And he said, "Yes! Yes! They mask it, the flavor of what they're cooking, they don't *bring it out!*" He was so excited. I didn't know till just then that I missed having dinners, and her asking me what I wanted.

I started announcing in my brain. I was way ahead of everyone else in the Dishwasher Putting Away Championships and I had only the top to do and that was easy, especially with the rack all the way out. *In the home stretch*, the announcer said. I felt happy, real happy. The quiet was gone and we were having a real dinner and her voice was normal and I was holding the tooth and winning. But then I dropped it, the Blue Willow sugar bowl, and I heard it, too, break, both the handles were broken off and part of the rim where the top sits. I couldn't see where one handle went, it must have shot under the dishwasher but the other handle was like a little C, a little kitten curled up next to the bowl. I stared at it and I shouldn't have 'cause the quiet moved in on me. David was the gluer, the one who glued things that broke, good things and anything Blue Willow. The quiet moved in all around me, like a dream is all around you when you're in it, and like how you can do bad things in a dream, I stepped down on it hard, on what was left, on the bowl, and I crunched it under my boot. I liked it, too, 'cause how it sounded and how it felt crunching under my boot. It was like the tooth, how I couldn't stop 'cause I liked it ripping, it was the same, I couldn't stop, I stepped on each piece that wasn't all the way broken just so I could feel it crunch again under my foot.

When I looked up, she was staring at me, but I was in the quiet, it was all around me, like a blanket of air all around me, nothing could reach me, even her. Even when she said "Face me," in her hardest voice, I did 'cause nothing could reach me, I didn't duck when she hit me, my face stayed completely straight without my even holding it, and she hit me again, and I didn't duck again and I thought, *She's not waiting for Dad.* And I spit out my tooth onto my palm and held it out to her. I thought it was a gift I was holding out to her but then it came, I could feel it come over my face, the smile, it curled the side of my mouth up and it was the bad smile, I knew, and I looked at the tooth and I knew it was bad, too, but it was too late, she saw it, I couldn't take it back, she saw it and she saw the smile, and her face turned, her mad face turned into a face I had never seen, and I thought she was backing away from me again, backing toward her room, but she didn't, she sat down on the floor, she was holding herself on the floor and then she curled onto her side and covered her head with her arms. The quiet broke and I screamed, "Mom! Mom!" but she didn't look out from under her arms. I tried to pull them away from her face but they were too strong. I kept screaming, "Mom!" but she didn't say anything, not even a cry and she didn't move an inch till Dad walked in and knelt down over her and she rolled onto her back and he held her elbows tight to her sides and the veins popped out in his hands each time the jolts ran through her body, they shook even her feet. It wasn't till way later that he let go and she said the words. There were three of them. "Her or me." And I said, way underneath my breath, I said, "Me."

I WAS WAITING in my bed, waiting to leave. I had already packed. As soon as I heard the words, the three words, I packed. I found a little square suitcase from their old set in the back of the hall closet. It was the same size as the new one she'd carried in from the hospital.

I could see in the dark the large shapes my legs made under the blanket, and for just a second, I wanted to go into her bed and kiss her and say good-bye and give her a present and get one, too, but it was just a second. I was only her size for just a second.

And I didn't need her to give me a present, I had one already. I packed it first, on the very bottom, her book. *Dear Heart's Sonnets.* We had always known she was writing poems but even David didn't know she sent a whole group away to be published into a book in New York City. It wasn't till we walked in one day from school and she was dancing to her favorite music—Glenn Miller—and she danced up to us both and sang to us, over the song's words and not at all with the music, she sang, "It's finished! It's finished!" And she waved her book of sonnets around. It had come to her in the mail and the brown paper and the string were still on the kitchen table where she had ripped the package open, she didn't wait even to throw the paper away, she put the music on and started dancing, holding her book to her cheek like it was Dad's face.

And that night Dad put *The Best of Glenn Miller* on the record player and they danced together in the living room and drank champagne. David was looking at the record jacket and I was looking, too, but then, because of their faces, we didn't stay in the room. We watched them from just behind the dining room door. Their faces were right together, touching and resting on each other's shoulder, but her eyes were wide wide open and Dad's were closed. They were swaying back and forth back and forth till all of sudden he picked up his head and whipped her around and she was smiling 'cause he caught her again, and his fingers spread out on her back so that between them her shiny blue blouse bunched up like waves.

There were nine books, and Dad and David and me, we all got our very own copies and Dad made a big deal getting a special pen for her to sign them and David talked into the saltshaker again and made her appear on *The Ed Sullivan Show* but all she could do was laugh even when he just asked her where she lived. But she got very serious when she opened the first book to write her name for Dad and he turned to us and put his finger to his mouth, *shh*, and we were both quiet as she wrote. Under the black print that said

PUBLISHED
FOR LOVERS EVERYWHERE

she wrote, *For mine. Yours.* And after Dad kissed her on the forehead, he made her sign her name, her whole name, *Florence Benham Buell*, right under where it was already printed on the title page.

And then she did David's and then mine and she stayed very serious for each one though she said the same thing in both books on the very first page, which was all blank. *For my own David. For my own Eudora. Love forever and ever, Mother (Mom).* And then she turned to the title page and signed, and on David's, her signature touched just the edge of the two printed *l*'s, but on mine, she wrote right over, right through the big black letters. And then, all at once, as if a spell had broken, she laughed.

Some days, especially in the spring, she used to write sitting on a little stool out in her garden. If we saw her there when we came home from school, sitting with her pen and her notebook, we wouldn't even wave, we'd go right in and have our toast and cereal. But this year, she didn't even go out to see the red tulips that she planted last fall in a heavy rain just so the bulbs wouldn't have to wait one more day in the garage and maybe mildew. Even when Dad picked one and brought it in to her, she looked up at him and said, "Is this one of mine?" and he nodded yes and she didn't take it, she rolled her head away from him, in toward the back of the couch. He put it in a glass of water though and she hated that it was just a glass, so later when she was up, she climbed on a chair to reach the very top shelf in the kitchen where she keeps vases and she picked out a small thin one and put the tulip in the center of the table. But Dad didn't bring any more in, even though there must have been fifty blooming at once, and they stayed, too, getting more and more open each day, the petals didn't fall onto the ground for it seemed a month.

She never went this year to Tappen's Greenhouse to get what she called her "usual"—petunias, pansies, and geraniums—even though she'd always come home with more, 'cause she could never say no to new colors, especially dark purple. She'd bring home anything that was dark purple. Every single time, she would complain she had gone hog-wild, and now, how could she possibly plant it all? And then she'd plant right into the night under the porch light. First, her hanging baskets, then her planters and her pots, and then she'd stick "the leftovers," she called them, into her garden where the perennials were or in front of her roses.

But now, there was nothing on the porch. All the pots were still stacked up in the back of the garage. And in her garden, there were big blotches of empty dirt. Most of the perennials were all finished blooming and were brown because she never went out and cut off the old flowers. Only some of the roses were blooming, and the phlox. She loved phlox, even though each year she'd say, "They'll take over if you let them." Still, she would cut them and bring them in and smell them.

But she didn't love anything as much as peonies. She loved them more than even her roses, 'cause how big the blossoms were and how they smelled, and before, before David, as soon as they'd start to bloom, she would keep a huge vase of them in the center of the table. When one wilted, she'd take it out and add a different one so the colors were always changing little by little till they were all completely different from the first flowers but one was always older, almost wilted and ready to go out, and some were brand new. She picked a few "still in the bud," is how she said it, so she could watch them open. "You just can't have too many peonies," she'd always say. But no one brought any in for her this year.

It was almost time. I wanted to leave at midnight to make sure Dad would be completely asleep. I was all ready. My cowboy boots and my dungarees and sweatshirt were in my spot and my suitcase was under my bed.

I didn't have a place I could head to yet but neither did the man in black when he first would leave, he just walked away and kept walking till something appeared to him on the horizon and it wasn't till when he saw it that he knew where he was walking to.

I made it outside without a sound even with my boots on. I'd practiced so long not making any noise, it was easy now. And I was real careful closing the door. I looked at the road. I had forgotten about the streetlights. Even though there was only one real street to Langdon and no one was ever on it this late at night, except maybe a truck passing through, still there were streetlights. What if a car did come and they saw me, just a kid, under the light?

I stopped by her garden. I could only really see the white phlox. The dark pink and the purple phlox and the red roses that were left, they looked black, darker black than the leaves all around them. I picked up two handfuls of dirt from a place left empty in the front of the bed. I closed my eyes and splashed it like water over my face and then I picked up more dirt and rubbed it in to make my skin dark and easy to hide if I saw any lights. I could hide on the side of the road in the weeds. "Flowers in the wrong place," she used to say, "that's all weeds are." And then she'd name whatever she saw that was blooming.

I used to call her Mama Mountain when she would lie in bed curled under the thick covers. Her legs and her back, her shoulders, made all the hills that in some places were so steep they fell into the narrow valleys and hollows, but there were places, too, where the hills rolled down little by little onto the plains at the foot of the bed. There were gorges everywhere, and dead ends, and folds where rivers began.

When she shifted, it seemed the whole world was falling apart, and the bears and the big cats and the wolves, they'd run and run and run and even after she stopped moving, they'd run more till they found new hills with thick woods they could roam through and caves, too, they could hide in.

PART II

AUGUST 1958

BEULAH:

"Whatever come when the joe-pye weed's out, stays." Grandma was talkin' about sickness and all us girls knew never to get sick or even hurt when those dusty-rose blossoms, looked like a head full of seeds, went feathery. But *she* come right to our door and our front door, too—that ain't never used 'cept by the Jehovah's Witnesses, got orange daylilies growin' out of the stone step—she come right up the stone to that front door.

Tappen had just headed out to the barn and I was settin' down for my mornin' coffee when I heard the little knock. It didn't seem like nothin' much till it come again, not any louder but not stoppin' neither till finally I says, "That ain't no animal scrapin'." There hadn't been a soul come through that door in years but I didn't go to the back and yell "Come around!" I give it a good pull. And that little knock kept right on steady while I was pullin' and pullin' till I feel the bottom give, sounded like a icebox openin', and there she was, just standin' in the mornin' dark with the dirtiest face I ever seen. And the first thought come to me was, *The joe-pye weed's featherin'.*

She look up at me but she don't say a word. "Aren't you the little Buell girl?" I say but she don't say "yup" or nod, even. Instead she put her head down and walk in through the door like she's on a rope, one tiny cowboy boot goin' right front of the other, the little pointy toes pokin' out from her dungarees. She go right to the kitchen. She was holdin' a square vanity case must've come from her mother. And she got two big bulges comin' from her pockets and I say, "What you got in there, honey?" But she don't say nothin'. I don't push. I pull out a chair and she set the case down real careful. I say, "You come all that way—you must be mighty hungry." And I don't wait, I get out the Cheerios and milk and I feed her one, two, three bowls and after the third bowl she leans her body back from the table, she only take up the edge of the chair, and she goes into them pockets and pulls out quarters and more quarters and she lines 'em up in eight stacks on the table, eight dollars of quarters, and she says in a voice too low for her size, she says, "That'll pay for my food the first week, ma'am. Then I'm mighty willin' to do chores for my keep."

Now there were some things I knew right off. First that this was no accident she landed here even though there was no reason to it neither, at least that I could see. We're in Sweet Hollow, eight miles from Langdon, and dead end at that. Everyone knew hers was a troubled family ever since the boy got killed but I didn't know how bad it had grown.

And so I says, "If you're gonna do chores, you'd better be gettin' some rest." I take her up to the front bedroom next to Laureen's 'cause it's the quietest if Tappen starts on the north side of the new greenhouse. I pull the sheets back and she says, in a voice even lower than before, "I'll sleep right here on the floor, ma'am. I wouldn't wanna wreck your sheets." And I says, "No sirree! I have never let a cowboy sleep on the floor." And she get in under the

blanket and I don't say a word about them boots and filthy dungarees she keeps on.

I leave the room and I can't think of what that child's name is,
though I must've heard it plenty, all them times she come along
with her ma for flowers and at the service they done for the boy. I
walk straight out to the barn and tell Tappen in ten minutes he's
gotta be inside ready to talk. I give her ten minutes but she was
asleep by the time I got back in, I snuck a look. And Laureen, too,
my five-year-old, she was still sleepin', too. Popsy, he wake up
early but it take him till almost nine to get out of bed and down
the stairs and he don't hear nothin' much.

Tappen come into the kitchen and I'm fussin' here and there
and he knows sump'n big is up and for two reasons: Things were
gettin' clean *and* he had to come in, I didn't talk out there, in
his land.

I says, "We got trouble."

He says, "Whose is he?" He straighten his back up from the
sink though he ain't finished scrubbin' his hands.

"So when did you see her?" I say.

"Comin' up the driveway. It's a girl? Didn't see no hair."

I hand him the brown towel before he grab the red and white.
"She's gotta be the Buell girl. It's pulled back in a ponytail."

"She don't talk?"

I glare at him.

"Well, if you know, how come you ain't called them yet?"
he says.

"A girl don't run that easy. And she's been plannin', got a suitcase even."

"Ain't you ever gone with a suitcase?"

"And eight miles outta town and up our hill, I just don't see . . .
and filthy. Now, there is something big goin' on and—"

"Well, we gotta call." He stay leanin' against the sink pickin' his calluses, like the "we" means *me*.

I says, "Go ahead."

He says, "Now Beulah, you ain't thinkin a hidin' her."

"You can use a phone good as me."

"And with people comin' up here buyin' plants all day?"

"Go ahead. You wanna call."

Tappen move slow to the phone. Even slower pickin' it up. "Gladys? Tappen. I need the Buells down in Langdon.

"They ain't, huh? Well then, give me Esker.

"Jimmy? Clay Tappen here. You missin' someone? ... Yut. Wouldn't be the little Buell girl, now would it? ... Right here, yut. ... This mornin'. Walked right up. ... That's right. ... Okay, yut. We ain't goin' nowhere."

Tappen hang up the phone. I don't say a word. He knows though, I ain't emptyin' the drainboard for nothin'. It don't have any good pots in it though. Only dishes ain't good for slammin'. Poor little thing walked all night.

"Well, you ain't thinkin' of keepin' her."

"Well, I ain't thinkin' of Jimmy Esker drivin' her off in that car of his, probably turn on the siren, screech through town."

"You think a kid can just set down where she want and start livin' like she ain't just a kid? Think if it was Laureen."

"It's probably all over town already, like she's a outlaw. ... And it ain't a *flat* eight miles neither." The drainboard's empty so I move in on the sink and Tappen move off to lean against the icebox. I start in on the silverware that's always left in the bottom of the sink. "Laureen ... she'll never run, she ain't the type. And I sure wouldn't want Esker savin' her."

"Esker is all we got."

"All we got! All *you* got, you mean." I'm pointin' a spoon at him but I sure wished it was a knife I was holdin'. "My God, she's just a little thing, a tiny thing, not a whole lot bigger 'n Laureen! And she's fast asleep and you think we need the name of the Law comin' through here, his belly rollin' on in front like, like . . . he's ridin' it to glory."

Tappen turn and walk out.

"You're crazy as Esker."

He don't like bein' called crazy, and he don't like I compared him with Esker. And he don't like bein' in the house when he's got a argument on his hands ain't goin' his way.

I don't follow him out there, but I do yell after him, "Probably come carryin' a gun, too, like at the church suppers."

He keeps walkin' and I don't know who to call to make sure Esker don't come. I don't stick with the silverware. I move the toaster out from the wall, clean all the crumbs dropped below it. Then I start on the legs of the drainboard, the mildew that's built up, then I go to the windowsill and move the pile of little strings I got there and the pile of rubber bands, too, and I dust everything. I got pins, safety pins, straight pins, bobby pins on the right side and I move all them, too, makin' sure I don't drop none, and I'm glad of the little dust balls 'cause it make it seem right, then, to be cleanin'. At least as right as just settin' on the fact that a runaway child is sleepin' upstairs, just settin' on that and waitin'. Waitin' rather than rushin' off callin' Esker. "What do we do? What do we do?" Like that is the only question in the world that means sump'n. And like if sump'n ain't done NOW, the world's gonna blow. And ain't nothin' would blow but the men, they can't set on nothin' without blowin'. The pins was all back so I grab the broom and I'm cleanin' between the icebox and the counter findin' lots of stuff, enough Cheerios for a bowl. I've a good mind to give Tappen a bowl of that for his next breakfast. Oh and

Esker, give him a chance and boy, he'll run right inside a Western faster 'n you can say. Yup, Old Big Gun puff up right into
John Wayne. Yeah, he'd like to save Laureen all right—give her
about ten years. I was almost done with the broom scrapin' down
the cobwebs alongside the icebox, in the inch between the two
walls, when I feel maybe Laureen was woke up. I turn around,
but there *she* is instead in the doorway.

I say, "You ain't done much sleepin'."

"Want me to chop some wood for you, ma'am?"

I say, "Nope, but you can go for a bucket of water." Like I was
crawlin' into the Western myself right along with her—we got water comin' right through the tap same as anybody. I hand her the
bucket I use for scrubbin' from under the sink and I say, "For the
chickens," like that explains it.

"The brook ain't far, just right side of the greenhouse." I point
to it from the door. It was so low, bein' August, I didn't know if
she could get any water into the bucket and kept there, but that's
good, I think, her bein' too little to carry much anyway.

She start over the grass holdin' her elbow up so the bucket
don't drag. I wonder if Tappen's lookin' on from his end. He's
gotta come around, though come around to what, I don't know.
But callin' Esker. At least I knowed this wasn't gonna have a easy
solution.

She come to the back door with about a third of a bucket.
Now that's pretty darn good and I tell her, too, as I lead her
toward the coop. I jerk open the gate to the run 'cause it don't
open more 'n a foot if you don't jerk it, the bottom of the frame
gets stuck against the dirt. Then you gotta jerk it to get it closed,
too. The chickens, of course, think we got a bucket of peelin's. I
pour out their tin bucket and she pours in the new water.
"There," I say, "that's a treat for 'em, water from the brook." But
the chickens don't see it as a treat, fussin' all about our legs wantin'

food. I turn around to leave so she don't notice. I lean down to take the bucket from her but she don't let go, so I start on back out the gate and she follow along.

As she hand me the bucket front of the sink, I say, "Now what name do you go by in these parts?"

She look at me, she can't be a drop over ten, and she squeak out, "Eudora." But then she says louder and deeper, "Eudora," and then, "Shane. Eudora Shane."

"Eudora Shane. . . . Ain't that a pretty name. Now are you still hungry?" and she nod and I give her her fourth bowl of Cheerios, which was the last of the box. "From now on, it's ham sandwiches, ain't too early to eat a ham sandwich, not with the miles you've traveled. You like ham?"

She nod. *Yes-and-no questions*, I think while I wipe off the counter, *stick with them and give her a breather*.

The chair scrapes and she is standin' right up, her arm stretched out straight toward the doorway. There is Tappen. He ain't tall but he's wide and he seemed even bigger with his greasy overalls on, his shoulders almost touched the doorway when he come through to the kitchen. He stretch his hand out, too, and they shake. And she says, "Your wife has been mighty kind to me, mister. I'm much obliged." Tappen can't hardly hide his smile but he try and he says, "Yup, that's her way, and what can I do for you?" She sets down and I see her swallow but she still comes out with, "Work. I'd like just a little work for my stay." Tappen nods, stands there, nods again. Then he says, "Well, we got that. You finish up eatin' and we got that. We always got work for the willin', don't we, woman?" *Why, he's crawlin' in, too*, I think. *We're all settin' inside a TV, like three settin' ducks for Jimmy Esker. Drive right up and switch the channel.*

But instead, Eudora she says all in a breath, "I ran away, my mom, she's crazy and she hates me and then she . . . well, but

I ran away first but I can't go back and she doesn't want me to either, I know." Then she put her face back down into her cereal bowl again, look like she's waitin' way down below and we're up above.

It's Tappen who speaks first. "Now don't you worry," he says, "you come to the right place. Don't you worry." He don't look at me. I know he's mad hisself he called Esker. He keeps sayin' it, "Don't you worry, we ain't gonna let anyone take you where you don't wanna go, don't you worry," until he stop short 'cause before we heard the car we heard the police radio blowin' loud up our road.

Tappen's jaw was makin' a decision. I watched it harden till it set. He looked back at me and throwed his head toward the pantry door like we was supposed to hide in there. I didn't move. He throwed his head again toward the pantry and then he looked at the back door Esker was comin' closer to. I grabbed Eudora up, hurried in, and closed the door. It was pitch-dark but I set down where I knew there was a box of dog food, against the back corner. She was on my lap and I felt like the runaway or the criminal myself, 'cause she wasn't big enough to be hidin', her legs danglin' either side of my lap.

"Clay, Clay, you in there? Hello." Esker was callin' from behind the screen, but Tappen wasn't walkin' toward it. Esker, he walked in anyway to the kitchen. "Boy, it has been a mornin', I'll tell you, what with the lookin' and searchin' before your call, and the kid's mother, she's off to Burtrum, loony as all get-out, so poor Mike, he don't know what to do even after I informed him we had found his girl."

I was startin' to see in the dark. The shelf straight ahead got ketchup, Tappen always got a spare, and the last three or four jars of tomato from last year, and a big space where the applesauce was, then a lot of currant jelly that don't move so fast, wouldn't want to see the year marked on that, and cans of tuna. She don't move a muscle, got her hand restin' on my arm. She's so light, too light to squeeze.

Tappen didn't say nothin' back. I was waitin'. Even Esker who could go on forever was waitin'. Tappen didn't say nothin' though. I closed my eyes.

"Well, Clay," Esker finally says, "where you got her? In the barn?" and he laughs.

And Tappen don't. And he don't talk yet neither. I tighten up my arms around Eudora, just a little. Her belly hits my arm each breath, then sinks into bones. I see the basket of early potatoes front of us on the floor and I think, *I could grab one, and if Esker open this door, he'd get it smack in the face*. But I don't. I whisper, "Don't you worry, Dorrie, ain't no one gonna take you you don't want."

Tappen still don't give a word. I even think myself, *Say sump'n, Tappen, come on*. I could barely stand it. But he don't. Esker don't know what to do, so he says, "You have coffee? You wanna give me a cup a coffee? It *has* been a mornin'."

Tappen open the cupboard. Damn, if he ain't gonna spoon out the instant. The kettle's always on warm so we ain't gotta wait too long for it to boil. But he ain't puttin' up the flame 'cause he's already pourin' the water in the cup. Then I hear the spoon. *He's gotta at least spend time stirrin'*, I think, but he don't much, the spoon rounds the cup maybe three times before the cup hits the table. Ugh, must be mostly warm mud at the bottom and probably ain't dissolved yet on the spoon, and poor Esker has to drink it 'cause there ain't nothin' else to do in front of Tappen's quiet, 'cept leave.

Oh, Tappen he know Esker would never search this place. Suddenly I can't help but smilin'. Everybody think Tappen is so kind, so wonderful, Santa for the 4-H and all, ain't no one seen him as a foe, Esker don't have a chance. And he's in a fix, 'cause you can't yell at a man when you're settin' in his kitchen drinkin' his coffee, but with Tappen not talkin', he might as well be settin' back in his own car, but he ain't.

"Well, Clay, I guess this ain't a good a time, how about we come back after lunch and then you'll have her all ready to come along back to her daddy—I don't think that mom will ever be straight." And he give half a chuckle. He's tryin' for a in, tryin' to chuckle his way in, usin' a crazy woman to chuckle his way in, and all he's doing is hardenin' up old Clay, my old Clay, lettin' nothin' seep in.

The chair scrapes, Esker is up. "So you think after lunch? I won't push you, Clay, after lunch and I won't ask no questions, don't you worry. Won't even mention I was here." Esker at his best, handin' out them favors. Won't mention he was here 'cept it's already been all over town. And he seen only the tip of his foe.

But the police radio goes on down our road, and I come out from the pantry carryin' little Eudora, her face white as ice through the last of the mud wearin' off.

"WELL HOW LONG *you* been here, child?" I say, 'cause Laureen's settin' on the stairs in her pajamas, her face squished up against the spindles, peekin' out. I pull her away from the banister into my arms. She don't answer. She fuss with my hair instead. She love to pull it back over the top of my head with both her hands, though it don't go far, it's short. But then my hair falls flat again 'cause she points to where Eudora is but she don't look at her. She look at me. She's got bigger eyes than any other kid I ever seen. I put her down and I say, "Meet Eudora Shane, Laureen. And this is Laureen, Eudora." But I don't even get out that

"Eudora" before Laureen run off and jump up into Tappen's arms and bury her head.

Now, one on one, you can't get Laureen to shut up. Mostly birds. She talks about birds and chipmunks, squirrels, little animals. She don't take to the bigger ones, the cows. But even if there's just Tappen here with us, then there's nothin' comin' out but them eyes. If her eyes was a mouth it'd be goin' all day in one big long question.

"I'm showin' Eudora the bathtub, Laureen. She's a travelin' cowboy and she needs a hot bath to soak them weary bones."

Eudora starts like she's been poked for her cue, but she don't take them hands out of her pockets. As she reach the stairs, she turns to Tappen, and to Laureen, and she nods to 'em. "Nice to meet you, Laureen," she says in about the lowest voice she come up with so far. I think, *a hat. She needs a cowboy hat and she'd be tippin' it right now to Tappen, biddin' him "Good day, and to the little missus, too." A hat. We gotta get her a hat. And we need more Cheerios.*

From upstairs I can hear Tappen open the screen to bring in Charlie so he can let down Laureen. Charlie's twelve and deaf and Laureen is *his* kid. People think kids got to have dogs but it ain't true, it's that every kid should be had *by* a dog. And Charlie bein' deaf is perfect for the job 'cause he don't have to hear an order and Laureen has learned real quick she don't have any sway over him, and no one does, not even Tappen, and if Tappen was a dog, he'd be Charlie. Charlie just live right along happy, completely outside her yellin', slappin' her thigh, tryin' to pull and push him here and there. He mosey along goin' his way, ignorin' her absolute rule, or anybody's rule, and he don't just go puff, neither, when she turn away. But that don't stop him comin' inside, beggin' biscuits—she won his heart with biscuits—and *always* there ready for huggin' and pettin' and scratchin'.

Eudora's gettin' a clean pair of dungarees and a shirt out from her suitcase, and I get the water runnin' and I set a towel and a washcloth out on the sink and then she just stands there, waitin'. And I'm waitin' for her to give me her old clothes so I can get 'em out on the line to dry before supper, and I'm waitin' and she's waitin' till I figure out she's waitin' for me to leave. "Well, here's your towel and a washcloth," I say. "Now, the hot and cold are backwards." And I show her which is which and I say, "Just throw your clothes out in the hall so I can wash 'em," and then I wait outside the door for a handful of clothes so this little thing, this scared little thing that was settin' on my lap in the dark can take a bath private.

Tappen was already thinkin' *Call Burtrum General*, before I said it when I come through the kitchen carryin' Eudora's clothes. That got him from the thinkin' to the movin' and he gave them a call and got Mike Buell on the phone.

And then he's sayin', "Yup, Mike, we just want you to know your little girl is fine. Beulah got her in the tub now, yup. . . . She's happy. *Eatin'* us out of house and home, too, yup." And then just as easy, he says it like it was nothin', "We'd be happy, Mike, to take care of her for a while, till everything's eased up for you. . . . Yup . . . yup. . . . Nope, it wouldn't be no trouble, we got a five-year-old now . . . yut, and my father here with us, too. . . . Nope, no trouble, no trouble at all. . . . Yut, and you know no one takes to kids more'n Beulah. . . . Till it's straightened out some, yeah, okay, we'll call you 'bout the clothes, yeah. . . . Okay, bye, bye now."

Bye. That simple. I stood there front of the wringer washer in the back room off the kitchen, just starin'. The water gone off upstairs. I start loadin' her dirty clothes. Bye, that's it. And wouldn't no one know what that man would do if *anyone*, and her dad included, took Eudora against her will. And I guess now no one's gotta know. But now, I feel almost nauseous. No fight and I turn weak. And she don't have any clothes here, just the one change probably, ain't much could fit in that vanity case. We gotta call back. And call Esker, too, so he don't come and he'll call Mike sure enough, still keep hisself a hero. Oh Grandma, the joe-pye weed's featherin'.

I lean down on the washer just finished fillin'. "You want a cup of coffee, Mr. Tappen?" I say. I hear his "yup" aimed at me, and a long breath out. He's leaned back against the sink with his arms crossed, starin' at Charlie gettin' one more biscuit, probably his fourth. "Yup, woman, I do." It was my turn to smile and we both knowed each other was smilin' though neither of us looked to check.

FLORENCE, SHE LIKED purple and red together, and every year she'd buy a flat of red geraniums and a flat of purple petunias for her front porch boxes. But then she'd never stop with just that, she'd buy anything bloomin', the big yellow marigolds. She got every new rose we ever grew, and boy, she loved peonies. If any of them was out, she'd lean over and smell 'em first thing 'fore she even say "Hi." Sometimes little Eudora'd come, and she smelled everything right along with her ma, followin'. But purple was always Florence's favorite color. The first time she seen a purple-and-white petunia, she stop right in her tracks and let out a "aah." Even Tappen said when she gone, after spending more'n a week's pay, he said, "Ain't no one love flowers like her," and then quieter he said, "like Elmer and his drink."

But then this year after the boy died, she didn't come up and I thought maybe of bringin' her the two flats of purple and red but I didn't want to push 'em onto her, might of made her think of them roses on her boy and all gone into the ground now.

Then we started hearin' things, how she wasn't copin', and how she gone in the hospital, and at first it seemed just natural for that time but then people started sayin' she really was crazy, that it was in her blood from the beginning and it just come out now after the boy and she might even have to get the shock. But I never heard nothin' 'bout Eudora. Mike always been such a kind man, and his business kept on okay and no one ever said nothin' 'bout his little girl.

Eudora was so long and quiet in the bathroom I started to get worried she was drowned in there but I knowed I couldn't open that door. From the kitchen you can hear every step taken upstairs 'cause the floor bends so, even under Laureen, less than fifty pounds.

As soon as I hear a scurryin' down the hall, I gone upstairs and yell at Pop's door like I always do in the mornin', make sure he ain't dead, but now I wanna make sure Eudora hear me, too, so I don't just come up on her. "Feel better now?" I says as I near the door.

I seen her hair first from the back, chopped flat against her head, little patches of dark and straight lines where the scissors cut. She didn't even nod, just set down on the bed like a thing caught, didn't even look up. The top of her head had no hair left either, it was all chopped flat, didn't look reddish no more, just blotches of brown but then some parts was so close you could see her scalp right through. Here she was all clean and with clean clothes but she got her boots right back on again. And her suitcase right at her feet.

I says, "Ah honey, you can just rest now, just set down. You don't have to go nowhere."

She still don't look up. I wanna run and pick her right up and hug her but I hold back, I stay at the door.

"You're safe here now. Esker, he ain't comin' back. Don't you worry about *him*," I says. "And Tappan called your dad and he's with your mom at the hospital and he said, too, your dad said you can stay right here for a while till everything's all squared away with your ma and . . . and you know we'll feed you as long as you want. We'll feed you up fat."

She look up then and I see she left a tiny bit of hair at her forehead. It stuck straight up and out.

I can't hold back no more. I walk in to set down beside her, not too close up though 'cause I don't want her to crack, but I says, "Ain't no one gonna take you where you don't wanna go." I look down and she got a eyeful of tears she's fightin', she don't want to drip nothin'.

I says, "You know every cowboy worth his salt cries, don't ya?" but she don't nod. "With all that's happened to you, honey, you can't go through all that without cryin', your brother and then your ma, 'less you're stone, and cowboys, they ain't stone. I know that, they ain't stone." And then I see the line of tears come down her cheek. She still got little bits of cut hair, quarter-inch long, all over her head didn't come off in the tub. *Where is all her hair? I'm thinkin'. What'd she do with all that hair? Her ponytail?*

I keep talkin'. "I just want you to know you don't have to worry, Dorrie, okay? You don't have to worry, Dorrie." I put my arm on her shoulder and give her a squeeze. "Okay? Okay?"

I'm lookin' at her, waitin' for her to look up, and she does and even with the tears the littlest grin start up and she peep out in her own voice, "A worry-dorrie."

"A what?" I says.

"A worry-dorrie."

"What?" I says quieter and lean toward her 'cause it was like being let in on a secret, she was tellin' me a secret.

She start in slow. "You said . . ." And then she stop.

"I said what?" but she just look down again, don't say nothin'.

"Tell me, honey, 'cause I don't know. Talk as much as *I* do, can't keep track. Tell me."

"You said, 'Don't you worry, Dorrie.' A worry-dorrie, like worry beads."

"Worry beads?"

She nod and then she come out again a little louder now, but still every word comin' out careful, "What my grandmother used to call her rosary sometimes." Then she say, slowly again, "Her worry beads. I just thought a worry-dorrie."

"Yeah," I says, "a worry-dorrie. I like that."

She shrug her shoulder and she says, "Something you could get in a store."

"Like a little doll you can hold," I says, and give her another squeeze. "And here I didn't even know I called you Dorrie—you sure I said Dorrie?" And she turn serious as the Law and nod real slow and big. Her front hair though, it look like a little horn from the side. "You sure?" I says again, smilin'. I wanna see her nod again, boy how that hair stick up, like she's a little goat buttin' its head.

I says, "Don't that beat all? I don't even know what come out of my mouth. Don't that beat all?" and she nod again but the little grin is comin' through and just like them tears she didn't wanna drip before, this grin's holdin' back a big smile she ain't gonna be able to help.

"You like the name Dorrie?" I says, and she nod quick and turn her head so she can look up at me.

"The name Dorrie? You like it? You wanna be called that? You wanna be called Dorrie?" And she keep noddin' away. "Your head gonna bounce right off, girl." And her face break right in half, 'cause she got a smile ear to ear. "Then Dorrie it is, Dorrie's your name. Dorrie Shane. It's very nice to meet you, Dorrie Shane."

And she stand right up and turn to me, settin' on the bed, with her hand stuck out ready to shake and she say slow and clear, "Nice to meet you, too, Mrs. Tappen." And I shake her hand. She set down again beside me.

"I tell you what. You call me Beulah. It don't fit, you callin' me Mrs. Tappen. Will you do that for me? Call me Beulah? Will you do that?" And she nod and then she says it real slow, "Be-u-lah," with every letter soundin'.

"You're a careful girl, ain't ya?" And I think, *How she learn so young to be so careful?*

We just set there side by side. She didn't seem to mind silence none and I didn't either. It was a while till I started up again.

"You know, Tappen he cut his own hair, he don't let no one cut it but hisself, and after all these years he still ain't too good at it neither, 'specially what he don't see."

She don't say nothin' but she touch the very top of her hair back and forth, back and forth, look like bristles to scrub with.

"You like the feel of it?" I says and she nod, but slower, seem almost scared.

"Can I feel it, too?" I says and she put her hand down and wait a long time. We both wait a long time but then she nod, real slow she nod.

"I'll be careful," I says and I touch down onto what I think are gonna be stiff bristles and it is soft, so soft like my fingers is landin' onto a little bird, a reddish-brown bird, a robin, and I says again, "I'll be real careful," before I see the tears drop onto her wrist.

BEULAH WAVED TO Mike from the back porch, the dish towel still in her hand. "Come on this way! Come up to the back!" Maybe it was that she couldn't remember him ever bein' there, at least not with Florence when she come for flowers, or maybe it was just how clean and quiet his car was, and two-toned like she seen new in front of Fancher's, but all of a sudden she seen nothin' out the back window but a mire of undone work she didn't want Mike to get lost in. Even now, she couldn't see him or half his car behind the pile of tires Tappen saved up more 'n a year, story-high and spreadin' almost to the hollyhocks which was spreadin', too, juttin' straight up from the yard. Every year they changed colors till now most of 'em was a wine red, only a few left pink. And there was the TV antenna Jerry left off here never got hooked up front of the old greenhouse Tappen gave up on fixin'. Instead, he hung scrap pieces of plywood over the broke glass on one half of the roof where they throw boxes and plastic pots, some old buckets still good for plants. The back stands open, the floor just ground, dusty except after a rain, with only a few tufts of crabgrass, pineapple weed, and dock. Beulah never pictured dock without seein' its taproot, too, taperin' down into 'less you take a bath," she said, "and get on some clean clothes, too." He didn't care much about the church part, but afterward pies got served in the back and he loved mincemeat more 'n he loved drink. Now Pop didn't go as far as soap but Beulah didn't quibble. He's incontinent and even with the bathroom right off the back room, with his one leg that drags, it's still not as near as the cushion he's settin' in.

Now, almost every week, Beulah stands by his door and yells like she did that first New Year's Day she decided as long as he's in her house, he's gonna have clean clothes. "Hand over them long johns, Pop," she yelled. And Pop peeked open the door a crack and said, "These ain't long johns, Beulah, this here is a union suit." And she said, "Oh it is, is it?" "Now you should know that, Beulah. They smell like the whole U.S. of A., don't they?" "Yut," she said, "and I don't see why I bother carryin' 'em neither. They could walk clear to town if they had a mind." Pop mumbled a whole week about women cleanin' and how it ain't natural but smellin' like the whole country is. But Beulah is stubborn, and whenever she does a rag wash, almost every week, she stands by that door again and "waits for the goods," she calls 'em. She even use extra water, 'cept through August when the spring gets low.

Beulah yelled, "POP!" loud enough so he could hear.

"Yut, boss," he said, chewin' on his pipe in the same steady rhythm as his cows used to chew.

"This here is Dorrie Shane come to stay for a while," she yelled.

"You're too late, Beulah," Pop said. "We're old friends by now, ain't we, boy?" And Dorrie yelled back, "YUP!" even louder 'n Beulah, and Maxwell jumped clear.

"She's a girl, Pop!"

"Nope, she ain't," and he started laughin', his pipe shakin' along with his shoulders. "She don't got no hair. Gotta have hair be a girl, don't ya, boy?" And Dorrie yelled again, "YUP!" top of her lungs.

Pop stretched his chin up toward the sunlight comin' through the window and what was folds of skin became a plain of white stubble. "Hold there, Pop," Beulah said as she checked his neck for new lines of dried blood from his razor. "Just countin' your wounds."

"Back when I was a little girl . . ." Pop started in on a story just like he used to with Laureen before she stopped jumpin' up on his lap. 'Cause of the smell. *Horses*, Beulah thought. Mike said she been around horses, has a talent for horses, and Pop, too, all that time drivin' and carin' for his workhorses.

"Carry on!" Beulah said. A car was comin' up, could be a customer. City folk. No local people would come this late, with only a little over a month left before a frost, and all the vegetables needin' harvestin'. Just the zucchinis could keep you tied makin' relish.

Dorrie was still back there visitin' Pop when Beulah carried in a armful of carrots she picked still small as a treat for supper. And the first corn, too, twelve ears she set down by Pop's seat. He husk it for her while he's waitin' at the table, even though he don't see to silk it good and he make such a mess. Tappen'll eat five of 'em and Pop'll eat three even though she gotta shave it off for him 'cause he only got the one tooth.

Beulah called Pop in from his rocker 'cause of how long it take him to get to his place. "And we got new corn!" she yelled in. *Be a good night for Mike*, she thought, *don't get better 'n first corn*.

Beulah's come to count on Pop comin' through the kitchen while she's peeling' or cuttin'. Soon as he hit the linoleum and his hand come around the corner reachin' for a hold on the counter, she finds herself waitin' for it, the slide of his right boot along the floor. The step with his left is quick and she knows it hurts but the long slide of his right as he drag it up even with the left, that slide comforts her, like hummin' or the sound of bees buzzin' in the thyme that's supposed to be lawn.

Pop was at his place still huskin' when Mike come in and Beulah knowed the way he hung by the screen that it was the smell keepin' him there. *Damn that Pop.* Always seemed worse when visitors came but at least they could close the door on the back room. And what if Mike thought she don't have a home clean enough for his daughter? And his daughter hidin' upstairs.

"Dorrie?" Beulah opened her door just a crack—"Dorrie, honey?"—before she gone in all the way. "Your dad's downstairs waitin'. He wants to see ya, honey. He's waitin' to see ya."

Dorrie was scrunched up with a pillow over her head, her cowboy boots still on and the suitcase right up next to the metal bed rail. "He wants to see you, Dorrie. He loves ya. You know that, don't ya? He loves ya."

Beulah set down on the blue chenille spread and Dorrie's body moved like a rowboat top of a wave. Beulah put her hand on Dorrie's neck. "He don't blame ya for runnin' off." Maxwell come from behind the bed, his tail up like he was stalkin'. "Don't ya wanna come down and see him?"

The pillow lift up just enough so Dorrie could shake her head underneath. White pillow, white T-shirt. Beulah start rubbin' her back, almost Laureen's size, but tight as a wire. Muscle, bone, nerve, not a hint of fat. Like Tappen once was, in high school. Even under his baseball uniform, his skin seemed thin as paper, and all his veins showed in his forearms. Beulah kept on rubbin' and Dorrie's head finally start to slow down till it shake back and forth along with Beulah's hand goin' up and down.

"He brought clothes for you." She heard Tappen come in downstairs. He was talkin' to Mike while he wash his hands.

Thank God, Beulah thought. Dorrie's gonna take her time, and Mike just standin' there with the smell, and the water stains. They already come through the wallpaper they put up last winter to hold up the ceilin'.

"Your dad wants to be with ya, Dorrie. He does more'n anything, he wants ya there at home, but he knows it ain't right there for ya, with his business and havin' to go to the hospital every night and you'd have to be home all day alone all summer, on summer vacation . . . why, its just summer vacation here. Ya come here to vacation."

Maxwell had gone, probably toward the attic door in Beulah and Tappen's room. He waits for mice or sometimes a bat to come out where the plaster's cracked.

Dorrie had stopped shakin' her head but Beulah kept on rubbin' her back till she started to peep out from under the pillow. Beulah's hand floated up to Dorrie's hair, reddy-brown, rubbed the top that looked chopped-off and prickly, but was so soft it still made Beulah smile. *Like a surprise*, she thought, *that softness come again as a surprise, and her little grin, too, pokin' out the side of her mouth like she can't help it.*

"Let's get on down to your dad, huh? He's been waitin' a long time."

And Dorrie nod, as hard as she shook her head before. She walk in such small steps from the stairs to the kitchen, *Could take as long as Pop*, Beulah thought.

Soon as Mike saw her, he knelt down and opened his arms and Dorrie walked normal then, even fast right in to his chest for a hug but she didn't hug him back till he squeezed her tight and his eyes closed.

"They have cats here," Dorrie said, and Mike nodded, his eyes still shut. Over and over he nodded, just like his little girl, but slower and bigger.

"SWEETEST CORN EVER grew," Pop said. "And still white." He don't like it once the kernels yellow.

"Don't even need butter," Tappen said, but he already got his knife in one hand and with the other was grabbin' a slice of the white bread Beulah buys when they got corn. He buttered the bread thick and rolled the cob in it.

"But it won't hurt none," Tappen said. "Butter won't hurt."

"Mike . . . he should've stayed," Beulah said. Dorrie had looked so intently at Tappen rollin' his corn, Beulah handed her a piece of bread.

"Ain't every day ya get new corn and baby carrots," Pop said. "Ain't that right, Laureen?" Knowin' she hate anything called a vegetable. Cereal and bread, Beulah didn't even try for more tonight.

You couldn't hear nothin' then but chewin', Laureen on her Rice Krispies, everyone else on the corn. Beulah loved these moments at the table. Made her remember the first night Tappen took her out to Pop's barn. They was both bundled up settin' there on the bench by the milk tank holdin' each other's gloves and listenin' to the cows chew.

"Yut," Tappen said, though no one knew to what. Then he turn to Eudora. "How do *you* like your corn? Beulah here, she go like she's on a typewriter. Me, I go around and around, in neat rows."

"Like you're sowin'," Beulah said. "I mean crops, sowin' seed."

"Who's sowin' their seed?" Pop piped up, corn leakin' out of his mouth 'fore he wipe it with his rag he call a "hanky."

"No one, Pop! Now remember, we got children here."

"Well, they got sowed, too, didn't they, Beulah?" She looked over at him. "Now why you got the mouth on and I ain't even cussin'?"

Beulah had tried for three years to stop Pop from cussin' front of Laureen but it didn't help.

"I waited a lo-ong time to be able to cuss," Pop had said soon as he moved in. "And all that time I saved up behind them words I ain't gonna give over to a ankle-biter."

"Waited heck! Probably started cussin' when you was five."

"Nope! We'd get the strap."

"You cuss, she gonna cuss," Beulah said, "and I don't want Laureen headin' off to kindergarten sayin' them words."

"Well don't let her then," Pop said, and that's how they left it. Pop still cussed and Beulah still sent him what he call "the mouth," which he don't see half the time anyway with his one good eye.

Tappen always try to keep the peace. "I think, Pop, we got sour cherry pie left over. 'Less Eudora here will snatch it up before us. You like sour cherry pie?"

Dorrie shrug her shoulders. "I don't know," she squeak out. She was still tryin' to figure out how she like her corn—trying half of it around, then the rest across.

"You ain't ever had sour cherry pie?" Pop asks.

And Dorrie shake her head.

"Well I'd run, too, if I never got sour cherry pie."

Beulah sent him the mouth again but this time Pop made sure he didn't look. He was wipin' more corn from his face, which only go into his hanky to get to the floor.

"Don't it beat all? This boy here run all the way from town, don't that beat all?"

"She's a girl, Pop." But he was already shakin' his head back and forth like it just come to him.

"Why, I bet"—and he stop his head toward Dorrie—"Esker's boys looked right over the top of ya." And that made him chuckle.

Beulah looked at Dorrie all nervous. "Don't you listen to him." And she waved Pop off but Dorrie was lookin' right at him and with that grin on.

"Yut, that ma of yours must be mighty crazy make you run, such a little boy to run away from his ma."

"She's a girl, Pop." Beulah look at Tappen but his head was down onto his third ear of corn. He wasn't gonna help stop Pop.

"Drive ya right out into the night, won't they, boy? Ya run in the night, right?"

"YUT!" Dorrie yelled loud enough for even Tappen to pick his head up.

"Smart as a whip. Tiny thing he is, but smart." Pop's head was still goin' back and forth. "Beat all." And Dorrie was still grinnin' with half her mouth.

"Now Pop."

"Must be crazier 'n . . . got her tongue rollin' out, does she?" and he stick his tongue out to Dorrie just like a dumb kid, flappin' his tongue around and goin' "ahahhhahhah."

"He's *your* father," Beulah said toward Tappen but he didn't look up at her.

"She's in a hospital," Dorrie said to Pop.

"You hear, Pop?" Beulah yelled. "You're talkin' 'bout a woman in a hospital."

"And probably her ma, too. She's crazy, and her ma and her ma 'fore that. It's good you run, boy, probably the whole lot's crazy. Crazy as a loon." And Pop drop his chin down onto his chest. "Crazy as a loon," he mumbled again before he throwed his head up and back all the way and out come a loon call loud enough to hear to the end of Close Crick Road. And it lasted and lasted, he made it last long enough so it no longer seemed like a sound but like a river, braidin' its different waters as it move through the air, so that even after it was over it didn't disappear. It had cut through the room and had separated everything that come before from what come after.

Tappen was first to land 'cause he answered. Not as long or as loud but he answered and Pop take off again.

Beulah set there. She give up. But just as she give over the final bit of herself, Dorrie, the child she was scared for, the child with the loony ma, starts tryin' to loon-call herself. She throws her head back and croons, and she come out with every sound in there but a loon. And then Laureen start in, too, with a plain old yell. The four of 'em. You could barely hear Pop's clear call, hoverin' alone above the rest.

Then Tappen, he stops, shakes his head, and says, "Nope, nope," shakin' his head "nope" till Pop stop. "Nope, Eudora, Laureen. That ain't it." And then louder he says, "Ya gotta go to school for this, right, Pop?"

And Pop nod. "That's right, yut, school."

Then Tappen says still real loud, "Ya gotta go to Professor Barnwell. Elmer'll start ya out step by step."

"First step the whiskey," Pops says.

"Oh Dorrie," Beulah says, "they're teasin' ya."

But Tappen set up straight like he's serious now. "Now Beulah, ain't no one learned a good loon call around here ain't been taught by Elmer." And then he yell, "Ain't that right, Pop?"

"I taught Elmer."

"Elmer says he taught you."

Pop shake his head. "I taught Elmer. Taught him everything he knows." And then he chuckle again. "Yut, ya come to the right place, boy. Beulah's cookin' here . . . good enough for a minister."

"Now you just tryin' to make up to me for wreakin' havoc."

"Nope, I ain't." And he chuckle again. "I never did like them ministers."

Beulah wave Pop off but she got a big smile on her face. "Ya gotta watch it here, Dorrie, they're always teasin' ya." She takes up Laureen who's come knockin' at her lap. "Don't they, honey?" she says right close to her little one's nose. "They tease."

"But boy, Beulah make good food. Right, Laureen? She make good Rice Krispies, don't she?"

And Laureen nod to him smilin' and holdin' on to Beulah's arm.

Pop wipe his face off again, the callin' made him sweat. "Good food," he says again while he wipe. "That's if I don't gotta chew it." And he jut out his jaw to Dorrie and shows her the one bottom tooth he got left. "I don't like them store-bought teeth."

Beulah look onto Pop's plate and he's got a extra helpin' of carrots on Dorrie's side, must've come straight from her. Beulah was so busy watchin' her face for trouble, she didn't even catch it. And Pop was too busy loon-callin' to mix 'em in with the rest of his supper like he usually done with Laureen's.

"Eat your carrots, Pops," she says. "They're breedin' there on your plate." Dorrie give her a look but Beulah smiles. *Ain't gonna scare her over carrots.*

"THERE ARE TWO kinds of people in the world," Elmer said, "them that drink whiskey and them that don't."

"And which're you?" Pop asked.

"Neither." Elmer set back down in the one lawn chair by the rocker and take his bottle out—a old brown medicine bottle—and throwed his head back.

Elmer's same age as Pop. Pop says eighty-nine but Elmer says ninety-two, and you can't believe neither. Tappen, he says eighty-six or ninety 'cause they was born one of the years Grant got elected but he don't know which. Elmer's still got both eyes but he see just about the same as Pop see out of the one. He can walk good though, and he stand up almost straight.

Elmer didn't talk till he was seventy, 'cept to his dog and his ma, not even to Pop, who lived three farms down. They both walked to the school in Big Hollow, though Pop stopped when he turned ten. They had thirteen kids in the family and only his younger brother could go. But if anyone asked Pop if he still went to school, he'd say, "Yut, I bring Will lunch when he forgets it." But Elmer, he stayed till he turned thirteen or fourteen. The teacher would ask him if he understood sump'n they was studyin' and he'd nod or shake his head and that's how she'd mark him. But later he learned from his ma how to write and he was always known then for how beautiful he make his letters. And if anybody asked him a question he liked, he'd write 'em long notes. Pop, he couldn't write but he could talk his way anywhere so they was best friends. But then Elmer, he turned seventy, and his niece found him she thought dead in his barn, and after he wake up in the hospital, the nurses couldn't shut him up. He talk ever since.

Elmer stood up again, all six feet of him—even after he shrunk half a foot. He start in again like he was preachin'. "There are two kinds of people in the world"—he's pointin' his finger to the light—"them that think and them that work."

"Which're you?" Pop said again.

"Neither." And he take out his bottle again, but this time he hand it to Pop, who's chewin' on his pipe. It ain't lit, not since the day Beulah took his tobacco. "Med-sen," Elmer says. "You ain't feelin' well. I can tell." And Pop throw his head back and then shake his head hard.

"This ain't yours—this too good to be yours."

"There are two kinds of med-sens in the world—" Elmer start.

"Yut, them that are good and them that are yours," Pop butt in.

Dorrie was suckin' up the leftover milk from her Cheerios but she got one ear glued to the back room, her little suitcase again by her feet. "If you survive Elmer," Beulah said from the sink, but then she yell louder so they can hear, too, "survive Elmer, survive anyone." Beulah was smilin' with her head cocked toward the back room waitin' for what Elmer yell back but all that come was the loud breath he let out after his med-sen. Laureen settin' up on the counter cocked her head, too, then started wavin' the dish towel like a flag. Beulah whispered back to Dorrie, "Ain't never harmed a soul, that Elmer."

"The name's Shane," Dorrie said as she stuck her hand out to Elmer. In the other, she carry her suitcase. "Dorrie Shane."

"Barnwell," he said back, "Elmer Barnwell." You couldn't see how big Elmer was, settin' in the one chair, just his hands, the largest hands Beulah ever seen, wrapped around Dorrie's tiny fingers.

"Pull up them newspapers over there," he said to Dorrie. Customers dropped off more'n Tappen could ever use for mulch. Dorrie dragged 'em over by the balin' twine tyin' 'em together. "Need more chairs in here," Elmer yelled in to Beulah, back in the kitchen. "Osmer holdin' court here."

"Who's Osmer?" Dorrie said in a small voice, settin' down now, suitcase right beside her.

"Who's Osmer? Who's Osmer? Ain't ya even introduced yourself, Osmer?" Elmer said to Pop.

"Nope."

"This here's Osmer, but call him anything, he don't know the difference."

"Nice to meet you, Mary," Dorrie said.

Pop chuckle. "I told ya he was a whippersnapper."

"She's a girl, Pop!" Beulah yell in from the kitchen 'fore she gone outside.

"Yut, boss," Pop said. "Yut, you're a girl, ain't ya, boy?" and he chuckle again.

"Now Os, let me tell you sump'n." Elmer stood halfway up out of his chair and waved his hand. "There are two kinds of people in this world, them that are girls and them that are boys."

"And which're you?" Pop says.

"Neither!" Dorrie yelled out 'fore Elmer could, but he still took it as a cue for his med-sen.

"See? Smart as a whip," Pop says.

"Now where did all your hair go?" Elmer said, settin' down

again after he get the bottle back from Pop. "Didn't throw that away now, did ya?"

Dorrie shook her head.

"Hid it under your bed, I bet," Pop said.

"Some people's got money under their bed. Some people's got hair." Elmer hand over the bottle again. "Poor man's sick. Gotta make him feel better," he said to Dorrie.

Pop shake his head hard again, then lift the bottle to Dorrie. "You want any, boy?" Dorrie shook her head. " 'Bout the right age, ain't he, Elmer?"

"My hair's in here." Dorrie said and lifted her suitcase up onto her lap. Her fingers slid back and forth over the top, like she's pettin' it.

"Why, that one you been carryin' everywhere?" Pop ask and Dorrie nod, and her mouth curl up into her grin.

"Ever smell hair burnin'?" Elmer says, standin' up, "Mmmm-nnn, smell just like steak." He lean in to the kitchen, make sure Beulah gone out to the greenhouse and that she got Laureen, too. Then he says to Pop, "You gonna set here all day like a old cripple, or we gonna do sump'n?" He turn to Dorrie. "I told him not to go cripple, ruin all our fun.

"Come on, Os. Dorrie here gotta smell hair burnin'. Mmmm-nnn, ain't nothin' like it."

Elmer snatched up Pop's cane that was hooked over the back of the rocker and went to rope Pop's neck with it but Pop grabbed the curled end 'fore Elmer got it even close, and they were on both ends then fightin' for it, the cane jerkin' between them, Pop hittin' his chest with the fist he got holdin' it.

"Stronger 'n you used to be," Pop said when Elmer let go.

"Must be *some* trash we could burn. Or you still fired from that job?" And he grab Pop's arm to help him up. "Heavier 'n you used to be, Os."

"Only problem is matches," Pop said, 'cause the last time they asked for matches after drinkin' Beulah stood firm. "Boy, we need them eyes of yours." Pop got a handhold on the table by his rocker. "She got 'em high up 'cause she know we can't climb." He start to drag his leg. "You climb up on that counter and start lookin' till I make it in."

"I'll stand watch," Elmer said, and he edged his face in between Beulah's geraniums she got staked up three feet tall front of every south window. Elmer was squintin'. "The windows is cloudy. Full of webs."

"Yut," Pop said, "and your eyes is clear as a bell. She'd be in the door 'fore *you'd* know." He had already reached the linoleum. He gone a lot faster than when Beulah got peas to shuck.

Dorrie hiked herself up onto the top of the counter by the refrigerator. She only had two narrow spots to put her feet either side of the cuttin' board Tappen made. It was crowded out to the edge by little jars—hundreds, it seemed—full of dried herbs Beulah never used as fast as she filled. Dorrie could see all the way to the top shelf of the cabinet but she couldn't find even a space for a box of matches, it was so full. *Not like hers*, Dorrie thought, remembering how each item had to be organized so it was seen from the front and not even her dad could put the groceries away. But Beulah even had cocoa on two different shelves.

"Jump, son, if I spot her," Elmer said.

"He could jump off Denny gallopin'."

"Old Denny-do-no-wrong."

"Yup, we got a horseman here, Elmer. Does all that fancy stuff, too. Jumpin'."

"No! This little tyke?"

"They're not here," Dorrie said and twisted around toward Pop.

"The pantry," Pop said. " 'Course. Whyn't I think, they'd be in the pantry."

Dorrie hadn't been in there with the light on. She jumped onto the full box of dog food cans Tappen gets in bulk from Hubbard's Feed. Still, she could only see up to the third shelf. She reached her foot up to it and hoisted herself up enough to grab the top board. Perched like that, she could see where Beulah kept all her pickles and watermelon rinds. Dust covered all the dates. She stepped slowly around the edge of the shelves lookin', ready to jump if she heard Elmer. Three boxes of noodles, ten cans of tuna, six jars of mayonnaise. *Like a store*, Dorrie thought. She was just about to give up when she saw on the top corner not one but six boxes of matches covered, too, in dust. "Got 'em!" she yelled and let go the shelf to grab a box and jumped back onto the floor, almost landin' in the box of old potatoes. She pulled the string for the light and stayed for just a moment in the dark before she went out into the kitchen like the day Beulah carried her. The grin came on her face and she didn't lower her head, she waved the matches. "Got 'em!"

"That a boy," Pop said. "We're in business now. Got us a good 'complice, don't we, Elmer?"

"Yut, we need young blood to carry out my plan. Been thinkin'."

"Good, 'cause ya ain't been seein' nothin'."

Elmer headed Pop toward the old horse barn, away from the greenhouse. Beulah was pottin' up more starts front of the soil bin. The road used to go right on through to the farm the State bought after the Depression. It turned from gravel to dirt before it seemed disappeared into weeds, but not to Pop. He felt with his feet for the level and held tight to the old road. They was aimin' for the rock where the sun land just south of the barn. Outta Beulah's line of sight. "Till she see the smoke," Pop said.

Dorrie was hidin' out behind the barn with the suitcase and the trash, waitin'. She had gotten the grocery bag full of the burnable from under the sink. It was easy to sneak it out here. She leaned the bag against a old milk can, the bottom on one side rusted out, daisies and grass stretched up toward the hole.

Dorrie finally saw Joker, the pony that comes and goes as he pleases. Tappen had called *her* a little Joker last night at supper. "He come here on his own, too," he said. He was tied up in the Bradys' yard bottom of the road and no matter how many times Tappen led him back, he'd rip loose and be right outside the cow barn every mornin'. It took a whole winter before Tappen stopped throwin' rocks at him and gave him hay instead. The Bradys didn't want him. That was twenty years ago and he been here ever since, sometimes in the pastures with the cows, sometimes on the lawn or up back in the woods. He can get in and out of every fence 'cept one. Sometimes he stands right in the middle of the road under the white pine and customers have to honk and inch right up to him before he slowly strolls to the side. "He owns the place," Tappen said, "might as well pay him rent."

Joker stood there, chewin', as Dorrie walked toward him, up the hill behind the horse barn. He was the hairiest thing she ever saw. "Don't shed no more," Tappen had said, "too old." And then he added, "Part Shetland part dog." The hair on Joker's back was curly, perfect curls, just like a permanent Dorrie'd hate on a lady, and stiff, too, like it had just been sprayed. But underneath, his hair hung down from his belly almost a foot and was thick and soft except where it had caught some burdock. There was burdock in his fetlocks, too, and in the long hair under his chin that made him look like he had no throat. Dorrie had never liked ponies, but he wasn't like a normal pony, or like anything she had ever seen before. With that hair, he looked wild, like he had always been here, before horses even lived, and like he always would be here, too. She squatted down beside him in the tall grass and started workin' apart the bunches of hair caught with burdock, and he didn't move, not even when she got to his chin. He just looked back toward her and that's when she saw his eye, level with hers. It was tame, so completely entirely tame that *she* felt like the wild one.

The name's Shane, she said to him in her mind like she used to talk to Wink. *Dorrie Shane.*

"HARD, THE CRIMINAL life," Pop said as he lowered himself down onto the rock. Longest he walked in a year.

"Now where is that boy?" Elmer said just before he seen Dorrie run toward him, springin' like a deer, but with trash in one hand and the suitcase in the other. "Happy kid, that one."

Pop took out the matches from his pocket. Couldn't even tell they were in there, he got so much extra room.

"Okay, son, ready for business?" Elmer asked.

Dorrie nodded hard, a little out of breath. She put the bag of trash down on the huge rock. It was far enough away, though Elmer still made sure Pop was settin' upwind.

"Know the three rules of fire?" Elmer asked.

Dorrie nodded. "Heat, air, and fuel."

"Told ya, smart as a whip."

Elmer handed the matches to Dorrie and she lit one on the rock just like her dad had showed her. And she knew to put the match under the rolled-up papers or a napkin and not try to light any flat papers laying tight on top of each other.

"Keep it close for the heat," Elmer said, "least for a while."

"Till she fall apart," Pop add.

At first, squished together in the bag like that, it didn't seem like it would have enough air to catch.

"Here she go. Here she go!" Elmer said, his foot tappin' like he heard a beat. "Here she go!"

Dorrie opened the suitcase and got out what was her ponytail. It looked shiny red in the sun. She waited till both sides of the bag caught and the flames darted up. Then she laid the whole hank of hair down onto the wax paper on the top startin' to burn. She stared. Water drops squeezed out, rolled down the strands near the sides, vanished. Then all of it sizzled up and melted down. For a moment, there were thousands of skinny worms swimming over and under each other till all at once they turned to ash, worms of ash, before they fell apart and disappeared into the rest of the garbage.

It stunk! Oh, did it stink! Dorrie's face wrinkled up "Oooh!" and she covered her nose. But then she leaned over the fire again, kept her hand away. "Oooh!" Then again and again, she leaned over and sniffed, each time closer, just to smell how awful it was and wrinkle her nose. "Oooh!"

"Just like steak," Elmer said, "mmmm-nnn." Dorrie cracked up laughin'. "Uh-oh, here he go. He-ere he go." 'Cause Dorrie wasn't just plain laughin', she was laughin' so hard till she was almost cryin', laughin' and laughin' and holdin' her belly, she could barely keep sniffin' the air. "What do you say, Pop? We got a wild one here?"

Pop's head nod as he bang his pipe down onto some ash fallin' on his pants. Already got too many holes.

"Yut," Pop said, "he's gone, won't come to till she go out, till she's all out."

LYLE ORTON HUNG up another dead bobcat front of his garage. Tappen didn't like it. Pop hated it even worse, 'cause even though he used to shoot 'em when they came in near his calves, he always liked 'em, liked their sound, liked just that they were *there*.

Dorrie had never heard a bobcat and that was as funny to Pop as not knowing how you like your corn. "Where you been all your life, boy?" And then his shoulders shook how they do when he laughs with no noise. He didn't call her nothin' but "boy" now and Dorrie thought of it like a name: Boy Shane—it was her name just to him alone and she liked that, having different names for different people and then she even said her old name out loud in her head. *Eudora*, she said but it came, instead, in *her* voice, and Dorrie could feel the smile twist up her lip and she shook her head hard 'cause it felt bad again, for the first time since she had come here, it felt bad and she had to get outdoors.

It was only a few days later she got to hear the sound. Tappen heard it first. He always heard everything first. Even inside, even when he's eating, "he still got one ear out," Beulah says. It's his left ear 'cause all of a sudden, he'll stop chewing and cock his head till that ear points straight to it. Beulah stops chewing, and Dorrie, Laureen, till even Pop can hear the quiet and stops. Everyone waits, their faces aimed right at Tappen pointing, waits till he drops his head and says, "Porcupine in the barn," or "Plane," or "Cats," and then everyone starts up chewing again.

But this time he said, "Bobcat," and then, "Come on, Dorrie" and he scraped his chair back. Dorrie looked at Beulah, but she didn't need to. "Go on," Beulah said in a hushed voice. And then she whispered down to Laureen who came creeping up into her lap, "Why, the poor girl ain't ever heard a bobcat." Tappen grabbed the flashlight they kept on the Hoosier cabinet by the back door but he didn't turn it on. No one said another word, or chewed even, till they were both out beyond the porch in the almost dark.

Dorrie followed Tappen's exact footsteps and was so quiet, Tappen smiled. *We'll hear a lot*, he thought, *stays this quiet. How most kids tromp along, animals a mile away'll scatter.* The smell was comin' to them from the barnyard where the manure spreader sets till it's loaded and that was good, the wind was right, maybe they would get up close.

Tappen stopped. Dorrie stopped. The woods they were facing looked full of night, like the trees were holding night, but like they couldn't hold it much longer, it was spilling out into the pasture and yard, it was coming close to the buildings. And it carried a sound, the sound of the trees all together and all at once. But then it came, the screech of the bobcat, it ripped through the dark and that's all they heard after that.

It wasn't like anything Dorrie ever heard before but she knew it—it was cat, but big, too big, and scary wild, hard wild—a scream from the belly, nose, the teeth, aching for food, blood— and no milk anywhere. She held her elbows tight, she was wrong there. She was all wrong. She wanted to disappear.

It's unnatural, that sound. They were Beulah's words in her brain: *unnatural, that sound.* Like *her*, Dorrie thought. She shook her head, no. No. But it didn't help, shaking didn't help, the screeching was still loud and it was *hers* and Dorrie felt wrong, being there was wrong. She held herself tighter, but the sounds wouldn't stop, they kept pulling her, toward them, toward the air. She could disappear. Like *she* did. But then she remembered Laureen's fingers, how they'd close like doors over her huge eyes. "I'm gone! I'm gone!" she yelled 'cause she knew now it wasn't true, she was five now. And Beulah was behind her little daughter, holding her, nibbling at her ear. "My little chocolate cake. My rice puddin'." Dorrie closed her eyes, trying to cuddle in closer.

Tappen turned and put his hand on her shoulder. The sounds were going away, the sounds were gone. *She* was gone. "Eerie, ain't it?" he said and Dorrie nodded hard. Tappen turned and without the flashlight on, she followed his exact steps back toward the house.

Mike had called. Beulah said so as soon as they walked in. Dorrie said, "I know." She often said "I know" when she meant only "yes" or "yes, that makes sense." It just came out "I know," and adults thought she was lying.

Beulah didn't. Words could fly out of Beulah whether she meant 'em or not and she never minded if some didn't add up. And she had looked down at Dorrie's face and seen she was spooked, she'd come in spooked.

"Bobcat get ya?" she said, taking Dorrie into her arms. "It ain't a sound to sleep on." But then Beulah whispered, "You okay? You get scared out there?"

And Dorrie didn't nod but she meant to. "*She's* coming *here*?"

Beulah brought her in closer. "To visit," she said. "Just for a afternoon, to visit."

Dorrie squeezed her eyes as tight as possible. Beulah whispered right on her ear, "It'll be okay, everything gonna be okay, she gonna be okay, it'll all turn out okay." And she squeezed Dorrie tight but she couldn't squeeze back the tears pouring down out of Dorrie's eyes.

Laureen started yelling, "Dorrie's cryin'! Dorrie's cryin'!" and Beulah's hand chopped down hard behind Dorrie's back meaning STOP! Tappen picked Laureen up over his head so her yelling turned into screaming laughing 'cause she was flying and it tickled and Charlie came over and stood deaf but drawn right to Tappen's leg.

Beulah wiped off Dorrie's face with the bottom of her apron and more tears came and more. And she kept saying, "It'll be okay" over and over. She didn't hear herself but Dorrie heard it like rubbing, like a hand rubbing her ear, soft like air, rubbing, "It'll be okay" and she knew Beulah was right as long as she didn't ever hear that bobcat again.

Damn her! Dorrie thought. It was the first time she said those words even to herself, and she liked them, they were like a fist.

CAT GOT HER tongue again, Beulah thought. Ever since last night when Dorrie heard her ma was comin'. *It's her ma she's scared of.* They were comin' around two. Mike would drive her here from Burtrum General for a hour. A whole hour. 'Least she got new pants on Pop so he don't smell so bad.

"Who died?" Pop said.

"No one. Yet."

"Well, I ain't goin' to church for nothin'."

"You ain't goin' nowhere, Pop. Dorrie's ma's comin'."

"You mean the—"

"Yut, and she ain't gonna hear one word outta you. You're

gonna set in your rocker and you ain't gonna spout off one word, you hear?"

He didn't answer. He knows when Beulah means business. She swept out the kitchen first thing and with her good broom, too, and she swept off the back porch, around the doorless refrigerator been there since it broke so all the shelves filled up—hoses, coffee cans filled with bolts, old oil, dog blanket, jar full of gas. She picked all the rags off the floor and stuffed them in, too, a few newspapers. She even got Tappen to move the box of parts been there since winter meanin' to go out. He won't throw nothin' away.

"Well, they ain't stayin' long," Tappen said.

"It don't take more'n a minute see your junk."

"Ain't junk, it's parts."

"Junk." But he was already headin' to his barn, walkin' like he had a limp, droppin' the box down onto one thigh to hold it together, most of the cardboard rotted out.

Then Beulah beat what she could of the couch, trying to beat the fleas out 'cept the cushion that was ripped so bad, just plain old foam on the bottom, won't help to beat that. Then she got the carpet sweeper goin'. At least they ain't had loads of customers come. Nope, and no one showerin' 'em with money neither.

And the whole time Dorrie was hangin' around like a cat wantin' milk. Laureen on one leg, Dorrie on the other. Beulah turned on the stove. "How 'bout some hot chocolate?" They always want that, don't matter it's top of summer. Laureen clapped her hands and did a little dance, but Dorrie just nodded, didn't even peep out a "yeah." *Like Elmer*, Beulah thought again, *'fore he got sick*. But he had that silly laugh, she got the grin.

THE CAR CAME up the road slowly, so slowly like they were city folk sightseeing. Dorrie glued her face right up to the kitchen window, between the leaves of the geraniums, watching till the car stopped. Cream-colored with a white top. *She* picks the colors, Dad picks the models. That was their rule. Dorrie closed her eyes and leaned her forehead up against the cool of the window. The night they were deciding, *she* almost went for the turquoise but the cream she had said was more "classic." Dorrie backed away. The window had gotten warm, and he had gotten out of the car. He ordered their new Oldsmobile whenever the old one reached fifty thousand miles and then they'd go on long drives on the weekends before he'd trade it in 'cause he wanted to put miles on it. He got all his cars from Bob Dodge in Ashland and that was always their joke—they got an Olds from a Dodge. But all that was before, way before, and sometimes, if *she* wasn't with them, he would stop the car on some back road and he and David would trade places and David would drive even though he was only fourteen, and then fifteen.

Dorrie walked down toward them. Her dad had closed the door but he still stayed there by the car. He gave her a little kiss on the cheek. Then he knelt down on one knee, touched her elbow and whispered, "Mommy's going to stay in the car, okay? Can you visit her in there, okay?"

He leaned his head back to look right into Dorrie's eyes. "Okay?" She nodded extra hard. He was holding both her elbows.

"Talk slowly, okay? Sometimes she doesn't . . ." He shook his head. "Anyway." And he got up again to open the door for her.

Dorrie felt like she was a lady, he was opening the door for a lady and she sat down onto the driver's seat, his seat, a panel of black cloth surrounded by gold, black with thick silver and gold strands woven in and flashing like real metal. She heard the door close and her hand touched down on the gold heat of the vinyl, the gold surrounding both seats, *her* seat, too, her black woven seat. Dorrie did not look over or up. She touched the steering wheel with her other hand, followed its arc with the same gold color, the same heat, the same smell. Some cars didn't smell like their colors but this one did, it smelled gold and she let each hand rub separately its own gold heat.

"How's my sweetie?"

"Okay." Dorrie's eyes stayed straight ahead, looking up over the steering wheel. She could see the edge of the back barn roof, rusty, almost orange in the sun, white puffy clouds and bright blue. She could see under the top of the wheel, too, the sliver caught inside the arc over the dash. There was the hay door and a part of the wooden frame of the hay wagon. She smiled that she knew it was the hay wagon. It looked like only an inch of wood, she could blot it out with her thumb, but she knew what it was because she had helped Tappen hay and he had said, "Would you believe that?" just like Buddy when she lifted the bale onto the back all by herself. "And at her size," he said. At night she traced all the scratches from the hay on her forearms till she fell asleep.

It would have been "How are you?" but she couldn't ask that now. "How's my mommy?" it might've been once, before, and it would've come out right away so it echoed "my sweetie" and they would both laugh. But Dorrie sat there now with no words. She had planned to show her how she could feed the cats, stirring the hot water around the dry food till it melted the bacon grease and all the leftover scraps mixed in. And how all the cats would gather around her when she walked with the pan out to the barn, all twenty or thirty of them, meowing, and the white ones blind, trying to stop her but how she didn't slow down, she walked steadily till she reached the doorway and each time it seemed almost a miracle how she could put the tub down right on top of their squirmy backs but at the last second they'd get out from under it, the brave ones last and closest to their food. But now she sat. Even one or two words would help, would break the spell. Dorrie could feel her mother look, up and down and up at what used to be her hair. And then it came to her, suddenly, her mother was drinking her in, all of her, slowly in, and she closed her eyes and let herself be looked at. It turned easy, it was like letting herself be kissed.

TAPPEN'S EYES TRAVELED all the cracks in the ceilin' like they done every night while he waited on his back for Beulah or sleep. He slept always on *his* side of the bed, even the four nights Beulah stayed with her mother, the spread was still tucked tight under her pillow when she came back. Tappen would close his eyes with his face still straight up—looked so peaceful, but so formal-lookin', too, it always made Beulah think how he'd look when he was dead. *Almost like a king*, she thought, *in them days they was carried on their deathbed through town*. The thought didn't make her shudder as she got on her old flannels 'cause she felt so cozy, he was there now, with her, listenin', sometimes talkin', in the few minutes before they turn off the light.

"Even if you clean her hair up so it's all the same, all even—that almost bald spot on the top—why, it'll be so close, still won't help. The kids'll all still tease. I don't think it's growed any and with school comin' . . ." Beulah didn't finish 'cause the sheets on her side were like cold water to get into and she shook her head "brrrr" and curled in tight, pulled up the covers tight. "Where's the stove?" she whispered as she reach for Tappen's chest but he grabbed her hand, protectin' himself. Her hands was always cold.

He'd hold 'em there over his chest but away from his skin till the ends of her fingers were warm. Tappen didn't answer for a while but she could see he was takin' it in.

"Ain't a hint of girl in her 'cept her name," he said.

"Oh, she's a girl, all right. That little girl is *all* girl."

"Well, it don't show," he said and reached his hand for the light switch on the cord he rigged up so he don't have to move.

"Nope, I guess it don't." Beulah liked when it was easy to agree. She rolled onto her back, felt the breeze across her face from the window she keeps open 'cept in the dead of winter. She liked her face bein' cool when everything else was warm, and Tappen, already smilin' in the dark. She waited for him to say it, his words, "My big smoo-ooth engine, you're my big smooth engine," before she turn her face.

"HOW 'BOUT TAPPEN clean up that hair of yours some," Beulah said to Dorrie after supper, "while I wash the dishes"—which wasn't easy now 'cause they was haulin' water. The spring had stopped drippin' or was drippin' so slow you couldn't see it. "Drier'n it ever been," Tappen said, but Beulah heard that almost every year this time, late August. That way of thinkin', he don't have to change to a well. They drank water still from the house, but whatever they needed for dishes, and the toilet, and the wringer washer, they hauled that from the crick where it pools down the road. Tappen siphoned it into a sap tank so they had plenty, even for the cuttin's they started in the greenhouse—they hosed out a quarter of a tank for them every day. The cows and Joker, they got the stream runnin' in the one pasture, even though it was barely a trickle now. So they didn't have a actual *shortage*, it was just a pain in the neck to bucket and not hot either. But it had been two weeks now and Beulah was gettin' used to heatin' her big pans up each night and everybody, even Laureen, usin' only one glass a day. Dorrie liked it 'cause it meant she didn't have to take a shower. Beulah did before she gone to the store and then it took half a day before they had enough water again to fill a pot for corn. 'Course Beulah used that water the next mornin' for her geraniums.

"Gonna have hair short as mine," Pop piped in to Dorrie, rubbin' his head which didn't have no hair 'cept in the very back. It looked bright white curlin' over the collar of his blue work shirt. *Like them fluorescents*, Beulah thought. "You better go first, Pop," she said. "Been a long time since Tappen got *your* hair."

"Whatever you say, boss."

"TAP-PEN!" she yelled 'cause he already got up from the table and once he disappear, he's gone, got his nose in sump'n he's fixin', usually sump'n no good.

"Yu-ut," they could hear from upstairs seemin' from one of the back rooms full of boxes. That "yut" meant he'd come but he was in no hurry. Never was.

"You keep that boy of mine doin' his job." Pop was still rubbin' his head. "Been lettin' off on him and now *feel* my hair. Probably look like a girl."

"Yut, Pop, look just like a girl. Don't he, Dorrie?"

She stick her face right up to his. "Hi, Mary," she said. He jut out his jaw, show his tooth. That always made her laugh, probably how big it looked in there all alone on his bottom gum. "The lone soldier," Elmer called it once, "battlin' that meat." Nothin' Pop loved more 'n meat cooked black except the fat around it.

By the time Tappen come down the stairs, Beulah got a towel 'round Pop's shoulders pinned tight with a clothespin so he don't itch and she got the scissors and the comb she keep on top of the Hoosier and a glass of water on the table.

Tappen held up the box he was carryin' to show Beulah. "Clippers," he said, "Sears Roebuck." He knew he had them somewhere, probably never even been used, needed a little oil, maybe—that was right in the box, too. The Truesdells left them behind at what they called their "summer camp" on Henderson Road though it's a good house and not small neither. Like gypsies, how they traveled so much, must have forgot sump'n in every state, but they was good folk, liked animals. And Tappen, 'cause he mowed the field front of their house twice a year, he got their clippers, two rugs, some coats, and all their sheets—they left their sheets.

Tappen picked up the comb. It was Tappen's ma who cut Pop's hair and all the kids', too, before she taught Tappen. Beulah liked watchin' him 'cause he still done it just like his ma, dippin' the comb in the water and usin' small strokes to comb the hair straight without pullin' it. 'Cept the comb looked like a child's 'cause Tappen's hands was so big, and when his thick fingers ran up Pop's head between cuts, looked like black stripes in the bright white hair. The grease don't come outta them calluses even with Boraxo.

But when it come to Dorrie's time, Beulah set down. She didn't care she had to heat the rinse water again. Tappen hadn't even seen someone use them clippers, never mind doin' it himself. Closest he got was shavin' the hair around Millie's teat with Jerry's ear clippers when her cut flamed up. But he plugged 'em in and started 'em right up like he was a expert.

'Course anybody'd be expert compared to what was there: bald in one place, inch-long in another and hangin', not two places the same length. Dark, straight edges all over and every which way, made her head look like a patchwork quilt, shades of brown and red. Like Grandma's harvest quilt.

Tappen set the clippers down right top of Dorrie's forehead and run 'em back like he was mowin' a field. Dorrie squinched her nose and shoulders up, smiled big like it tickled. Thank God she couldn't see the almost bald road right over the top of her head down the hill to her neck.

'Course Laureen couldn't hold it in. She got one hand up to her mouth and one hand pointin' while she jump up and down, laughin'. "Dorrie's a boy-oy! Dorrie's a boy-oy!"

"Told ya that from the beginnin'," Pop said.

"Now you hush," Beulah said as she leaned forward and grabbed Laureen's waist from behind and pulled her back and onto her lap. "You hush," she said again into her ear. "It ain't done yet."

Beulah started strokin' Laureen's thin, dirty-blond hair. You could barely tell where it ended on her back below her shoulders. "Laureen, too," Beulah said. "She oughta get her hair cut, too, 'fore she go to kindergarten."

"No!" Laureen screamed, "No! No!" and jumped off Beulah's lap and run to Charlie like he'd protect her from her mean old ma.

But Dorrie was still smilin', squinchin' her shoulders like a cat bein' pet, like it was almost too much but she couldn't get enough either. One row wide, two rows wide, three rows wide, till it look like a half-cut field. After each row, she'd skim her hand over the top of her head. She wouldn't stop feelin' it, and Tappen would wait, before he start again a new row. The patches disappeared and she looked more and more like a boy.

"Gettin' you smarted up for school," Beulah said. Quick as it came out, she wished it didn't.

Dorrie gone white. That face that been smilin', tickled, in less than a second gone white, and blank, not even a cryin' face, but one of pure terror.

Tappen give Beulah a look: Thank you very much, Mrs. Tappen, please don't stop now.

"Every kid gotta go to school, sweetie," she said. But Dorrie's face stayed blank. Even Laureen was lookin' at her from behind Charlie, scared.

"Well, she could wear a hat," Tappen said. "Ain't no rule against a hat."

"You can't wear a hat in school."

"You can't?"

"My goodness, Tappen, your mother taught you nothin'? Ya gotta take it off soon as you step through the door."

"That's right," Pop said. "Can't pour nothin' into your brain if ya got a hat on." Even he didn't help.

Tappen would still wait after he finish each stroke back to her neck. But she just set there, her hand limp on her lap. *Like someone pulled a plug*, Beulah thought. *Me.*

"Ain't no problem go as a boy," Pop said.

"Heavens, Pop," Beulah said, "ain't a soul around don't know Dorrie's here. Esker take care of that."

"Well, nobody gonna believe she's a girl."

"Thanks, Pop."

"Won't be at Kaatersville for more 'n couple of weeks anyway," Tappen said, "before she probably go home."

"Who's she? The cat's mother?" Beulah hated them talkin' like Dorrie wasn't settin' right there. "See, Dorrie, you'll be goin' to Kaatersville while you stay with us. We're in that district, right on the border. The bus come right down there, to the mailbox at the end of the road. But it ain't probably more 'n a few weeks before your ma'll be home and okay."

Like Beulah was talkin' to the air. Dorrie didn't say nothin' back.

"There!" Tappen said. "All done!"

She looked the spittin' image of her brother when he was young—cute, tight, wiry. Even how she sat hunched looked more boy 'n ever. Beulah got out the hand mirror she keep in the top drawer, her junk drawer, and she show Dorrie front and back, feelin' Dorrie's head, ooh-in' and ah-in', and she pull her over close to Pop so he could feel it, too. "Nicer 'n mine," he said, rubbin' his own, and then hers again that got just a quarter inch more fuzz above the scalp. But it didn't work, Dorrie look at the mirror and her face stayed blank, even when her eyes filled up, it stayed blank. Then just as she look like she was gonna crack, she turn and run off up the stairs. Beulah closed her eyes, waitin' till she hear the door slam.

EVERY NIGHT BEULAH gone in to Dorrie's bed, tuck her in. She rub her hand on the covers over Dorrie's belly 'cause in bed is when she's the littlest, but also when she talks, or asks questions. Like the time she ask, "How come Laureen doesn't have a nickname? Like *Laurie?*" Beulah had to shrug. "Just never called her that. She just don't seem like a Laurie." Dorrie shake her head with a big smile, "No, definitely not. She needs that *eeeeeeen.*" Beulah smile. "Well, it ain't any good without the *Laur* part, too." And Dorrie nod, smile, too, before she squiggle down lower inside her bed and curl up. *Never seen a kid love bed so much,* Beulah thought.

But now, she could see Dorrie in the dark before she reached for the light on the bedside table. She was still in her clothes on her belly, pillow over her head just like the first day. Beulah stroked her back. "It won't be bad. Really," she said, but she knew she was lyin'. "Oh hell, it's gonna be horrible!" Beulah didn't think, it just come out. "First, them kids on the bus makin' fun of you for lookin' like a boy. Then all day in class—gonna be straight hell I know and if I had the power, I'd keep you home."

Beulah sat stunned from tellin' the truth. But Dorrie turned right over and pulled the pillow down, the grin pokin' her lip up.

"You don't think I been worried?" Beulah asked as she leaned toward that crooked smile.

Dorrie nodded slowly.

They were both quiet then, Dorrie on her back and Beulah's hand on her T-shirt, almost same size as her belly. Dorrie's eyes was still wet and red but the spell makin' her face blank was broken.

"I could hide," Dorrie said.

"Now you listen here!" Beulah said, sharp. "You ain't gonna hide, hear?" She lifted her hand up and set it down on her own thigh. "Run and hide. Run and hide. You ain't gonna turn coward now, girl, I don't care how bad it feel, them makin' fun of you. You gonna show your face that's pretty enough anyway, don't *need* any hair. You're a pretty girl, hear? Hear?" She waited for Dorrie to nod. "You hear?" And then Dorrie did, slowly, very slowly. Dorrie had never heard Beulah's voice like that.

"You're gonna walk in that room, hold your head up showin' your face and you gonna say, 'I am Eudora Buell, I don't care what you call me, boy girl Peter Nancy.' "

"Dorrie Shane." She looked straight into Beulah's eyes.

Beulah looked right back. "Dorrie Buell."

"Shane."

"Buell. Dorrie Shane Buell. You're Dorrie Buell and you can play games but don't you ever ever forget your last name."

In a way, Dorrie thought, Beulah looked ugly, compared to *her*. The skin on her cheeks drooped and she was big, with a big stomach that pushed tight against her dress when she sat down, and her arms drooped, too, like her cheeks. Beulah looked so much older than her, but she wasn't. She was the same age almost. It was old though, to have a five-year-old, but they had tried fourteen years to have Laureen. Beulah said that a lot, and each time Laureen would smile.

"You come from good stock, hear?" Dorrie nodded right away. "You don't got nothin' to be shamed of to anybody." Beulah stopped, lookin' at Dorrie's cheekbones. "Such a pretty face," she said, soft again, almost to herself.

"They're gonna know she's in the hospital," Dorrie said and turned her head toward the window. It looked, without a curtain, like black rectangles, four black rectangles. "That she's crazy," she whispered.

Beulah traced her finger along Dorrie's forehead, where it met the reddish brown fuzz that used to be her hair. *My new little boy*, she thought for just a second.

"Look at ya," Beulah said, her voice still soft, "bright little kid. Take a good ma do that. And feedin' and clothin' you, too. It ain't easy. And she ain't committed no crime neither. Bein' in the hospital's no crime.

"Everybody talks, you know, they talk big, but they ain't just had their boy die. And they're all *still* strugglin'. Don't show it straight to ya, but they are. Every one of 'em. It ain't easy just to live, never mind through sump'n like that."

Dorrie nodded. She didn't mind it was true, that living was so hard, she even wanted it true, 'cause Beulah said it, to her, in her bed. *The harder the better*, she thought for a second, as long as Beulah could be there with her and see it, and say it, and still, knowing it, run her hand up and down Dorrie's belly. It almost tickled.

"I *hate* that I have to wear a skirt again," Dorrie said.

Beulah smiled. "You know what my grandma used to say to us? We was four girls, all in skirts, and she said, 'You still got your two legs underneath, don't ya?' 'Course that usually meant work. We had to git to work, couldn't set around no more."

Dorrie smiled. "I was the fastest girl in my class, faster than Peggy Weaver and she's almost a foot taller than me."

"You better go pee and brush your teeth so I can tuck ya in."

BEULAH TURNED FROM the stove to get milk for her mornin' coffee, and Dorrie gave her a start. Like she just appeared, leanin' against the door frame to the kitchen, smilin'. Looked again just like David used to.

"Guess what Pop gave me?" Dorrie said, beamin', holdin' her hands behind her back.

"Now what in heaven's name?"

Dorrie jumped into the kitchen and whipped his red wool cap around over her head. "Brand-new."

Pop never worn it, Tappen's Christmas present to him last year. Even though his old cap's almost black, he likes how it feels, looks melted right onto his head. Dorrie pulled the bill down onto her forehead, it was too big but she didn't care. Beulah gave a low whistle, as good as she could in the mornin'.

"Dorrie Shane Buell." She stuck her hand out to Beulah, with the grin on.

"Mrs. Tappen," she said as she shook it, noddin' and smilin' both.

IT WAS ONLY a week later, Dorrie came down in her skirt and button-down shirt for the first day of school. Laureen, too, in one of Shooey's girl's skirts. Beulah just finished the hem the day before. Laureen took a beeline right toward her brand-new lunch pail, not even filled yet. They gone all the way to Miller's to get that.

There was a pail with a horse on it and a red barn, and Laureen picked it up thinkin' 'cause it's a horse, Dorrie's gonna like it. But then Dorrie shake her head. "Dumb," she says and Laureen shake her head, too, and says, "Dumb." And then Dorrie, just like she's goin' on forty, explains, "A horse's legs can't go that way, not in *any* gait." And Laureen now is noddin' like "of course, how dumb," till she seen a pail with a pair of fat robins on each side settin' on a limb, a little squirrel underneath, fat, too, a few acorns. And she picks it up like it's made of gold and then she remembers Dorrie there and looks up almost scared what Dorrie's gonna say but Dorrie nods "yeah" and Laureen's whole body giggles and she don't stop dotin' on them birds the whole way home.

Dorrie don't want a pail for herself, only a paper bag to take her sandwich in. Lucky she ain't growed none in the short while, they didn't need to buy her clothes, or even shoes. She still fit in her saddle shoes ain't been worn since last day of school. *Guess I could've asked Mike for the money*, Beulah thought, *ain't really no shame in askin' Mike.* Lucky, too, they'd had some downpours, 'cause both of the girls got clean, Laureen in a bath and Dorrie in the shower.

She had called the school but Sharon Boyce already knew, even had Dorrie listed under Mr. Stevens, the sixth-grade teacher. And the bus route was no problem, they changed that back in July to pick up Laureen goin' into kindergarten. Now they'd have two kids waitin' down there, end of the road. *Good all around*, Beulah thought. Kids can walk there by themselves. Be good for Laureen to walk that far, a little under a mile, without her ma. And be good for Dorrie, too, bein' the older and more sure. Maybe sump'n start sparkin' up between 'em.

Dorrie seemed all bright-eyed. Even after Beulah told her she can't eat her Cheerios with her hat on, and she gotta take it off at the school door. Can't wear her hat through the door. Dorrie just nodded, laid it down beside her bowl. She seemed so happy eatin', Beulah kept lookin' at her. Both of 'em was finished, bowls in the sink, teeth brushed, by quarter of seven, plenty of time to walk down there. Beulah handed them their lunch—egg salad and two cookies for Dorrie, and a piece of toast for Laureen and oatmeal with sugar and milk in a plastic icebox container. She don't care it'll be cold, that's what she wanted. Beulah leaned down and gave Laureen a kiss and then a hug, another kiss, and then she turned to Dorrie and that grin poke up and Dorrie flashed up her skirt quick as the wind but Beulah seen 'em— shorts. She got shorts on right under her skirt, and happy as a lark, she skip out the door and whip on her hat before she turn and take Laureen's hand. Beulah smiled. *Ain't nothin' to be worried about with that girl.*

"A CAP'S GOTTA have a good bill," Pop had said the day he gave it to her. Dorrie nodded but without looking up from the thick, rough tips of his fingers roaming back and forth across the red-and-black checks. "Just big enough," he said. Dorrie thought maybe he was changing his mind, but then he went on, "Now when you wear this cap, boy, you keep a mind where this bill's headin', hear?"

"Okay," she said quick, looking up, "okay," before he handed the cap over to her. She didn't put it on though, till she looked at which windows the sun was pouring through, and then, like Beulah, she stuck her right arm out straight east so she was facing north.

Dorrie knew right away Pop meant the direction. It drove Beulah crazy 'cause Pop (and Elmer, too) wouldn't ever say left or right, even inside. Pop was either headin' north through the kitchen or south into the pot or he'd answer her about where he'd set her box of rubber bands, saying, "West of the newspapers" — which were usually in the south end of the back room. Outside, it was easy for Beulah but she never got the hang of it inside.

She'd set her mouth. "I don't have all day," she'd say, and blow out hard. "Can't you ever make sump'n simple?"

"See, Dorrie," Beulah said once, "I have to go each time from start to scratch." But then she added, " 'Cept if I'm in the kitchen. There I know the sink's east. I get that on my right and I'm set."

Beulah always figured out north and east first. Even if she was facing her south windows, she'd turn her back to them so she was heading north and stick her right arm out east. Tappen grew up with it so he knew directions perfect but most times he'd say left and right to Beulah if they were in the house.

It was hard on the bus 'cause it kept turning and it took all Dorrie's concentration to keep the direction she was heading in her mind. She kept her face glued to the window. She could hear all the kids talking, though it wasn't as loud as her old bus, or as crowded. She was glad Laureen was beside her on the seat and happy just looking 'cause then no other kids could sit there. If she had to turn and say hi, she'd completely lose track. Still, Dorrie lost the direction two times. Once when a girl named Nancy got yelled at for chewing gum just as the bus was turning and once when a boy—he was older, a few seats behind them—started saying, "Cock piss suck cock piss suck" over and over, just the perfect loudness so everybody but the bus driver could hear.

Both times, Dorrie started over like Beulah did, "from start to scratch," though it didn't make her mad 'cause she *did* have all day. She checked the sun, which was coming from the east but in the southern half of the sky. She'd been practicing for a week and she didn't have to turn her whole body north anymore. The bus was mostly going south but it would change all the time, a little east, then southeast, or all the way east, or a little west, then southwest, even north sometimes 'cause the road was so curvy.

The bus came right up to the back of the school. Laureen's teacher was waiting, gathering all the kindergartners. Dorrie winked at Laureen as she let go her hand. Then she turned. The door faced south. Dorrie was heading straight north into the school. It seemed easy, with east on her right. There were kids all around, behind her and in front of her, all talking. She got as close to the door as she could, right up till she reached the doorsill, before she lifted the bill of her cap. It turned quiet behind her. *I am Dorrie Sha . . .* she tried to say it to herself like she practiced but she couldn't, it was dumb, pretend, crazy pretend. The quiet spread out behind her, stone quiet. She stared ahead, not seeing anything in the darker light, she stared straight north, followed the noise in the hall in front of her north. But the quiet kept spreading behind her, it followed her from the south. Her tears, too, they were coming from the south. She closed her eyes over and over to keep them back. She couldn't run back. She didn't know the number of the door she had to go to. She knew only north, she followed the noise north.

DORRIE WAS WALKING slower and slower toward the office at the end of the hall when the woman at the desk saw her and walked out to her. "Eudora Buell?" Dorrie stopped, looked up toward her, WEST, started to focus on the woman's face.

"Eudora Buell?" she asked again. Dorrie just looked. "You're with Mr. Stevens, room one thirty-seven, Mr. Stevens . . . Here hon, I'll take you."

Dorrie followed her, EAST, third door. The woman stopped and turned. Dorrie slowed. "Right here," she said to Dorrie and then louder, into the room, "Got one of your students here." Dorrie turned north and took very small steps through the door.

Mr. Stevens looked up and smiled. "Thank you, Mrs. Boyce," he said in a booming voice. And then almost as loud, "Who do we have here?"

Dorrie just looked at him. "Eudora Buell," she heard the woman behind her say. "Eudora Buell, a new *girl*." The room was quiet, very quiet.

"Hi, how ya doin'?" Mr. Stevens said and looked down at a sheet of paper on his desk. "Come right on in! Buell, Eudora . . .

yes." Then he turned back to her. "I'm Mr. Stevens, your teacher, but I guess you know *that*." Dorrie nodded.

Mr. Stevens smiled at her again before he looked back down to his sheet. "Let's see here . . . you're fourth row, third seat back."

Dorrie looked for the seat. There were kids, sitting, they were there but it was quiet, absolutely quiet. She stared, she stopped seeing anything but the seat. Her ears stared, too, so she couldn't hear any *one* thing. She walked toward her seat, WEST. She sat down, stared forward, EAST, her three new notebooks and her cap in front of her on the desk. She felt the cool of the chair against her legs till it was gone, it was warm.

"Okay!" Mr. Stevens said, loud, clapping his hands together. "We got everybody here?" "Yeah!" Kids were yelling.

"You all glad to have made it through another dull summer? And *finally* be back at school?" There was loud groaning from all over the room.

Mr. Stevens was smiling. He pointed to his white shirt. "You know what *my* name is?"

"Mr. Stevens!" a few kids yelled out. His sleeves were rolled up and his collar open so his thin dark tie hung down below it like Dorrie's dad's used to at dinner. His smile looked like it could break into a laugh at any moment.

"Well, there are two new kids this year." And then he said, "Carl Hoffman," and everyone looked over to a blond skinny boy with glasses in the first row. He turned so his back was to the window and smiled shyly, gave a little wave. Mr. Stevens said her name then, "Eudora Buell," out loud in that booming voice, and everybody looked, they turned around and looked at her, and she stared, hard, EAST.

"Well, time to get to work! Huh?" Mr. Stevens picked up the chalk and wrote on the board in huge letters as big as his voice:

STRATEGY. And then he drew four X's in the shape of a diamond. Dorrie could feel her lip poke up. Baseball. He was talking about baseball. She could tell by his smile. She looked over to the desk next to her, NORTH. The girl had written down *strategy* carefully at the top of her clean sheet of paper in her brand-new notebook. She was copying the X's, too, looking up, then down, up, down to make sure she had them in the right place.

"First off is the pitcher." And he made another X inside the diamond. A large boy a seat ahead and to the right of Dorrie leaned back on his chair and crossed his arms like an adult, looked all around with a huge smile on his face. There was the sound of a few pencils put down and chairs moving, breaths being let out.

There were X's for every player, even the outfielders, and then Mr. Stevens made arrows. He made them quick, sloppy quick to mark each player's territory and some went right on top of others. "Let's start with some hypothetical situations," he said, and then he wrote the word "hypothetical" on the board, too, but in small letters and only the girl beside Dorrie copied it down. The diamond got messier and messier and more and more full of arrows everywhere 'cause he was showing how each person would move for certain hits and the ball made dashed lines across the board.

Almost a half hour had gone by when Mr. Stevens chalked a dashed line that went all the way from home plate to the top of the board before he went onto his tippy-toes to keep the ball going off onto the yellow paint of the wall till the big boy with the folded arms yelled out "HOME RUN!" and everyone laughed. And then Mr. Stevens erased the board with the same quick sloppy strokes so that little bits of arrows and dashes and X's were still left behind him.

Every single day they'd play, he said. Recess, eleven, before lunch. Softball but with mitts. There were nineteen baseball mitts he had collected or been given. There were seventeen in the class. How many lefties? Five. Five! He'll work on getting another leftie mitt. The mitts stay at school, in *that* box. He would pitch. To both teams. Dorrie liked how his booming voice could change in a word from laughy to serious and back again.

The more Dorrie listened, the more she felt the hardness of a rock inside her. But it didn't feel bad, it felt good, it felt like she was good and she'd have her chance and she would show she was good. She could play baseball. She even liked the waiting 'cause the rock kept on hardening, it almost shined.

The baseball field was out the side door, WEST. They didn't need to line up in the hall. She put on her cap as soon as she reached the door, and started to run. All of them were running west down the steps and out to the field. Mr. Stevens walked behind but when he stopped near home plate, everyone started to gather around him, smacking their mitts. He picked the teams. Dorrie's team was first up. The big boy was named Billy Schmidt. He was on her team and he acted like the captain. He told everybody who was up when. He pointed to her, fifth. No one said anything to her, or said her name. She sat at the end of the second green bench, holding close to her rock. She watched the field, WEST.

There were nine out there, eight on the bench. Billy was first up. Everyone started yelling his name. He took some practice swings before he stepped to the plate. He looked like he was good. He hit first pitch. A double. Everyone was yelling. A few kids kept on, "That-a-way, Billy!" even after a girl named Amy got up. She struck out in three pitches, giggling. Kevin, a tall guy but a little fat, hit a single. Billy stayed on second. A small, skinny boy was next, but the team was yelling again, "Come on, Ricky!" "You can do it, Ricky!" "Let's go, Ricky!" He had a good swing. A pop fly to shortstop. A girl caught it. "Out!" Mr. Stevens's arm flew up and back. "Good catch, Pepper," the first baseman yelled. She gave a nod but didn't smile. She looked tall.

Dorrie was up. The bench was quiet. She walked toward the bat with her shorts on under her skirt. She loved how the bat felt, its weight, the shiny blond wood, where it was warm already and where it was cool, and how firm she held it, and comfortable. She stepped right up to the plate, moved back and forth just a little bit from one foot to the other like David had showed her. "Take enough time," he had said, "not all day but just enough." And then she focused her eyes hard on Mr. Stevens, SOUTH-WEST. He pitched. Way high. She backed off, her bat falling to swing loosely near the ground. "Good choice," Mr. Stevens said. "Sorry." And then he yelled officially, "BALL one!"

The next pitch was perfect, like one of David's, just enough above her knees and a little outside, it was made for her, for the rock, for the bat, it hit solid, perfect. Low between first and second, but hard and far, far. She ran, throwing her cap off, she ran fast, she knew it was fast. She could feel the hardness of the grass cut close to the ground underneath as her feet landed and each stride seemed to go longer, farther as she rounded first, arcing toward second, and everyone back on the bench was yelling. Billy was home! But she kept watching, watching, like David had taught her, she could make it to third, she could slide, she was just fast enough, just little enough, her feet slid in to the bag.

She stood up in the small cloud of dust as she heard the ball land in the boy's glove ten feet from the base. They were still yelling from the bench. She brushed the dirt, the red dirt on the side of her calf just a little, just so her hands could get dirty, too, before she rested them on her hips to wait. She breathed fast and easy. Her teammates held out their hands for Billy to slap as he walked by both benches before he sat down.

A guy named Wayne was up. Big. "Let's go, Wayne!" "Come on, Wayne!" "Let it go, Wayne!" "No hitter! No hitter!" from the first baseman. She bent down, loosened her shoulders like David, readied herself again to run. NORTH. Her foot against the edge of the bag, she waited, ready, her hand on her thigh, she could feel the shorts through her skirt as she watched.

He hit. Right over second. Plenty of time, she slowed near home, springing up on each stride like a horse in a collected, springy trot, she looked down as her foot bounced on and off the plate, easy, she slowed to a walk. A boy, small, dark-haired, handed her her cap, smiling. They were saying her name "Eudora." "Dorrie," she yelled out as she put on her cap. "Call me Dorrie." And they said that, too: "All right, Dorrie," "That-a-way, Dorrie," "Way to go, Dorrie." *Like they know me,* she thought. The smile poked her lip up and it was David's and hers both as she slapped fast the line of hands.

"YA KNOW, I know you." Pepper swung her legs over the cafeteria bench, shaking her finger at Dorrie. "Don't you ride the Petersons' horses?"

Dorrie nodded. "Well, I used to." Pepper was huge, bigger than Peggy.

"You were at the county fair last year, weren't you?"

Dorrie nodded, "Uh-huh."

Pepper opened her carton of milk. "Don't you want to get one?" she asked. "They're right in there."

Dorrie shook her head, "Nah." *Maybe Beulah forgot*, she thought. *And ice cream, too.* She had no change for ice cream.

Pepper shrugged again and took out her sandwich. Hers was in a paper bag, too. The wax paper was folded very neatly and Scotch-taped so it was still square like the bread. *Like* she *used to do*, Dorrie thought. Beulah had rolled her sandwich up so quick.

Joanne Tully, who had been on Dorrie's team, sat across from Pepper. She said "hi" and some of the other girls did, too, or they smiled quickly as they set their trays on the table, farther down, and stepped over the bench. Most of them bought lunch.

"Yeah." Pepper turned to Dorrie. "My dad made me watch you. He made my sister, too, and he talked about your riding the whole time. Your heels, your legs, your seat, your hands, your posture . . ." she threw her eyes up but then she smiled. "And then you went and won the jumping."

Dorrie nodded but she didn't smile.

Pepper showed her sandwich to Dorrie. "Bologna." She shrugged again. "Not my favorite but—"

"Egg salad," Dorrie said, showing hers.

"Ich!" But then Pepper smiled.

"But if you ever bring tuna fish," Joanne said to Dorrie, but smiling at Pepper, "watch out!"

"I'll trade for that," Pepper said.

"Yeah, right!" Joanne said and then she smiled at Dorrie. "Steal it more likely."

"You make such a big deal outta that one time." But Pepper was smiling. "I'm gettin' a Fudgsicle *now*," she said, standing up. "They always run out."

The boys were all huddled together at the next table, like in football. Billy Schmidt turned around and all the others looked over. "Hey Pepper!" he yelled. "How's your new boyfriend?"

"Stuff it!" she yelled toward them and walked off.

Joanne leaned toward Dorrie. "He's only a jerk sometimes," she said quietly. "Not like Kevin."

When Pepper came back, the boys didn't say anything. She was already eating her Fudgsicle.

"Hey." She tapped Dorrie on the shoulder as she stepped in. "Did you know Kenny Telford? He's Western but—he was my sister's age, she really liked him, you know, *like* like." Her mouth looked cold, she was sucking on her Fudgsicle as fast as she could, taking in as much cold as she could. "He had a beautiful quarter horse named Cooper? You remember? He always won the Western Pleasure?" But Dorrie kept shaking her head. "Well anyway, he hung himself this summer."

"Wha-at?!!" Joanne said loud, slapping her carton of milk down.

"Yeah," Pepper went on, "from a tree. They think he stood from his horse."

"Why?" Joanne said.

" 'Cause it's higher!"

"I know that! I mean, why did he do it?"

"Oh." Pepper laughed a little. "No one knows." She shrugged, turning to Dorrie, who was looking from one to the other. "He seemed happy. At least that's what everyone keeps saying." Joanne shuddered. "My dad and my sister went to his funeral. She said everyone was really a mess. Especially his mother. She was a *total* mess."

"What's she *supposed* to be?" Joanne said, and then she stretched her neck and stuck her chin up with her lips pinched together. "Oh dear . . . dear, dear," she said in a high voice with a fake English accent. "My son killed himself today. Toodleloo!" She gave a little wave with her hand cupped tight. Pepper laughed. Joanne kept going, "Oh no, I *forgot* my lipstick. I couldn't bear"—she pulled her lips all the way back—"be-ar to be without my lipstick."

Dorrie started to laugh along and Pepper stretched her neck, too. Her face looked like a bird's, tilting back and forth. "What should I wear to the funeral? My red dress, or let's see, maybe my blue?"

"Black and blue," Dorrie blurted, but it came out hard.

The two girls both stopped laughing, turned toward her. "I ride, too," Pepper said, "though not . . . not like you."

"You some kind of champion or something?" Joanne said.

Dorrie shook her head. "No."

"She could be," Pepper corrected her. "That's what my dad said."

"I don't have a horse," Dorrie said. "And the Petersons moved."

"You should come over. You can ride one of ours. We have four, Western but . . . my dad wants us to start English, too, so we can jump. Uh-oh. Time."

Dorrie turned around and saw a woman swinging back the two doors. "Sixth," the woman yelled and waved her arm. She was about to blow a whistle.

"Who's she?" Dorrie said as they were getting up.

"Senior bitch!" Pepper said, low. And then she pinched her lips and said through her teeth, "Miss Murphy."

Joanne turned around—she was normal tall—and said, "She makes each class line up. Even sixth. It's so dumb." Everyone paired up, NORTH. Dorrie stayed with Pepper. She put her hand flat on her head and keeping it at the same height swung it over to just under Pepper's shoulders.

Billy Schmidt was in front of them. He turned around to Dorrie. "So do you piss like a boy, too?" he said, just low enough.

Dorrie looked up, feeling Pepper there beside her. "Yup," she said, looking straight into his eyes, "I do." He turned back around.

"Shut *him* up," Pepper mouthed to her. "Can you really?"
Dorrie nodded.

Pepper cupped her hands up to her mouth and leaned down to Dorrie's ear. "Standing up?"

Dorrie nodded again. She felt like Elmer but she didn't know why 'cause he never lied.

"That's so neat! You gotta show me!" Pepper whispered low.

And then she turned back to Joanne behind her, whispered to her in cupped hands, too, while Joanne looked at Dorrie and started to giggle. They all started to giggle.

"Show me, too," Joanne whispered, still giggling, she couldn't stop.

"Girls!"

They all stood up straight-faced, turning straight forward, looked forward.

"Ma-arrch!" Dorrie said, like David imitating Mrs. Klepp, but it came out too loud.

Pepper and Joanne both slapped their hands to their mouths but you could still see they were laughing. Till the woman, Miss Murphy, stepped toward them, looked right at Dorrie.

"*What* did you say?" she asked.

Dorrie looked straight ahead.

"What. Did. You. Say?"

"Nothing," Dorrie said. "*Always* say 'Nothing,' " David had said after the first time she got detention. "They take it kinda as you're sorry even though you aren't."

"You better watch out, Missy," the woman said, "I know your type."

Pepper pushed her elbow against Dorrie's shoulder. Dorrie looked straight forward, NORTH. She stayed blank-faced, but she pushed back.

"All right," Miss Murphy said, and then louder. "Go on.

"One thirty-seven's out," she said to a younger woman following behind her, writing on a pad. And then Dorrie heard, low, "It's the Buell girl."

Pepper pushed again and their arms stayed together till they were all the way out of the cafeteria. Then Pepper looked down. "See?" and she mouthed, "Bitch!"

Joanne sat in the front row. Pepper's desk was even with hers but three seats over. *Like Pop and Elmer,* Dorrie thought. Even though they were the same age they were three rows apart by the time Pop stopped because each row was a grade and they always kept Elmer back.

Some kids were still coming in from the bathroom. Billy Schmidt. He pushed his chair back—it looked too small for him—and he turned around, stretched toward Dorrie. "You gonna show me how you piss, too?" he said, a big smile on his face.

Dorrie looked straight ahead, EAST.

"Huh?" he said. "Baldie? You gonna show me, too?"

She kept her eyes east, pushing both her fists forward into the bottom shelf of her desk, like it was a ship steering east, or like Elmer the time he tracked east five whole days with no food, just his compass and his dog.

"Huh, baldie?" he said again louder, but Dorrie didn't look. She could still feel where Pepper's elbow had pushed against her shoulder as they both faced north and began to walk.

DORRIE LEANED BACK as far as she could but the pee sprayed out everywhere and down her legs. It seemed hopeless. She stepped, SOUTHEAST, into the creek to wash, but pulled her foot right up out of the too too cold but then put it right down again up to her shin. She loved how the water was dark but the cold felt bright and made her move quick—her feet going up and down, up and down, like she was running away and wanting the cold all at once.

It took a long time, though, before it seemed, not warm, but not too cold to splash her legs and her privates clean and then it took even longer, jumping up and down shaking each of her legs over the rocks, to dry off enough to get dressed again without water sticking to the inside of her pants. She had goosebumps now everywhere on her legs and arms.

A crack! A branch, she was being watched, she knew it, she froze, her one sock still on the rocks with her sneaker. She didn't move at all. She waited. SOUTHWEST. Then she turned, just her head, EAST, toward where the branch had broken before there was nothing again, no sound again. She squeezed her eyes tight to see in among the grays and blacks of the trees, the ground, through the plain dark of the air. She saw nothing move. She waited. She could see more, farther, but still nothing moving. She waited and waited. And then she laughed. It was Joker, gray, too, shades of gray but round, and curly, little curls like miniature waves against the straight lines of the trees.

"You scared me!" she said out loud, putting on her other sock and tying her sneaker in the air.

She jumped rock to rock across the creek toward where he stood so clearly now but had looked so invisible before. Still, he didn't move. He was resting his left hind. She walked up to him as quietly as she could, reached to touch the top of his neck and even then he turned his head only enough to keep the whole of his eye toward her.

"Joker Joker Joker Jo Kerjok Kerjok," Dorrie said, scratching her fingers into his mane. "Kerjok, little Kerjok. Whatta *you* doin' here? You lookin' at me pee? Huh? Huh? Little Kerjok?" She kissed his nose.

Dorrie pulled on his neck just enough to tip him off balance so he'd move and then keep moving if he wanted to. He did. It had become almost night in the woods. They walked together SOUTH, SOUTHEAST back toward the high pasture and then down toward the few windows already with lights, both toward supper, his from Tappen in the cow barn and hers from Beulah in the house.

IT SMELLED THICK with meat when Dorrie walked in. Beulah stood at the stove, then moved to the sink, the icebox. *Her triangle*, Dorrie thought, thinking of the shapes on her brand-new math book. Beulah was wearing her kitchen apron, which she wore more and more instead of her garden one, now that customers only came for mums, pumpkins, any surplus vegetables they laid out, sometimes a few shrubs.

"Meat loaf," Beulah said, "for your first day at school. You and Laureen. Meat loaf and mashed potatoes. It's the *one* thing you *both* like."

Dorrie smiled at Laureen at the table, then squinched up her T-shirt like her belly had a mouth. "Mmmm-nnn."

Laureen hunched over to hear her own belly. "Mmmm-nnn."

"And I got ketchup, too, for ya." Beulah got the bottle out of the icebox and set it down on the counter like it was for right then. " 'Course Laureen will only eat it with gravy. So I'm makin' that." Then she whispered, "Check Pop."

Dorrie looked into the back room and nodded to Beulah, which meant, *He's coming.*

"Takin' forever tonight," Beulah said, too loud.

Pop yelled back, "I'm comin'! I'm comin'! She's always hurryin' me!" He looked up. "That you, boy?"

"YUP," Dorrie yelled. "A LITTLE WEST OF SOUTH."

"That's my boy. Keepin' track."

"YUP." Dorrie didn't say any more 'cause then he'd stop again and Beulah hated that. She didn't like *anyone* to start Pop talking till he was sitting at the table. "He'd talk to the moon if it meant he didn't have to walk," she said once. And she was already starting the gravy.

"Could you run tell Tappen five, at the most ten minutes. Probably the cow barn."

Dorrie ran. It was her job and she loved it, running from the light and smell of the kitchen and from Beulah as fast as she could through the not-quite night into *his* barn where Tappen would be standing at the workbench that was covered in junk, one bright bulb aimed and shining on some piece of old metal the same color as his hands. Or Dorrie would see the light in the cow barn where the five cows Tappen had left would be already chewing, their heads straight forward and steady, chewing. "Professional chewers," she once said and Tappen laughed, almost out loud. She knew he'd be carrying hay or a shovel or a block of red salt and that he would look up and smile.

"Okay," he said, before she said anything. "I'll be right in."

She paused. The beams had been painted white once but now every corner and along every beam was covered in cobwebs, hanging and stretched like curtains colored in shades of brown.

"How was school?" Tappen asked. Dorrie looked over, surprised. "Any kids tease?"

"Mainly one. Billy Schmidt."

"Schmidt, huh. . . . His dad, must be his dad, maybe his uncle, it was Jeff, he was a year below me."

"Was he mean?"

"We all was."

"You were, too?"

"Not *all* the time. But we was all mean to *some*one."

"Who were you mean to?"

Tappen smiled. "Teacher. But you got Mr. Stevens, don't ya? You'll like *him*."

Dorrie smiled. "I got a triple, first inning. I was the only one the whole game. Well, we only played three innings. But I was second baseman and I caught every ball thrown to me so I know he'll keep me there."

"Yup, bet you can play all right. That'll show 'im, that Schmidt fellow."

Tappen was standing on the stone sill, nodding. Dorrie moved up beside him. He was looking out toward the house, southwest, but then he reached back and hit the lights and pulled on the huge barn door which squeaked and rumbled as it slid halfway closed. "Guess that's enough," he said. "Ain't gonna freeze tonight, that's for sure."

She followed his steps. Going in to supper they were bigger, she had to spring and stretch from one to the next.

"Your hair's gonna grow soon enough. Don't you worry," Tappen said before they reached the back porch where he sat to untie his boots that smelled just like the barn. "And you're gonna look back one day and you're gonna like it, that you gone and cut it off. You're gonna tell people and they'll all smile, you mark me."

"Pepper Benton thought it was neat."

"The Benton girl?"

"Yeah. Pepper's what she likes to be called but she's really Patricia. They have *four* horses."

Tappen got up. His socks were quiet on the cement. "You ain't goin' up there, hear?" He looked back and down at her. "You hear me?"

She nodded. She didn't ask why. She just nodded, before Tappen opened the door into the thick smell of Beulah's cooking.

IT TOOK DORRIE almost two weeks, holding her pee in and practicing whenever she could in the shower or after school out at the creek. Each day the water seemed colder and colder. Finally she could shoot the pee out so that it didn't drip on her legs at all, even at the end. And she found out, too, that if she pulled both pieces of skin up and out, just a little, exactly even, the pee wouldn't fan out but jet right straight ahead. The hard thing was to do it wearing her pants and underpants and not get any pee on her fingers.

"I'm *dying*," Pepper said, waiting to see. Every single day, Dorrie had to make up another excuse, but she was good at it. "Inspired," was the word Mrs. Klepp had used. Dorrie could remember each excuse, too, just like it was real 'cause she'd picture it in her mind. She could still see some things even from last year, like her homework left on the seat of her dad's car, it was so clear that she couldn't remember if she'd made it up or if she had actually left it there.

Finally, Dorrie said okay. She was holding her pee in. Pepper thought the bathroom *before* recess would be clear but Amy and Colleen were smoking in there 'cause they hated baseball. They always dragged themselves out the door last and onto the field when the teams were almost all picked. Dorrie had to keep holding it in during the whole game, especially running. But after recess, after everyone headed to lunch, Joanne stood guard at the door and when it was all clear, Dorrie lifted the seat and stood back by where the stall door used to be. She lowered her underpants, planted her feet, held her skirt up with her elbows, leaned back and shot, perfect, the pee streamed straight into the bowl, only the tiniest bit sprayed sideways.

"Wow!" Pepper's jaw dropped and Joanne started to giggle. "That is the neatest!"

"How'd you DO that?"

"Practice," Dorrie said and they both cracked up laughing.

"You gotta come over," Pepper said, "and show that to me, how to do it. And we could ride, too."

"Yeah," Dorrie said, and walked to the sink to wash her hands. Only a few drops got on her fingers.

"I'll call you tonight, okay? To ask?"

"Yeah." Dorrie nodded quick, pushing her shoulder against the door. "I'm starving," she said, and they both followed her out, Joanne still giggling.

THE WHOLE NIGHT Dorrie stayed by the kitchen near the phone. She always did her homework on the table under the light 'cause her room didn't have a desk and it was really small. She finished in a half hour, but she still sat there, staring at her math book till all the numbers turned to fuzz. Then she'd draw back and they would separate out clear again. She did it over and over till Laureen stuck her hand in front of Dorrie's face. Dorrie grabbed her. "Pinky poo pinky poo pinky poo," she sang as she pulled Laureen onto her lap and tickled her. "The little pinker, little pinker poo." Laureen screamed and giggled.

After Dorrie stopped, Laureen lay there looking up and smiling while Dorrie stroked her belly. Dorrie knew it was coming—her Charlie face, Tappen called it, like she was begging biscuits. Laureen sat up. "Cost a nickel," Dorrie said, shaking her head but smiling. "A whole nickel."

"Oh ple-ease. Ple-ease. Ple-ease."

"Wel-l-l"—Dorrie loved to draw it out—"okay. Just this one time."

Laureen was all ready with her cupped hand. Back and forth, back and forth over Dorrie's head, feeling her hair.

DORRIE DIDN'T KNOW the phone number to give to Pepper. "Don't worry, I'll just look it up," she had said, shrugging. "It's under 'Tappen.'" But they were all finished supper now. Beulah had dished up the ice cream, spumoni, Tappen's favorite. She kept saying she didn't like it and wouldn't give herself a bowl but she still kept eating it off the scoop. The phone rang. Dorrie's chair scraped back. "I'll get it!" she said.

"Hello," she started carefully. "Oh hi! . . . Yeah. . . . Yeah, I'll ask, okay? Hold on." She put the receiver down, waited at the basement door for Beulah to come back up from the freezer. She spoke low: "Can I go tomorrow on the bus to Joanne's and stay over? Joanne Tully's?"

Beulah smiled. "Don't see why not. Sure. Joanne's ma knows you comin', right?" She started to fill the dishpan at the sink.

"Yeah," Dorrie said, nodding real quick before she ran back to the phone. Beulah kept smiling, squirting the soap, feeling the water get hotter.

"Yeah, I can," Dorrie said. "Yeah. I know, a note for the bus, yeah. I won't forget. . . . Okay. Thanks. Bye." Dorrie let out a little breath as she put down the phone. Then the smile came. But she went back to her place next to Tappen and finished eating her ice cream.

"THANKS," DORRIE SAID the next morning, picking the note up with her lunch bag. Beulah was already starting to can tomato sauce. "That means you'll have to get Laureen down at the mailbox, doesn't it?"

"Oh, sweetie. Don't you worry about *that*. I ain't gonna forget about my baby." Beulah wiped her hands on her apron and grabbed Laureen and lifted her up to give her a little kiss. "I ain't gonna forget about my baby," she said again. Then she set her down and pulled Dorrie in close and squeezed her. "I ain't a mother for nothin', ya know?"

Dorrie nodded. "I know," she said, fingering the stains running over the tiny flowers on Beulah's apron.

PEPPER POINTED TO a man standing by the door of bus number 26, nodding to each kid getting on. "That's him," she said to Dorrie, "Mr. Halcott," and they both ran up and Dorrie handed him the note and started talking right away really fast, waving her hands: "But my mother, just my temporary mother, Beulah, she got the name of Pepper, I mean Patricia, wrong and now its—"

"Ho-old on. Hold on. Calm down girls," he said, smiling, raising his hand and then lowering it: SLOW DOWN. "Why don't you let me read this note first and then you can tell me what the problem is, all right?"

Dorrie nodded fast, "Okay." She looked at Pepper, who looked back, crossed her fingers in front of her neck.

Mr. Halcott looked up from reading. "Okay," he said slowly.

Dorrie pointed to herself, "I'm Eudora." He nodded. "Patricia Benton's friend," and she pointed to Pepper who nodded hard. "And I'm supposed to go to *her* house and I just read my note right now and Beulah, she's my mom, sort of, just my temporary mom"—Dorrie started talking faster and faster—"she got mixed up about my friends. She said Joanne Tully—who *is* my friend but not where I'm supposed to go tonight." Dorrie waved her hands. "She *always* gets Joanne and Pepper mixed up and I didn't see it till just now so I couldn't call her and now it might be too late."

Mr. Halcott looked at Pepper. "She supposed to go to your house?" he asked her.

Pepper looked much older to Dorrie all of a sudden. "Yeah," she said calmly. "Her mom, I mean Mrs. Tappen, just got it mixed up."

He smiled and tilted his head toward his bus. "Get in. We'll get ya there, Eudora. You can settle down now."

"Oh, thank you *so* much," Dorrie said.

"Thanks," Pepper said, still older, and she followed Dorrie onto the bus.

BEULAH STOOD ON top of the manure pile in her big black rubber boots. She'd been meanin' to harvest all the pumpkins that sprouted there on their own. Every fall, they throw what's dead in the fields onto the pile, but it's always the pumpkin seeds that take. These ones had such a cute shape, Beulah was hopin' they'd get just a bit bigger and orange up more before frost killed off their leaves. It was a couple degrees warmer on the pile and that helped a few nights, but this last frost, that got 'em—Damn that Tappen! This is how they fight, always have. She start whatever she's been puttin' off and he start bangin' away and cussin' some metal, some blade been broke all summer.

Why in heaven's name would that girl lie? was all Beulah could think at first, after she called Marleen, Joanne's ma, for no real reason, just 'cause she was feelin' excited herself when she come in for lunch. She just couldn't see Dorrie lyin' like that out of the blue, and she was right, she found out when she talk to Tappen, it wasn't out of the blue at all, and she must be with the Benton girl. Still made her blood rise up.

"You ain't gonna hold her here," Beulah said. "Not like that you ain't."

Tappen had stopped bangin' but he didn't look up from the vise. He spoke so low Beulah could barely hear him. "It's you told me about him first. After Marge cleaned up there. Seen how he come out that girl's door."

"Well it ain't *her* fault!" Beulah yelled. She didn't care Tappen was closin' down toward his fuse. Beulah looked away. "Poor Benton girl. God knows she gone through enough."

He started real slow, talkin' through his teeth, "I didn't say it was her fault. Now you go puttin' words . . ." He stepped one leg back, head down between his straight arms leanin' against the workbench, lookin' at the floor. Then he flung his arm up. "You ain't fit to fight."

"Well, you ain't fit to father no girl!" Beulah yelled back as she throwed open the door. But she only got about ten steps out when she turned back and yelled, "Can't even play with her new friend." She was throwin' *her* arm now. "And she don't even know why!"

But nothin' came back from Tappen's barn, the metal door still the color of primer.

"Start tying her up, why don't ya? Like a dog. Be good as what you told her!" Beulah was yellin' at the barn from the middle of the lot. "Yup, just get a hold and and and and . . ." Tappen kicked the door shut, opened it, and kicked it shut again. The battens that were still nailed onto the side shook. "Yut, do just about as good as that," Beulah said as she turned around and walked toward the pile been waitin' for her. How it just sets there. She started hackin' away at the pumpkin stems with her garden knife, used to be her old butcher knife till it started rustin' too much for meat.

It wasn't that she didn't like the half-green pumpkins, but they don't sell, so every Halloween they have twenty or thirty unripe or flat-sided pumpkins on their stoop. And she found a few acorn squash must have come from the seeds in the kitchen garbage that didn't go to the chickens, and then what she calls "the unnameables" she wouldn't feed no one—she left them to set and rot, do their job that way.

It had been about a hour since she had got Laureen, fed her a bowl of Cheerios she loves now since Dorrie does. And now Beulah was hurryin' to finish 'cause Laureen was at her limit not gettin' attention after school, half dancin' half whinin' at the bottom of the pile, comin' in close as she could bear before she jumped away again, goin' "Ick! Ick!"

"I'm gonna go git her." Tappen was lookin' up to where Beulah was workin.' "I'm gonna go git her."

Beulah stayed bent over, fingerin' for the stems, choppin' 'em off so they don't break close. "Nope, that's right. You ain't gonna talk, or nothin' like that. You just gonna drive up there, git her."

"Ain't nothin' to talk about. She's the one lied."

"Nope, nothin'. Nothin' at all. Never. Oh, go on!" She threw her arm and a little orange gourd flew up in the air. Laureen started to get it but it landed still in the manure. "Drive right up there. Cause a scene, why don't ya?"

"I ain't gonna stand here while she's up there at that place, lyin'."

Beulah stood up, looked down at Tappen. "She didn't just up and lie for nothin'. She got a reason, don't you see? You can't be too dumb to see that?"

"Oh, you're diggin' low now, Beulah. And just 'cause you won't see nothin' come out of that girl ain't shinin' golden." And he walked off, slow and steady toward his truck.

Beulah hosed off every pumpkin front of the greenhouse before she lined 'em up, settin' 'em in groups accordin' to their weight. She didn't actually put 'em on a scale, just picked 'em up and guessed, but she had to persuade Laureen not to move every one she set down. "Now, we'll put this one over there with his family. . . . And this one here *wants* to be over, right about here. . . . Yut, he does. Asked me personally." It was almost dark when she could head in, one hand in Laureen's and one holdin' her apron up carryin' gourds, squash, and the ugliest of the pumpkins to cook.

DORRIE ROLLED THE wheelbarrow into the stall while Pepper moved around each horse, scraping the piles of manure together before she shoveled them up. "How come you don't do it after you let them out?" Dorrie asked. "It'd be so much easier."

" 'Cause of my dad," Pepper said, rolling her eyes. "We have to do it before we ride, *or else*."

The barn was full of air and the wood was light, like it had just been cut. There weren't any cobwebs on the ceiling or in the corners—even the floor was swept perfectly clean.

Pepper grabbed the box of Ritz crackers off the top of the feed bin and handed it to Dorrie. "They're a little stale but . . ." She took the cover off the new jumping saddle. "You can ride Jupie. My sister's horse. She's . . . cheerleading," she made a face to Dorrie.

Pepper led Sis out into the aisle and snapped the cross-tie onto her halter. Dorrie stood back, eating the crackers, looked Sis over. She was an Appaloosa with big brown spots on her rump, maybe fifteen hands. Little compared to most of Mrs. Peterson's horses. Pepper played with Sis's lower lip, which hung relaxed, made a funny blipping noise with it. Then she laughed and put her face down onto Sis's nose. "My Sis! My BIG BIG Sis."

Dorrie opened her palm toward Sis with a cracker on it, "She like 'em?"

"Loves 'em!"

Dorrie scratched Sis's mane while she let her nibble, lick the salt off her hand. She turned to Pepper, smiling. "I gotta pee."

"Finally!" Pepper said. "I can't hold it in much longer!" She led Sis back into her stall. "Come on out here, out the tack room door. By the hose."

Pepper took off her pants. "Your underpants, too," Dorrie said. "Just at first."

Pepper started to giggle. "Oh God! Lucky Mom's never out here."

Dorrie unzipped her dungarees, pulled down the front of her underpants, leaned back and peed. Not even one drip! Pepper covered her mouth and started laughing again. "Oh! Oh no!" she folded over and squeezed her legs shut. "I'm gonna die if I don't pee right now!"

"Well, lean way back and you gotta hold your, the two little, the pieces of skin up and just a little away, okay? You got 'em? Okay?"

Pepper was trying to stop giggling and concentrate.

"You gotta really lean back, farther, yeah, as far as you can and now, really PUSH it out. Like you're . . . SHOOTING it out. Yeah. OOPS." Dorrie started to laugh.

"Yuck! It's . . . all over me!"

Dorrie was laughing so hard, she could barely get words out. "That's what . . . that's what happens . . . in the beginning." She held her belly with both arms watching Pepper walk with her legs wide apart to the faucet. Pepper sprayed her legs down

and then—just quick!—flicked the hose toward Dorrie. "HEY!"
Pepper ran after her, holding her thumb over the hose to make
the water spray but she started laughing too hard to aim well and
Dorrie ran out of reach. Pepper acted like she was giving up, like
she was turning off the faucet behind her but she was really turning it up. Dorrie walked in closer till . . . SPRAY!! Dorrie's hair,
shirt, her right leg were soaked! Pepper couldn't stop laughing
and the water sprayed out everywhere.

It took a long time before their laughing seemed all the way
gone, for good, and they turned the water off. They walked back
into the barn, Pepper carrying her clothes and shoes. Her butt
was bright red, cold, and her legs were full of goosebumps and
shiny wet. She put her stuff down on the feed bin and started
shaking out each of her legs to dry them. But then she froze, her
eyes fixed. "Oh God." Dorrie turned toward where she was staring. A big man that must have been Mr. Benton was up the ramp
and opening the bottom half of the door.

Pepper straightened up, her mouth open. She covered her privates with both her hands.

He shut the door behind him before he looked at Pepper, it
seemed a long time, his hands on his hips. He was smiling! His
face was smiling, dark dark red and smiling. "Ah, you trying to
hide it, huh? Trying to hide the little kitten, huh? Huh?"

Pepper's face turned white. She looked over at Dorrie. Dorrie
swallowed, looked from Pepper back to him. "Hidin' it, huh?" he
was still saying but he was turning his head. He saw Dorrie,
stopped smiling, stared at her like he didn't know what she was.
Then he turned back to Pepper and said, "Well, you little whore.
You little disgusting whore."

Pepper ran, but he caught her, he caught her but he didn't yell
or hit her, he was just saying, "You whore, you disgusting whore,"
before he pushed her toward the tack room, toward where she

was trying to run. Dorrie ran, too. They both ran out and up the hill behind the barn and the house.

Tappen stared out of the truck window. He had just pulled onto the new macadam when he saw the Benton girl, pantless, and Dorrie, behind her, scramblin' up from the barn through the rocks and scrub. And then him! Walkin' down the barn ramp and comin' toward the house. Tappen kept his eyes fixed on him as he reached slowly back for his gun, opened the truck door, cocked the hammer.

The kitchen door slammed, but Tappen's eyes never moved off Benton, who had stopped halfway across the lawn. "Ain't my business the kind of stuff goes on here, ma'am, but I ain't lettin' my girl stay."

"What?!" Pepper's mom said.

"Dorrie," he called, just loud enough. "Get in the truck."

Dorrie saw the gun, saw Mr. Benton standing on the lawn. She didn't run, she walked down the hill away from Pepper, who was crying, hiding behind the hardhack.

"What's going on?" Pepper's mom kept saying. "What's going on?" Looking at Tappen, then her husband. Benton didn't answer. He was staring at the gun. Tappen still didn't move.

Dorrie walked toward the rusty green door of the truck. "Get in," Tappen said. He backed into the driver's seat. "You ain't gonna get away with this, Benton!"

Dorrie climbed onto the once-white rug covering the seat springs, stained now with cat piss and grease.

"NO, IT'S YOU that's in trouble, Clay. Pull a gun on a man in his own driveway," Esker said. "And a rich man at that."

Tappen just set there, lookin' into his cup steamin' up. Beulah had just poured 'em both hot coffee. She kept one eye on Tappen but her head was cocked for little ears on the stairs. She had made him wait till nine to call Esker, didn't want to drag Dorrie through more. Poor girl couldn't talk through supper, didn't even fight back at Pop when he land a spoon of squash on her plate.

"So he gonna just get away, just like that, get away," Tappen said.

"I'm tellin' you, Clay." Esker put a second teaspoon of sugar in. "As a friend. You didn't see nothin', hear? That man got more lawyers than you got . . . than you got . . . cows."

Tappen just stare at his coffee, black.

Esker lean in close. "You shouldn't of pulled a gun, Clay. It was you done the wrong. Legally. You gotta just set tight and you didn't see nothin'. *He* ain't gonna stir the water."

Beulah watched Tappen set his jaw. "Wouldn't be good for Dorrie neither," she said, "to be drug through more."

Tappen stood, his thick fingers wrappin' the cup. "Okay," he said, "I didn't see nothin'. But she ain't ever goin' *near* that place." He poured his coffee down the sink and walk out the kitchen toward the stairs.

AIN'T GOIN' ANOTHER *night cold*, Beulah thought as she climbed the wooden hill—what Pop called the stairs up to the attic. She opened the chest Tappen made, got out Grandma's harvest quilt for their bed and then the two thickest, the army blankets, for Laureen and Dorrie, both sound asleep.

Tappen still had his eyes open, starin' up. "Don't like it," he said as she walked in.

"But there ain't nothin'—"

"I know. But I don't like it."

Beulah nodded as she whipped the quilt over the bed. She pulled her wool sleepin' socks on before she got in, but still she had to hold her breath some while she waited for the sheets to warm. And for her hand, too, tucked between her thighs till it warmed enough to touch him, hold his arm.

He turned off the light, but she knew his eyes was still open. She waited as long as she could holdin' his arm in the dark but then she rolled over into what she call her fightin' position—on her belly with her one leg pulled up and her head toward the sliver of open window blowin' in the cold. Her hand was even with Tappen's then and without either of 'em havin' to reach, the sides of their pinkies touched. But she still waited till she heard his breath go long before she let herself drift off.

THE NEXT DAY, Saturday, Beulah cooked up the last of the late apples on the stove, two pots' worth Pop spent the mornin' quarterin' at the table. Dorrie backed herself up against the oven door. The oven hadn't been on since the apple crisp come out but it hadn't cooled much and she leaned right up against it and waited as long as she could before it got too hot through her shirt. *Still ain't talkin'*, Beulah thought, *though at least she got the grin on, ever since Tappen come in.*

Dorrie was eatin' her second feedin' of Cheerios and Tappen walk over to the table, look down, and her head sink lower and lower, almost squish into the bowl, and he reached for his jar of honey that she drown every bowl with and he says, "You didn't forget my honey, now did ya?" And she peeked up and she seen Tappen's smile and she shake her head back and forth hard. He was waitin' for that grin before he gone back out to mow. And there it was, spreadin' across her face.

Beulah made the apple crisp after Mike called. Wasn't no extra trouble. He said Florence been home two days now and she was so much better. "There's not even a comparison," he said. "It's like having the old Florence back." Dorrie was gonna go see her at home, first time, tomorrow, Sunday afternoon. Apple crisp would be sump'n simple Dorrie could bring.

Beulah started mashin' the applesauce through the colander into the big yellow bowl, and Dorrie run right over ready with a spoon, stealin' it as fast as she could once Beulah dumped in the sugar.

"Might not have any applesauce left for the jars, Pop." Beulah played like she was gonna hit Dorrie's spoon with the potato masher.

"What? That boy stealin' again!" He was settin' just close enough to hook Dorrie from the side with his cane. He kept jerkin' her back from the bowl so she had to lean to reach with her spoon. Then he'd pull her back even farther and she'd stick out her tongue and pant.

"Now why in heaven don't you want me to dish you up your own little bowl?" Beulah was smilin' as she shook her head. "Now Laureen, she always gotta have her own bowl or she won't touch it." Laureen was outside now, settin' on the tractor front of Tappen while he finished the last of the old fields don't get hayed no more.

"Ain't gonna be nothin' left," Pop said, but now Dorrie was laughin' so hard from the cane jerkin' she couldn't do nothin' but wave the spoon around wild. *Gonna even talk soon,* Beulah thought.

SHE WAS DRESSED. Her blouse had big red flowers and some green, too, leaves and stems. That was a good sign, they had said before, she was out of her bathrobe. And she wore lipstick, smiling with her bright teeth. She was already sitting at her place at the table. She pointed at the cheesecake in the middle. "It's for us," she said, reaching her arm out for Dorrie to come into. She had matching pants on, more flowers and leaves. Dorrie hugged her and then pulled out the chair and sat down, in her dad's place, where he sits at dinner. There were two plates and two forks and one knife.

Her hands were in her lap. But then she said, "Well," and stood, picked up the knife. "Shall we?" Dorrie nodded. She started to slice the first piece. It wasn't her cheesecake that everyone always talked about. It was from the store. Her hand was shaking. Dorrie stared at it, but not at the shaking, at her nails. She had quit biting them. They were polished, clear polish.

She had always bitten her nails. Sometimes when they were going out and she got all dressed up, she'd keep her fingers bent so her nails were tucked into her palm. Then she'd say again how she was going to stop so she could wear her mother's old rings.

Dorrie kept staring at them. Each nail with its little white half moon. When she used to read to Dorrie in bed, after she closed up the book and put it by the lamp, just before she tucked Dorrie in, she'd lean over and kiss her and then she'd take Dorrie's hands and bite her nails, too. And Dorrie would pretend-scream and play pull-away and she would say, "One more, please. Please," and they would laugh 'cause she would say it again and again till all ten were gone. "Just one more. Let me have just one more." Dorrie'd squeeze her eyes shut and hold out one finger and she would get a good grip so she could bite down without catching Dorrie's skin and then she'd pull off what was left and say "ahh" like it was great and Dorrie would laugh again 'cause *she* was the kid Dorrie was letting be bad just the once more.

Dorrie started to eat, one bite, two bites, but then it was like a lie that just blurts out, it came too quick for her to stop, but it wasn't a lie: "Tappen has a gun." *She* nodded and kept chewing. She looked down at her piece, cut another bite with her fork, a tiny bite, like for a kid's mouth.

"He rides around with it. In his truck," Dorrie said. Her legs were crossed and it seemed like they were eating out at a lunch place in the middle of the day, everything nice and her taking small bites and swallowing, nodding at Dorrie. "They're bullets in it, too. But he calls them shells." *She* was taking longer and longer to swallow even though her bites were still real small and Dorrie thought it was how polite she was, and that Dorrie should do that, too, spend time between bites, but then Dorrie realized the cake was like peanut butter or like thick glue in her mouth, she didn't like it, and she had a whole half piece left. "I saw him take it out only once though." *She* just kept swallowing, she wasn't even holding her fork. "At the Bentons'. He was taking me from the Bentons'." And then Dorrie was telling her about Mr. Benton stopped on the lawn and the gun pointed right at him and her getting in the truck and how Tappen drove away with the gun across his lap till they were a little ways down the road and then how he stopped the truck and uncocked the hammer. "That's what you call it," Dorrie said, "the hammer." But *she* didn't ever stop swallowing. She was calling for Dorrie's dad, "Michael," and then a little louder, "Michael," and then he was there and he was lifting Dorrie by the elbow, walking her out of the kitchen, out to the car. But it wasn't him that was going to drive, he was staying there at home, with *her*, because she hadn't stopped saying it, "Michael. Michael. Michael. Michael." Dorrie could still hear her inside the house. She was calm saying it, over and over. She never stopped, even when the neighbor, Mrs. Nardley, came to drive Dorrie away.

"A VERY REPUTABLE school, Mike," Father Bob was saying on the phone. "And just for a year or two, while Florence gets more stable—well, it'd be just one year probably. . . .

"No, no, more like a prep school. . . . Yeah. . . . No, not *delinquent* children. Just children with parents that aren't available, you know, for one reason or another, either they've died or . . .

"About an hour and fifteen minutes south of here. . . . Yes, a *very* good reputation. They have counselors, and they're all specially trained. . . . Just *exactly* for situations like this, yes. And that's in addition to all the teachers and the rest of the staff. See, they try to . . . they set it up in a real family atmosphere. . . . Yeah, that's the most healthy. . . .

"Well actually . . . *very* expensive. I'm not sure the exact . . . I know. Unless the State pays, but in your case . . . just one year, yeah . . . yeah, absorbed, yeah. But just to get her out of that situation, Mike. . . . No, I know, it's *not* just the gun. . . . Right. Very kind, I know. But it's just not the right place for her. . . . Yeah. Who knows what else? And then Florence would be through her . . . in a healthy state by then. . . .

"Oh, I'm sure they could. They take on new kids all through the year. . . . Yeah, right away, this week. . . . Sure you do. I'll give Tom McGuire a call. . . . Yeah, the director. Right away, yeah . . .

Beulah had hugged me about six times kneeling on the floor and then after she stood up she hugged me again. My dad was already in the car waiting with my suitcase. I pushed the door open with my shoulder 'cause I was still looking back at Beulah, and Tappen, too, behind her, when she stuck her hand out to me, with her cup, she stuck her cup right out to me, the cup she used every morning for coffee. She didn't even say, "Here." She just kept her arm stuck out like that with the cup in front of my arm. The door was only a little open. I took it from her. I thought I was supposed to take a drink. The cup was empty, but she was nodding and kept nodding like I had done the right thing. I thought then but real slowly, She's giving me her cup. She must have just done it quick, it wasn't even washed.

PART III

NOVEMBER 1958

"A CUP." IT just came out. But once I said it, I knew it was a mistake. Mrs. Garno shifted. Just like Mrs. Klepp used to when I said something that was "ornery, just plain ornery."

The room we were in Mrs. Garno calls "the Family Room" but none of the kids call it that, they call it 109. We're grouped into families here and it's the room where we're supposed to get to know each other. That's what Mrs. Garno said and she's who does it. There are usually ten in each family but there are eleven in ours now with me. I came in on the day the topic was about what you believed in, but how Mrs. Garno said *what*, everyone knew it was about Jesus Christ or God.

She had said never to talk about what she told me about God. Just like after she told me about dying, she said, "Never never tell anyone."

Most of the kids said "Jesus Christ" till one girl said "God" but down into her arm and so fast I thought she said "red" but Mrs. Garno nodded and went on to the next kid.

But now, she didn't go on, she turned her head and then her shoulders right toward me. She said, very very slowly, "What kind of cup?"

All the kids fell quiet, even the bigger boys leaning against the back wall. "Dorrie?" she said. Everybody was looking straight at me but I still answered, I said, "It's from Howe Caverns."

The smile came back. I put my head down to hide it. I looked at my arm just like the girl did who said the "God" that sounded like "red." Mrs. Garno could still see it though 'cause when she said "Did you get the cup there, at Howe Caverns?" her voice was hard.

I shook my head. I wanted to disappear. I should have said "red." Maybe that girl really did say "red," and Mrs. Garno just didn't believe it.

I could see the kids back over my arm smiling, but not mean smiling. They probably thought I said it on purpose just to make a joke and make Mrs. Garno mad. She *was* mad now and I was scared but seeing them smile made me almost happy, like we really *were* a family.

WHERE WE EAT is called "the D.U." That's short for "dining unit" the man said who took my dad and me all around when I got here. The D.U. is huge and bright and has big windows that start high up so you can't see anything out of them except sky. The tables are all in rows and ours is by the far wall so I have to walk by all of them, maybe thirty tables, to get to it. We get our food first though 'cause the women wheel it out to the walls on shiny metal carts. Then as they put the serving pans down on each table, they roll the carts back toward the kitchen.

Each family eats together, so everybody at the table is called your brother or your sister. Mrs. Garno is called our "family mother" but she eats in another room, the F.D.U., "faculty dining unit." The youngest kid is Freddy. He's only eight. The oldest is Rocky but no one knows how old he is, and no one calls him

Rocky except Mrs. Garno. Kids call him Four-Eyes. He's huge and he doesn't go to school, he works instead. Mostly, he washes pots after supper. But here they never say supper. I can call it dinner again, like before.

The girl who said just "God" sat beside me. She had dark hair pulled back with a blue headband. I think she liked me 'cause she thought I was being funny saying "a cup" and that was okay 'cause I liked her 'cause I thought she said "red" when she didn't really so we were even. Except I didn't know her name, and everyone knew mine. I was the only one new when I got introduced. As Dorrie.

I was trying to remember her name, but then someone asked her for the saltshaker they wanted for a trick and she didn't answer or pass it and then a guy, bigger, yelled, "JU-DY"—real loud—"the SALT."

"I like the name 'Judy,'" I said to her, low, so no one else could hear. But the same guy who had just yelled, he was across from us, he said, "Judy the Jew." She didn't look down at her arm though, like she did in that room, she looked straight at him but more with her chin than with her eyes and I did, too. I gave him my chin, too.

But then the food came and Judy grabbed her fork and turned to me and said, "Noodle Disgusto."

"Whose turn?" someone yelled, and a girl on the other side stood up and starting dishing food onto the plates.

"At least it's not as bad as the cat food we get on Fridays," Judy said to me.

JUDY WAS TWELVE but she'd already been here two years so she knew a lot. The guy that was across from us, his name is Mark, he's been here the longest. Except for Four-Eyes. But he didn't count, he'd been here *forever*, Judy said. I wished Judy was my roommate instead of Mary Ellen. She was older than Judy, thirteen, but she'd only been here for six months. Judy pushed up the back of her hair and made a snob-face when she said Mary Ellen's name.

Judy could tell me a lot 'cause it was Rec Time, which was the hour after dinner. Most of the kids watched TV in the rec room, but the TV was broken now so it looked like just a big room with lots of folding chairs and a table stuck up against the wall. There were bunches of kids around, hunched over chairs or sitting on the floor, but they were all talking low, including Judy. " 'Cause of Fogey," she said as she plopped down in the corner. She pointed with her eyes to a woman in dark blue slacks and a white shirt walking back and forth. "She makes sure no one smokes or *anything*," Judy said. "Used to work in a prison."

Rec Time was almost over when Judy hit my elbow and whispered, "Hey, she's here. The Fish." I turned. Garno stood in the doorway looking across the room. She seemed taller and she had pants on now. "The Fish," Judy said again. "Cat food," I said, and Judy laughed. But Garno's eyes stopped when she saw me. She started walking toward me. Her nose pointed down, straight at my face.

"Come to my office," she said but then she added, "Just to talk," but Judy still gave me a look as I got up and she mouthed "cat food" and it made me smile all the way to Garno's door. *It's really Judy's smile*, I thought. *I've got Judy's smile.*

The chair across from her desk that I had to sit in was for parents or for the people who bring in the kids, my feet didn't reach. Even if I was bigger, regular size for my age, I'd still only fill up half of it. It was black vinyl. *She* hated vinyl, she called it "cheesy." There was a jar of butterscotches on the corner of the desk right by the chair. I didn't ask but Garno said, "Go ahead, have one."

Garno looked different in slacks. More like *her*. Beulah never wore anything but a dress, a housedress, but *she* only wore a dress when Dad took her someplace special, out to dinner or to see a ballet. But then Garno was behind the desk again and she looked just the same, the Fish.

"Eudora," she said. "I mean, Dorrie." I bit down on the butterscotch hard, I crunched it loud in my head. She smiled, "Is there *really* a cup?"

I looked at her, but I didn't see her, I saw Judy instead. But it didn't make me smile. Instead it made me shake my head. Then I said it, "No," and again, "no."

"I thought so," she said. She was smiling again. "You can go now," and then she explained, "for your quiet time in your room." I was almost out when she said, "Eudora?" I stopped and looked back at her but not at her eyes, just at her mouth. She said, "Thank you for telling the truth."

I ran all the way back to my room. Mary Ellen's light was on and there was a book facedown on her bed. *Probably in the bathroom smoking.* I got out the smaller suitcase and opened it. The cup was still there in the side pocket. It was cold. On the front, under the name "Howe Caverns," there was a lot of brown for the cave and it had a blue stream running through it and a little rowboat with a man in a red shirt rowing. I leaned back on the bed and held it up so the light shined on the blue. It looked more like water then. On the inside, on the bottom rim, it was all black and smelled from the dried-up coffee. *Like a little cave,* I thought.

I heard Mary Ellen at the door and quick stuck the cup between the mattress and the wall.

"So you had to talk to Garno, huh?" Mary Ellen said as she came in. She had nail polish on, bright red.

I nodded but I didn't say anything. I didn't want to talk. I closed up the suitcase and put it back in the closet and started to untie my sneakers. I just wore my same T-shirt and underpants to bed. I laid with my face right up against the wall so I could smell the dried-up coffee. Mary Ellen waited a long time, until 9:59, the last minute, before she turned out the light.

Without making any noise, I got the cup from its spot. *That's where I'll keep it*, I thought. Popsy said that he hid all his money under his mattress in an envelope. Elmer, too. They both seemed so far away, and Pepper, Tappen, far far away. Laureen, I couldn't even see her face.

Everyone seemed gone except Beulah. I could smell her hugging me in the dark. I squeezed the cup and curled in so I could feel her arms surround me, they covered every bit of me.

IT WAS JUDY who told me Four-Eyes had snakes. At first I thought it was a big secret and she was the only one who knew, but at lunch, Jerry, who sits all the way at the end, said, "Four-Eyes even got snakes crawling in his bed." Then Mark said, "Yeah, one crawled out his pants, too. Scared Eileen, boy, to death." They were laughing and Jerry kept looking at me. It was a family secret. Even Freddy knew not to tell anyone else 'cause snakes weren't allowed here. No pets were allowed and even though snakes aren't pets, aren't anything even *like* pets, they call a pet anything that's not human.

Four-Eyes didn't scare me, even though he was six feet two and about three hundred pounds and it was hard to look right at his eyes 'cause his glasses were so thick his eyes popped out just like a straw under water pops out closer and huge. But it was even harder to look at his teeth. They weren't real and they moved when he talked, and when he opened his mouth and smiled, which he did all the time, you could see the top half of them were all black. But sometimes I could forget they were teeth and I'd see just a black and white stripe.

After lunch, I hung back even from Judy so none of the kids

could see me sneak into the kitchen and up to the big sink where Four-Eyes was washing pots. His blue shirt had dark rings of wet on each side of his back and a long skinny ring like an island coming down from his neck. *Like countries*, I thought.

"Four-Eyes?" He threw his head back, surprised. But then he turned and looked down at me. Like a large, calm horse. And his eyes could look the right size if I fuzzed out the rest of his face. I didn't let myself look at his mouth at all.

"Four-Eyes?" I said again even though he was already looking at me.

He nodded.

I stretched up onto my tiptoes so I could whisper close enough. "Can I see your snakes? I mean just sometime, anytime."

He kept looking down at me, but he didn't say anything or nod.

"I love snakes. Even though I'm a girl, I really do."

I know he smiled then even though I wasn't looking at his mouth. I kept glued to his eyes.

"You ever touch one?" he asked. I could tell his teeth moved. It was very hard not to look at his mouth.

I nodded. "My brother and I used to have one."

"After dinner," he said. And then he went back to his pots and I ran back out the kitchen to catch up to Judy and the other kids.

David and I probably just had a garter but it seemed more special 'cause it had a bright yellow ring all around its neck that looked like shiny paint or plastic. We kept it behind the garage in a shoebox full of grass and then David made me a box in shop for its home but then the snake started to look like it was dying so we let it go. I never put another snake back in though I still kept grass in there and I had a rock, too, and a dish of water I'd even change to keep it fresh.

I thought Four-Eyes might say something through dinner but he didn't. Afterwards, all the kids were going to the rec room 'cause the TV was fixed. TV was allowed unless you had demerits. I stayed right outside the kitchen. Two men with aprons wiped up the tables with huge sponges they'd dip in a bucket and another one started sweeping right near me.

Finally, Four-Eyes came out. He walked right by me and then without looking back he waved his hand for me to come but he never said a word. I followed about ten feet behind. I thought maybe he knew I didn't want to be seen with him.

But once we were in the hallway of the boys' section, he waved for me to come up next to him and when I did, he leaned down and said, "You can't get caught here." I nodded. Garno had told me everything that was illegal.

It wasn't like the girls' section at all. Our section was new. These doors were brown and heavy and narrow and they were all about a foot in from the wall, like caves. We passed about ten doors and each one I thought was going to be Four-Eyes's but he didn't slow down.

Then he stopped, froze. He turned and shoved me into a doorway and stood there in front of me facing out. I heard the talking, too, grown-ups, about to walk down the hall. I was glad it was like a cave then. I put my arm right up against the tile wall 'cause it was cool. Four-Eyes bent over and fooled with his shoe, pretending to tie it. Even bent over he covered my whole body though I still bent my knees a little so I was extra sure they couldn't see me. I heard Mr. Gessley's voice—my counselor—but the others I didn't recognize. They were coming closer. Four-Eyes looked up and said "Hi" in a drawn-out way and smiled, too, right at them. I knew how his teeth would show, that black and white stripe moving up and down through the whole long "Hi-i-i."

Two of them said, "Hi, Rocky," but real quick and not toward him, toward the end of the hall. Not even grown-ups could look at his teeth.

Even after they went into the next section, Four-Eyes still waited there in the doorway. The tiles turned warm against my arm so I moved it over to feel more of the cold. Then Four-Eyes said, "Okay," and we came out into the hall. We were almost at the end ready to walk through into another hallway but then he pushed me into the last door, I thought people were coming again. He shoved open the door quick and followed me in. I thought we were in a closet or a storage room waiting for more people to pass but then he hit the switch and it was his room. It was tiny, only twice the size of the bed. He had a table but it was covered with clothes just thrown on it and shoeboxes piled up halfway to the ceiling and an old metal bucket. The lamp was on the chair by the bed. It didn't have any shade.

Even though the room was a lot smaller than the girls' rooms, it had the same kind of closet, built in one whole wall. Four-Eyes slid back the door, and the closet had no shelves or drawers like ours did, or clothes. It had a box big enough for even him to lie down in. It was made of wood scraps painted every color, or some peeling or just raw.

He turned off the switch by the wall and it was pitch black again. I could feel him walk near and then he was past me, touching something in the back of the closet. I didn't move and then a long, skinny, very white light started in fits and bursts and then shined right into the snakes. He lifted off the four rocks on each corner and pushed up the screen. His hands looked blue moving back and forth under the light.

I kneeled down in front of the box. My eyes were just over the top rim. Right away I saw three. But then two more crawled out from inside a cement block. Then Four-Eyes lifted up a flat rock and there were five more under there. And all five started crawling out away from their hiding place making their curves.

Then, in the corner, I saw one coiled up tight except for its head rising up in flashes from the dried-up grass. At the top of its neck, there was a yellow ring, shiny, like plastic.

"That's the one, that's the one, that's just like the one—" I yelled out but I didn't finish 'cause his hand came down on my shoulder and his other slapped against my mouth and then his mouth came so close I could feel his breath and I didn't see them but I knew his teeth were moving, he said in a whisper but sharp as a scream, "DON'T TALK!"

The yellow ring got all fuzzy around the edges and the yellow ran into the brown and into the black and the grass, they all ran together. I didn't move. Then it was all clear again and the yellow and black were separate, like the yellow line on the road you're not supposed to pass over.

MY BROTHER AND I found our snake when we were playing in the leaves. Actually, it was his job, he had to do the raking and I'd play in the leaves and we had this game. I'd sometimes run and jump but mostly I'd just lie there and be buried, and I would listen under the dark to the sound of his rake coming closer. He was a fast raker, not like my dad who took longer and slower with each stroke. Then, just before his rake reached the pile with a new batch of leaves I'd open just a small hole and scream, "No! No! Don't!" and then he'd bury me new. And I'd scream as I dug in deeper pretending to be dead or not dead yet but buried alive.

Then he'd go back to where the line of green lawn hit the brown of undone lawn to start over and I would lie there smelling the dead leaves. They smelled both wet and dry together. If I moved, cracks of light would rip through the dark so mostly I stayed perfectly still. But then sometimes I'd stick a hand out through the leaves and I knew that soon I'd hear his shout: "Oh my God! It's a hand!" Then the rake would get closer and we'd do it over and over again until the whole lawn was done.

But one time as I was burrowing in under a new load of leaves, he yelled out, "Eudora! Eudora!" and he dropped onto the pile and started scooping the leaves out with his arms and I started looking, too, though I didn't know what I was looking for but it was only for a minute 'cause he caught the snake by the end of the tail and jumped up holding it out so it was dangling away from his body. I dumped all the leaves out of the garbage pail so we could put the snake in there. He let me hold it and right as I was lowering it into the can, it curled around and bit my finger. It felt more like a sting than a bite, like a really really sharp needle, but for just a minute.

We carried the can behind the garage so *she* wouldn't see it. It was almost five when she looked out and saw the big pile of leaves spread out over the lawn again. They had been packed so tightly in the can. She started to yell but my brother said to me through the side of his mouth, "Don't worry, I'll talk to her," and he did. He said he lost a silver dollar he had gotten at school and I was helping him look for it and she never did know what we found, that we found a snake with a yellow ring.

FOUR-EYES LET go but I still didn't move a muscle. I kept my eyes pasted on the yellow band even though I could tell that more snakes were moving out from places I didn't know about. It seemed like they were all crawling over and over each other warming up under the light. He must have had twenty of them but I didn't look enough to count. I kept my eyes on the yellow ring. The ring was lined with two very thin brown stripes, but the rest of the snake's head was black. Its small eyes looked out from the grass bunched up around its neck, hiding its neck so that its head seemed separate and so far above the rest of its body, like it belonged to a snake I couldn't see that stayed floating over the one below, the one coiled in the grass.

Four-Eyes didn't move either. Only the snakes were moving. But then all of a sudden, he pulled the light off, grabbed my shoulder, and yanked me onto my feet. He pushed me in front of him in the dark toward what I didn't know was the door till he opened it. Then he pulled me back and stuck his head out in the hall, looked both ways, shoved me out and said, "Run!"

I ran as fast as I could out the door, down the stairs and out through the dining hall, past the rec room through the older girls' section into ours. When I saw our hall empty, I don't think even at school on Field Day I ever sprinted so fast.

When I got back to the room, Mary Ellen was already in bed but I could still smell the smoke on her. She said, but not loud, "Where were you? She's almost here." I pulled my pants off, threw them in the closet, and jumped into bed. It was already 10:01.

I just made it, too, 'cause right then we heard her close the next door down the hall. The proctor turns off any light that's on and everyone has to say good night. You can't even pretend you're asleep. "Good night, Dorrie." "Good night, Mrs. Ellsworth." "Good night, Mary Ellen." "Good night, Mrs. Ellsworth." Then click, black. I thought she must be able to hear my heart pumping, but in the dark, the door shut.

"Where were you?" Mary Ellen said.

"Outside. I ran outside." I felt so happy I made it.

"Oooh," she said. "Good thing you got back in. Didn't Fogey see you?"

"No," I said. But the no made the happy go. It came to me: I had gotten so close, I had the chance but I didn't touch it, I had forgotten, I didn't even feel the yellow ring, I had just forgotten.

WHEN I TOLD Popsy about how Four-Eyes's teeth move up and down when he talks, Popsy dropped his own teeth right out of his mouth and raised them up in front of my face. And they were bobbing up and down, too, right at me 'cause of how he laughs, his arms shaking with his head and chest. Then he popped them back in. They were brand-new, his birthday present from Beulah and Tappen.

"I hate 'em, ate better without 'em but don't you tell Beulah that. She thinks they're dandy. Ninety-eight years I done without 'em, but no, she says they're grand."

Popsy had only the lone soldier left but now that was gone, they took it out. He'd brag almost every night at supper how it could rip a piece of meat till it was soft enough to gum. And every night, Beulah'd fire back, "Yup, meat I've ground and cooked to a mush, a baby could gum it, too." But Pop would just wave his hand or say, "Yup, boss."

We were alone in Tappen's old station wagon, parked in the visitor's lot. Beulah had gone on the one o'clock tour of the grounds. It was December 2, my first Visitor's Day. My dad called the night before to tell me that he couldn't come because *she* was going back into the hospital today. Tappen was going to come, but Beulah said they couldn't both leave and "I won," she said, after she stopped hugging me, which wasn't for at least ten minutes.

"I wanna see where you been livin'," Beulah said, checking her watch. She ended up late anyway. Even after she got out of the car, she kept asking, "Pop, you gonna be okay out here? You two gonna be okay?"

"Beulah, you'd worry if we was tucked in bed—wouldn't she, boy?"

"YUP!" I yelled so Popsy could hear. And then he turned back to Beulah, seemed serious. "Now don't you worry none. We'll be fine." He winked at me. "As long as Elmer don't appear."

I thought just quick out loud. "Elmer isn't dead, is he?" I looked at Beulah still leaning in through the window trying to break away. She shook her head. "Oh no."

Pop shook his head, too, his chin down on his chest. "Elmer ain't dead, but that don't stop him from showin' up wherever. But don't you worry, boy, Elmer ain't gonna die 'fore I do. Right, Beulah?"

It was already a few minutes after the one o'clock bell.

Pop kept on: "He'll make sure I've sized the place up first, done all the work. Laziest man ever walked."

"You're not gonna die either," I said.

"Nope, I ain't. Hear that, Beulah?"

"Now don't you two run off." She kissed me one last time through the window.

I watched her in her pink coat moving toward the tall brick building. I didn't want her to go inside.

I kept my hands on both sides of the wheel. It was so big, it was like a hug. The driver's seat is the best place in the car, even like this, even not moving. We could have gone into the lounge area but it would have been hard on Pop to walk and I liked it better in the car. Just the smell inside, like old ice cream or like butter, like Beulah, it made me feel far away from the halls, the family, Mary Ellen and the Fish, even Judy. Judy didn't have any visitors so I told her she could have some of mine like they were dessert and that made her laugh a little but she still stayed in her room.

I told Pop that I was supposed to call Four-Eyes "my brother" 'cause we ate at the same table and that made him laugh. I loved making him laugh. He looked different and not just 'cause of his teeth. He was dressed same as for church at Christmas, wearing new dungarees, still dark blue and they didn't smell. He wore his rubber boots though, and I know without socks. His feet had been too swollen for years to fit into his one pair of shoes. Under his coat, he had on his good pair of suspenders and a red flannel shirt I'm sure Beulah picked out. He had just shaved, too, and his face was bloody in three places.

"We're not supposed to have any pets or animals but Four-Eyes has snakes, not poisonous or anything, just regular snakes." I felt almost scared to say it out loud even though we had rolled the windows back up. Still, I whispered it. "I visit 'em every night, or almost, not Saturday or Sunday 'cause we don't have Rec Time then. He's got them in a HUGE box in his closet. It's as big as a coffin."

Pop didn't say anything so I kept talking. "If I got caught, I could get in a LOT of trouble. A LOT."

Popsy looked down mostly, rubbing his scalp with his hand, the smooth shiny skin. He moved his teeth around and up and down, too. He hadn't stopped playing with them since I mentioned Four-Eyes's teeth. I thought maybe he wasn't listening. "Just settin' there," Beulah always said about him, "thinkin' 'bout Ida or drink."

But then he started shaking his head back and forth. "In trouble for seein' snakes, in trouble for seein' snakes." He said it over and over. "In trouble for seein' snakes."

"Well, the snakes are illegal," I said, "but mostly it's me being in the boys' section. That's *really* illegal."

"In trouble for seein' snakes." His chin crossed back and forth over his chest.

"I haven't even told my friend Judy about seein' the snakes," I said. "But I probably won't get caught anyway. That's the good thing about being so little. And so quiet, too."

Pop stopped repeating. He was chewing his teeth instead. That was the only noise in the car. It was much louder even than the wind blowing the leaves all around outside. And Pop's hand kept going back and forth over his head. But then it stopped, lifted.

"If you're about to get caught," he said, "if you're about to get caught, you know what to do, don't ya, boy? I told you what to do, didn't I? Now didn't I?"

I shook my head.

"Didn't I tell you? Didn't I?"

I made sure he could see me shaking my head.

"You turn and face where you come from." Pop looked up and out the window again, said, "Snow tonight." The leaves looked like they were being blown by tiny tornadoes, circling and circling, then moving toward us, over us. But it was warm and still in the car, perfect, like Tappen's barn at night. And Pop looking out, chewing. Then he started laughing, his whole body shaking, but with no noise coming out.

"You turn and face where you come from. Sure I told ya." I kept shaking my head.

"The night Will and me, we threw a firecracker in the dance hall? I didn't tell you that?"

"NO!" I yelled, smiling.

"The dance hall top of Mount Pisgah, and full of people, and all dressed up? I didn't tell you?"

"NO!" I yelled, again.

"And how they was so mad, we run off down the mountain. Sure I told ya."

"No you didn't!"

"How we stop about halfway down? I told ya clear as day."

I shook my head as hard as I could.

"How we straightened up our coats? Hats? Looked all prim again, then turned around, headed back up?"

I started to laugh, but I had to keep shaking my head or he'd stop.

"And how all these men come runnin' down, just as excited, and ask us if we'd seen some folk runnin' away? And what'd I say then?"

"YOU DIDN'T TELL ME!"

"You just don't remember it, that's all. Me pointin' off to just where we seen 'em, sayin', 'Two of 'em. Just ahead of you men, and was they runnin' lickety-split!' And then they go through the whole story, and when we heard the horrible crime they done, we turn right around ourselves, join the chase." Pop was laughing again, his hands still moving back and forth over his head. "Never did catch 'em, though, never did."

"I wish I was an adult," I said.

"Yup," Pop said. "It's a lot easier."

"When I grow up to be an old man I wanna be like you, Pop."

"But with a eye," he said. "Keep the eye." Then he laughed again. "You can lose the teeth but keep the eye." Then he spit his teeth out again and held them right up in front of the windshield. The leaves were swirling around and around behind his new teeth.

"Take 'em," he said.

I didn't know what he meant.

"Take 'em," he said again, pushing them against my arm. His real eye looked straight at me. I didn't know what to do. I just kept looking at his teeth. They were a little yellow already. Maybe they were made yellow to look real.

"Listen here." He started wavin' the teeth around as he explained it to me. "You got 'em in your pocket, hear?" I nodded. "You see you're gonna get caught." He waited for me to nod and I did, big so he could see. "You turn around and start walkin' back toward this Four-Eyes's door, hear?" I nodded. "You got his teeth. He left his teeth somewhere, got it? You're just returnin' 'em, see? Got it? Got it?" I kept nodding and nodding. "Now here."

I took them, the two parts of them, from his hand, stuck them in the front pocket of my sweatshirt. They clicked together, sounded like real teeth.

"What's Beulah gonna say?" I said.

"I'll take care of Beulah. Don't you worry 'bout Beulah."

I TRACED EACH tooth over and over with my finger. I kept them in my sweatshirt pocket in a sock so they didn't click. But even through the cloth, I could tell the top teeth from the bottom. I kept my left hand touching them and then I felt it: *protected*. The snakes I held with my right hand.

Four-Eyes would come into the rec room after washing the pots and stand by the wall. Then he'd leave and I'd leave a little later. We did it that way every night now, 'cause then he could unlock his door first. He almost always kept a padlock on it only he had the key for. He could do that 'cause he worked here, he wasn't really one of us. That's why he had a single room and why he didn't get inspected.

If no one was in the hall and I was safe in the cave of the doorway, I'd open up the door just a tiny bit so I could see the blue of the snake light in the dark before I'd come all the way in. But usually I was running 'cause I heard someone coming. Four-Eyes never jumped though.

Once each night, Four-Eyes would lean over the box and pick up a snake and give it to me to hold by the neck. I'd hold it for a second and then drop it back in. But I never picked up any on my own. Four-Eyes knew each one. He'd whisper something like, "This is the orangey-brown snake that's got the thin tail." That's the only time he'd ever talk. I hadn't touched the yellow ring yet but each night Four-Eyes picked up a different snake and I knew soon he'd·hand me that one.

THEY WERE GOING to let me see her. Mr. Gessley, my counselor, called me into his office and gave me the message. Dad was coming Saturday morning to pick me up and take me to Burtrum General, the psychiatric wing.

I practiced talking to her in the mirror over the sink in the corner of the room when Mary Ellen wasn't there. I thought, *If I just ask questions, I won't make any mistakes.* First I looked in and said, "Hi," that's all. Then I said, "How are you?" But then I couldn't think anything else. So I started over again. "Hi." But I got stuck again right away. The mirror wasn't quite straight. It was hanging in the corner so it was fastened to both walls but it was lower on the left. There was a space behind the mirror, between the mirror and the two walls. A triangle. *That's where she is,* I thought. Just for now, just to practice.

A question came to me: "Where do you hurt?" But I didn't know if that was okay or not. Maybe that was pushing. "She pushes," *she* used to say. She used to talk about the pills the doctor gave her for pain but I never knew for where.

Then I thought of a better one: "Do you get to be outside?" That seemed okay. I asked that. Then more came. "Do you get to walk around?" The mirror was good 'cause it didn't ask me any questions back but then I thought, *I better think of a few answers or I'll screw up, I know, on answers.* So I tried a whole series of answers: *How are you?* "Fine." I said it over and over. "Fine. Fine. Fine." I kept trying to get my face happier, and the "Fine" longer.

Then she asked about school. "Do you like your new school?" I couldn't make my face do anything but blank. I tried to say "Okay," or, "I like it okay," but I just ended up staring. I started over again. "Fine. Fine. Fine." Each one got a little better. So then I tried to say "Okay, it's okay," but I went back to staring. My hair had grown since she saw me. It was really short still but it looked almost normal, normal for short.

But then an answer came: "I like it okay but I don't get to be outside enough." That was good, 'cause she probably couldn't go out much either. But that was as far as I got.

Not once the whole time I practiced did the smile come even though I tried to see her face look at me. I could almost do it, see it right there, behind the mirror, in that space. Still, the smile didn't come, so I tried to shape my mouth into it, to see if then I could stop it if it got started but the left side of my mouth wouldn't go up. The smile wouldn't come. It's like trying to tickle yourself, you just can't.

HER FACE WAS white, almost bright against her dark hair. She was wearing her blue bathrobe. The collar was crooked. One side was up, the other was folded down the way it was supposed to be. It had a little flower stitched on it, a rose, darker blue, that was set in deeper, closer to her skin. I was glad she didn't have to wear a hospital gown like the man in the wheelchair I saw going into the elevator. That was back in the main part before the lady at the desk said hello to my dad and unlocked the door into this side, and Dad walked me down the hall to her room and then nodded for me to go in 'cause he saw the doctor he wanted to talk with.

I walked in slowly, very slowly, till I was standing right beside the bed, but she didn't know it. She didn't hear me come in. I wanted to say "How are you?" like I had practiced but she was lying back on her pillow, looking at the ceiling. I knew that that was pushing, "How are you?" was pushing. I didn't say it. I didn't say anything. I stood there looking at her face. It looked so old.

She turned her head, smiled. She wasn't startled or scared, she must have known I was there. She smiled like I was supposed to be there, and I had been, for a long time. Her hand reached out from under the blanket, off the side of the bed. Everything seemed slow here, like the air was full of water, dark water, or a liquid thinner than water so you could still breathe but arms and legs moved slowly and wouldn't get hurt if they bumped against each other.

Her fingers were cold. I moved my palm up to her wrist where her skin was warm. "Small-boned," she once said about herself. I crossed the tip of my finger back and forth over the bone that stuck out. I thought then: *She can die.* I closed my eyes. I hated those words. I had never thought those words.

"Eudora," she said. I opened my eyes. She was looking at me, still smiling.

I nodded. I didn't practice just a nod.

"I mean Dorrie," she said. "You're Dorrie now." She said it over, "Dorrie." She looked up to the side as if the name "Dorrie" didn't come from her lips but was coming down from the ceiling toward her shoulder. "Dorrie," she said again, "Dorrie," like she was trying to hear it from her own lips.

The nurse came in. She was thin and pretty and she paused at the edge of the bed like she had just come to visit. "So this is your daughter, Mrs. Buell," the nurse said, smiling at me. She had thick, curly dark hair.

"Yes. Here's Eudora." And then she added, "Dorrie now. This is Miriam, Eudora, who takes such *good* care of me."

"Hi."

"This is your first time here?"

I nodded and smiled.

Miriam turned to her. "She's a cutie, the picture of her mother." She walked around to the side, close to the bed, to her other arm. Miriam looked so comfortable that close to her, like she knew her well. "It's that time again, Mrs. Buell." She gave her two pills and a glass of water. When she swallowed, the skin on her neck looked extra thin, like paper. "Be sure you come back now," Miriam said to me when she left.

I touched again the small bone in her wrist sticking out. She moved her hand, our hands, up and down. It was easy, being here.

She started looking at me close, my face, my hair. "My little girl's growing up," she said.

I shook my head, too hard. I looked down. She didn't stop looking. "Growing up too fast."

My eyes started to fill. "No," I said. "No." It used to be our joke. But the tears dropped on the bed beside her. I kept my eyes straight down. The tears wouldn't stop dropping. I backed up so they dropped onto the floor. I watched each one fall all the way to the floor, hit.

"Oh, sweetie." She said it to the ceiling. "You're still my little little girl."

"No," I said. "No." *I'm not little anymore.*

I didn't hear it at first 'cause she said it toward the ceiling but it was building up like she was moving closer: "Yes you are You are You are Yes you are." The words started shooting out hard. "You are You are You are."

I lifted my face, nodded as fast as I could. "Yes, I'm your girl," I said to her, loud. "I'm your girl," I said it again and louder and louder so she could hear it. She did, she heard me, and then she stopped. She was quiet again. But I still kept nodding. I wanted my nod to be a wall she could lean against.

She squeezed my hand very hard and then she looked at me. I didn't look down. I looked right into her eyes.

"You're such a good girl, Eudora." She lifted our hands up off the bed. "A good good girl."

THERE WERE TWO of them, Garno and someone else. They were looking at me. They asked me if Rocky touched me. I shook my head. They were both sitting, facing me. Did Rocky say anything to me? I nodded. But then Garno asked, "What? What did he say?" I didn't say anything. But I could hear him in my head: *Saved the best till last.* I couldn't say it. They kept asking. I put my head down. His words were getting louder: *Got a collar, just beautiful, a goldy collar.* He was almost shouting. I thought for a second they could hear. I shook my head. The light made my face hot.

"It's very important, Eudora," they were saying. "For your health, too," they were saying. Very important to tell them. I couldn't. I couldn't but I kept hearing him in my head: *Here he is—a black back.* He was holding up the snake. *And a goldy collar.* And for me to hold, too. I couldn't tell them. They looked at each other. "We're not here to hurt you," the other lady kept saying. I kept my hands together in my front pocket, tight. I had worn my sweatshirt, but it had no teeth. I had forgotten the teeth.

They asked other questions. "Did Rocky take you there?" I nodded. "By force?" I shook my head. I looked down. My chair was orange, orange vinyl but it was all ripped apart. The inside was spongy, dark gray. I traced the hole by my thigh. *What country is it?* I thought, but I didn't know. Even to guess, I didn't know.

It was Garno's voice. "Why did you go there?"

Their chairs were greeny blue, like pool water. But they had holes, too, gray, too. The other lady asked, "Why, dear, why did you go there?" Both of them kept asking. "Why did you go?" "Why did you go?" My face was burning up.

Four-Eyes must have thought of something, must have said something to keep them away. Three years, no one had been in his room. He told me that. Not even one of *us.* Till me.

Even when they saw me from down the hall. Four-Eyes heard them yell and came out, quick locked his door. But they didn't care about his room. They only cared about me, and him. Coach grabbed Four-Eyes's arm and took him ahead. He kept turning around smiling his big dumb smile. Coach yanked on him three or four times. At the end of the hall, I could still see his teeth, the black and white stripe. Coach grabbed him by his collar when they turned the corner. I had to go straight. I was between them, Garno and her.

"Why did you go there?" They kept asking.

I finally said it. "To hold the snake," I said. I had to, I couldn't think of any excuse. It was over. I wanted to cry but I couldn't.

I could see the box being carried through the door into the hall. It would take probably three or four guys to carry it. Four guys had to carry my brother. But he was 150 pounds, too, inside it.

But it wasn't over. They were asking me more questions. "Do you have another name for the snake?" I shook my head, slowly, very slowly. I had no name for him, I never named him.

"Can you talk about it, the snake?" the other lady asked.

I shook my head.

"Did you touch it?" Garno said.

I nodded.

"What did it feel like?"

I shook my head. They were looking at each other.

"Did it touch you?"

I nodded. Then I said, "It bit me." I was about to cry but Garno was asking, "Where? Where did it bite you?" The other lady was writing on a form. I shook my head. "No, it didn't bite me, no, it didn't, I didn't, I didn't mean that."

"What did—"

"No. No. No. No. No. No." I kept shaking my head. "No. No. No. No. No. No. No. . . ." But she kept writing.

I KNEW WHERE I was right away, even before I opened my eyes. The infirmary. The sheets were pulled very tight. They were stiff, too, against my chin.

I saw the branches of a tree first, through the window up from the bed. The glass was super clean, like hers, before she stopped cleaning. She hated smudges. "Hot water," she'd always say. "Hot hot water. That's the secret." It was important not to see smudges when the windows fogged up.

I couldn't see the ground, or even the trunk. Only two branches, shiny black in the sun. The leaves were mostly gone. A few hung on through the fall, yellow, bright yellow. Black and bright yellow. *The goldy collar.* I rolled over under the tight sheets. There was no window on the other side.

She came in, the same lady that was with Garno last night. She was in white. She was the nurse. Last night she just looked regular, like a regular person. My pants were gone. I got into bed with all my clothes on. They must have taken them off when I was asleep. She kept opening and closing drawers, opening and closing cabinets, too.

"Where are my pants?" I said.

She turned around. "Oh, you're up. They're right here, don't worry. Did you have a good sleep, dear?" I nodded.

She was above me, looking down at the chair beside the bed. My pants were there, folded. Then she looked at me. "The doctor is going to do a small procedure, dear," she said. She had the trash in her hand. It was important. And it wouldn't take long. She said a lot more, too, while she was doing things. She put the trash by the door and wiped out the sink. There was only one other bed in the room, and a table at the other end by a curtain. She said that my father would be visiting me afterwards, as soon as it was over.

"Am I sick?" I said. I sat up.

"No. No, dear, but it is hard what you've been through, very hard, I know."

I wondered if "dear" was spelled like the animal. I laid back down on the pillow. It made a loud puff sound under my head like it was breathing out. I wanted to run, run with Judy around the soccer field. The ground was so hard now, frozen, I wanted to turn the corner of the last lap and race toward the two goalposts broken at the end of the field. I wanted to push ahead and feel Judy sticking there right at my side. She'd never push but she never dropped back either. I'd push and push all the way to the post and she'd just *stick*. Then after our breathing started to slow again, she'd be so happy as we walked back to Mrs. Burke. I wanted her to smile and put her arm around me.

The nurse was cleaning scissors. At first they looked like scissors, but some of them had funny shapes. They were all metal though. She dried each of them, then lined them up on a towel. The wood of the cabinets was shiny. Blond wood, like our closets.

The snakes. Did they get the snakes yet? I didn't ask though. What did I say last night, exactly? I was trying to remember everything exactly, but I couldn't.

She was finished with the scissors, looking into the other room. "Hi, Doctor," she said. "We're up and chipper this morning."

I could hear him. "It turned cold out last night, huh? My wife was upset, she left out some planter"—I heard the hangers. He must've been taking off his coat—"and it cracked. Why she left it out *this* long, I don't know. . . . Anyway, she was sick about it. Dropped down to thirteen!"

"Down to eleven at my house," she said.

"Is this Eudora?" he said, coming into the room. He was Dr. Mallone, the doctor for Crestview.

I leaned up on my elbows and nodded. He came over to the foot of the bed. "How ya doing this morning? Good sleep?"

"What's wrong with me?" I asked.

He sat down on the edge of the other bed. He didn't have a white coat on. He looked just like a regular man. He had brown hair but the sides were a little gray. I thought of how my dad would always say, "The sides are turning first," and *she*'d answer, "That's because you can't see the back, honey."

The doctor, Dr. Mallone, said, "We're just gonna do a small procedure to check you out after what happened last night. Just take a look inside, that's all. You can just relax. It will all be over before you know it."

A *look inside where?* I asked in my head but I didn't get it out. I just nodded. Judy would have asked.

He got up and left but as he passed her he said, "Get her ready, Mrs. Brennon, I'll be . . ." and he pointed ahead out the door where he was going.

She came over to me and said, "You have to take off your underpants, dear."

"Where is he gonna look?" I asked.

"At your privates, dear. He has to, but it won't hurt."

JUDY! I screamed but in my head. Mrs. Brennon put her

hand on my arm like I needed help getting out of bed, but I was already sliding off. She said, "You'll be covered with a sheet, dear."

She held the sheet up in front of me. I stepped out of my underpants. The sheet was in front but I was still naked behind. I looked around. I could see only one of the branches. Black, very black, but it looked wet, shiny. And the few old leaves, too, looked lit up. She gave me the sheet to hold in front of me, it was partly folded so it didn't hit the floor. "Scoot over here," she said but I didn't feel like I could "scoot" anymore. I followed her over to the table. I remembered how *her* slippers would scuff the floor, the rhythm on the hall rug.

The table was black. The nurse leaned over and pulled out a stool from the bottom of it. I pushed myself up onto the table and then put the sheet over me again quick. She said, "Lay back, honey."

"Judy," I said.

"What, dear?"

I shook my head. "Nothing."

She was adjusting something at the foot of the table. She said, "Now scoot your hips all the way up to the front. All the way up here. That's right."

There was a white sheet underneath me that wrinkled as I tried to scoot up. "Farther, farther," she kept saying. I thought I reached the end but she said it again, "Farther." *Judy, Judy, Judy,* I kept saying in my head. *Judy.*

I was at the very end. My legs were hanging off. "Even farther."

"I'm gonna fall off."

"No, you won't, honey, only a little farther."

"What's he going to do?" I said.

"Just look inside. It'll be over soon," she said. "That's good, dear. Lay back now." But she was already turning to go into the other room.

I stuck my head just forward enough to see my feet and ankles sticking out from under the sheet. They looked like someone else's. I thought it out in my head, *You're the same feet that can run, really run*. I said it twice to myself, but they still seemed like someone else's. I leaned back onto my elbows.

They were speaking in the other room. Their voices went up and down, up and down. The doctor's voice was a little louder but not as clear. At first, I couldn't hear the words and it seemed like a song, or I heard words but they didn't matter, they were part of the up-down, or a drum. "Well no-o, it's ob-vious," and then it would go flat, very flat, the drum in the back: "I don't think so," and then back to a song: "We-ell . . . if ya think. But they didn't say *that*." Then *his* voice again, low, "Yes, her father did." *The bass*, I thought, *the bass*! David spent so long trying to get me to hear the bass and I'd always nod. But I *did* hear it, and by myself. "Her father did." It was low. "It's beneath the music," he used to say, "almost like a drum," but it was fuller, like it was carrying something. Then something sharp, very sharp came out of the song, woke me up, like I'd been asleep or in a dream. Just four words, her words, but they stuck into me: "Well, Rocky denies it. . . ." but then she was whispering, my head was whispering, all the voices in my head were whispering at once and none of them loud enough for me to hear. I wanted to run, run as fast as I could with Judy, run around and around the frozen field. Then there was nothing. Absolute quiet, nothing except for the four words that wouldn't stop, *Well, Rocky denies it*.

She came back in the room, quickly, like she was walking in from a long way off. "Okay, dear," she said, cheery. She was cheery. "Put your feet up here." She had her hands on the sides of the table, at the end. "These are called stirrups." She smiled.

"Just like on a saddle." But I didn't move my legs. The metal things were all the way to the side of the table. "They don't hurt," she said. But I just laid there.

She took my right heel. She was moving it up. My leg was bending. She was moving it to the side, she was going to put it in the metal thing, the stirrup. She was moving my knee out. I kicked. "JUDY!" I screamed. My leg went straight, hard. She flew back. "JUDY!" I sat up. "Judy, what are they doing to me?"

But only the doctor was there. I kept yelling, "JUDY! JUDY! What are they doing?" He didn't answer. Nobody answered. She was behind him. He kept saying, "Relax, relax." But I kept on yelling. She came out from behind him. They were looking at each other and then she took my hand but not softly, she was holding me down. "Relax," he kept saying. "It won't be like last night, relax, it's going to be okay. We have to do this."

I fell back on the table. "Judy," I said, I didn't yell, "Judy."

She was holding my arm and then my one knee down, the one that kicked. I closed my eyes. My heels were being put into the stirrups. My knees were all the way out to the side. I opened my eyes but it was just a ceiling, a white ceiling. I was wide open naked, but it was far away, down there was far away. I kept my eyes on the ceiling. It stayed far away. He was still saying, "Relax. Relax. It won't take long." And then something touched me. I flinched. It was cold. But she was gripping my knee. It was like spit. "That's just the jelly," she said. He said, "Okay?" "Relax, dear," she said and then she nodded to him. Something else touched me. It was cold, too, but hard. It was metal. Like the funny-shaped scissors, all those things she was cleaning. It wasn't touching me, it was moving into me. I tried to close my legs but she was holding the one open. The other was held, too, open. She was saying, "Relax, relax." It was still moving. I pushed even harder to close my leg against her hand. But it kept going into me, slowly, it didn't stop, like a tank on TV, with all the soldiers diving to the side, onto the ground. It didn't stop. I closed my knee as hard as I could against her hand. It stopped. The tank stopped. It stayed there, cold, waiting. Then he said, "Okay?" And she said, "Yes." "NO!" I screamed, "NO! NO!" But it was too late, it had already spread me open.

I PUT MY hands under my sweatshirt and my shirt, too. My fingers were cold. I spread them flat over my ribs, pushed them against my skin, pushed the cold in. I tried to picture my brother's face. It wouldn't come clear. I squeezed my eyes shut trying to see him. I could see his back. His shoulders, too, but only from the back.

They were both gone, the nurse and the doctor. I pulled my pants back on. It was different. My legs were different. My sides, my arms, my skin. They were all different. I looked through the doorway into the other room. The lights were on in there, long and skinny like the snake light, but whiter, plain white. The nurse kept crossing in and out of sight, back and forth across the doorway. I watched her. Like she was in a play, back and forth, crossing back and forth.

No semen, they had said. I asked her what semen was. "The secretion of a penis that transports sperm." Then she added, "Sperm is what fertilizes the woman's egg." The word "woman" stayed back in my brain and got bigger. It was like a room I hadn't seen yet but they were taking me in, I was going in.

I closed my eyes. *David!* Only his back. He wouldn't turn

around. *David!* Still, he wouldn't turn. I wanted to touch his shoulder. He flinched, ducked, rolled away, like when we used to wrestle. He taught me to roll just like that. "You're so little," he said. "You could be really good at it." I was, too. I heard him brag about me to Roger, "Eudora can roll out of *any* hold."

I stood up, felt it again—I was heavier, not any bigger, just heavier, like I was carrying something, or could. *The bass*, David said. I almost smiled. I wondered if *she* could tell, just by looking.

I stuck my hands back under my shirt. My fingers had become warm. Lines of warm. There was no more cold to push in. My fingers made warm stripes over my ribs on my skin.

I COULD SEE my hand again in front of my face. I keep my eyes open in the dark, after the light goes out and Mrs. Ellsworth's gone. I wait to see my hand. Then I close my eyes and go to sleep. But tonight, I was waiting till Mary Ellen started to sleep-breathe. I was waiting to open the box, the shoebox I found in my closet. No note. Just a box. It was way after ten.

THERE WAS A horse swimming in the water with his head turned toward me, looking at me. People were on the other side with cameras taking pictures and TV was there, too. But the horse was looking only at me. He kept his head turned toward me. There was a man saying that because of the current and the shape of the land, this horse was being swept away at seven thousand miles an hour. I was looking from farther and farther away, from far up in the sky. A rope was attached to him, a rope from a helicopter. His head was still turned. He was looking for me. They were going to take him out of the water, lift him up. They were going to save him. I knew that if they lifted him into the air going seven thousand miles an

*hour, all his bones would snap. I knew and they didn't. I needed to
tell them right away.*

I SHOOK MYSELF awake. Mary Ellen was sleep-breathing
steady. I slid out of bed, opened the closet door slowly. The night
was darkest inside there. I could just barely see the shoebox, the
stripe of the rubber band. I walked toward the window. There was
some light from around the corner, a streetlight or the moon.

The rubber band snapped up small when I got it over the edge
of the box. I was near Mary Ellen's bed but she was still asleep. I
lifted the top off. At first, I could see only a shape at one end. It
was hard, a rock. There was cut grass, too, and a jar lid. The
grass around the lid was all wet. Then I felt it, the snake, in the
grass close by the rock. It was smooth and not warm and not cold.
I couldn't see it. I felt along its back. I started to see then where a
darker line curled over the grass. I moved my finger down the
dark, down its tail becoming smaller and smaller until I reached
the loose grass again. Carefully, I closed my fingers around the
tip of the tail and lifted it up, held it black and curling against the
window. Its head arched up hard toward its tail and my hand, but
then it fell straight again, the last of its curve straightening slowly
down. And then it got ready again, to dive upward, to arch its
whole black body toward my hand holding its tail. The yellow
ring flashed for a moment before I dropped it back in, closed the
top, put the rubber band on it, and placed it back in my closet behind my clothes.

The night felt good, like the dark underneath my blanket
when it's all warmed up, the whole room felt like that. It seemed
like *she* was here, too, easy, like her name, Florence Benham
Buell. I kept my eyes open for a long time.

I KNEW I couldn't keep the snake for long, I had to let it go, but I wanted to keep it just till Saturday. I was going to see her again. The Saturday before Christmas. I wanted to show it to her. I planned out exactly how I could do it so she wouldn't be scared. First, I would just tell her that I had a snake and then I'd tell her about David, how we had one together just like it, black with a gold collar, but I'd say right away that we never brought it into the house.

Then I'd say the words, "I have the snake in a shoebox and I brought it if you want to see it, but *only* if you want." I practiced the words in the mirror, especially the "only if you want." And then maybe she'd say yes, but I'd still say, "Are you sure?" And if she said yes to *that*, then I'd bring the shoebox out from under my coat that I planned to have on the chair in the corner. Then I'd open it up but real slow and careful so that nothing bad would happen.

THE NEXT DAY, Thursday, Miss Reed—she's our English teacher that makes us say "yes" instead of "yeah"—she came over to our table at lunch and handed me a note. I looked at Judy.

"Open it!" she said. I held my breath, but it was only Gessley. I had to report to Gessley after school. "Ff-yew," Judy said and turned back to her plate.

When I walked in and sat down, Gessley smiled. But then all he said was, "Dorrie," just "Dorrie," before he started. "The doctor says your mother has taken a turn. . . ." I couldn't see her, not at all, I couldn't see her. "She's taken a turn for the worse." And the doctor had put her up to three times a week ECT, electroconvulsive therapy.

I couldn't look at him. I kept swallowing. He kept saying, "Only for a while, it's not permanent, you'll be able to see her again, it's only for a while." But I kept swallowing.

ECT, electroconvulsive therapy, the words kept going over and over in my head, *ECT*. It was "a demanding schedule," the doctor had said. Like she was going off to work.

I went to my room. Mary Ellen wasn't there, everyone was in study hall. I locked the door. Three demerits, so what. I took out the box. I could let it go free now. I wasn't going to wait for Judy, I could let it go right now, I was already missing study hall.

I opened the box. It was too still. I picked it up. I shook it. I kept shaking it. It didn't move. I lowered it back down. I lowered it onto the dried grass.

I backed up against the bed. The words "electroconvulsive therapy" had stopped, and nothing else had come, no words, or voices, not Beulah, not anybody, not even me. Just quiet, and the weight of the box on my leg.

I don't know when it was that I lifted my head and turned to look at the mirror. It wasn't the mirror. It was the space behind it. It was still quiet in my brain even though I was lifting the rock out of the box. Even when I threw the rock like I used to throw a baseball at David after he'd say, "Harder, throw it harder," even then, when I threw it toward the corner, I had no thoughts.

I heard sounds though, I heard the mirror smash. And there were pictures, waves against rock, green waves, David, I saw David looking at me, his face in front of the waves and rock. Smash. I heard it and then again, more of the mirror falling onto the sink. I heard it again and again. I didn't hear them unlock the door, though. But I saw them. I curled up. They were coming at me—tighter, I curled in tighter toward the box. They were trying to get at it but I was curled too tight.

BEULAH:

It was after supper Mike call me up. Tappen had gone out to the
barn for the final round. And Mike says Eudora ain't well. She
ain't in class no more, in the school. They got her at the State
Hospital down there, where the crazy kids go, and she ain't re-
spondin', he says. They got her on medication.

"Mike," I says, "you gotta get her out of there. Ain't no reason
she should be on pills."

"It isn't that simple, Beulah," he was sayin' but I didn't see why
not. An animal start failin', you don't just keep feedin' the same
food. But for them, simple is just plain dumb, we don't have the
schoolin' all them counselors got, so they think we can't tell what
a kid needs.

Mike just wanted to see if I would visit her, alone, just me, not
Popsy. "Well, of course," I said. "Tappen, he can keep a check on
Pop. I'll go down first thing tomorrow." Well, he'll have to check
with her doctor. She got a doctor now, not just a counselor, she
got a doctor to check when I can come say "I love you." No, it
ain't that simple.

But I got the phone call the next mornin'. I could go between twelve and one. And they didn't say I couldn't, but I didn't ask—I was bringin' Cheerios and milk and Tappen's honey, how she likes it best, likes it even more'n ice cream. She'd eat it mornin' noon and night and more'n one bowl, too. I got a bowl out and a spoon and I was ready.

I told Pop I was goin', and that she ain't well. I tell him he can't come, he'd have to walk up too far. "What, they got her in the Empire State Buildin'?" he says.

"Yut," I says. "Top floor."

"Ain't no tellin'."

"Nope, not there, there ain't," I says. "They got her on pills."

He shake his head. "Whiskey first," he said. That was Pop's rule: Whiskey don't work in three days, go to the doctor.

"It ain't that simple, Pop," I says.

"Nope, nowadays it ain't."

THE STATE HOSPITAL was only about ten minutes farther on than where you turn off to Crestview. Mike had told me that I would have to wait in the main office till the supervisor come and open up the door into the ward and then he said I'd have to wait again in what they call the "ward office." But I hadn't set two minutes where the woman told me to, before the doctor, Dr. Singer, come in and smile at me.

"Mrs. Tappen?" he said.

"Yes," I says, gettin' up.

"Thank you for coming, Mrs. Tappen. Mike tells us you're very close to the child." And then he added, "This means a tremendous amount." We was walkin' into his section, where they was keepin' her.

He looked at the bag in my arms. "Her favorite food," I says. "I brought her favorite food." He nodded, but slowly. "That's very nice," he said, but slowly, too. *Thank the Lord they haven't outlawed food for a kid,* I says to myself.

But he was tellin' me about the room she was in, about how they keep a watch on her. "Twenty-four hours," the doctor said, "just till she starts responding."

She was curled up tight as a ball, in pajamas on top of the bed, the blue wool blanket and white sheet pulled just as tight underneath her. Like someone got me with the stun gun, but still I walk closer, over right to her. There she was, my little Dorrie. "You cold, honey?" I says. "Curled up so tight." But she don't answer. She was starin' up. I pulled the chair up close so I'd fit there in her stare. Like she was seein' me but not seein' me, seein' somewhere through me, beyond me, but not lookin' on me at all.

"What are you seein' out of those eyes, honey?"

But she just laid there lookin' up, my Dorrie.

I keep on talkin', I say, "I got your food when you're ready. Right here in the bag," and I show them eyes the bag, I swing it right front of her fixed stare. "I got Cheerios and milk and Tappen's honey and I got a bowl and a spoon, too. So we got everything we need for a bowl of Cheerios."

But she ain't there. I come to see her but no one told me she ain't there, she's starin' in from somewhere far away. "You see big big Beulah, honey? I been gainin' the pounds all these years and I got it so now you can't miss me. Not even from far away, Dorrie, I'm big enough you can't miss me."

I put my hand on her hair, brush it back. I was tryin' to stop my tears. I says, "You miss your ma, honey? I know she loves you. And I do, and Popsy does, and Tappen does, and little Laureen, bless her heart, she miss you, too, ticklin' her." My hand touched just the side of her face and I felt her skin flinch just a little just once but then she gone to stone again. "And Charlie, he miss all them biscuits you snuck to him thinkin' I wasn't seein' nothin', thinkin' I thought it just magic how he followed you around close to that hand you was trailin', like you was a walkin' kitchen." I moved out of her stare but she didn't follow so I gone back in. "And Mike, your dad, I know he miss you. Everybody miss you, loves you, we all love you." I was lookin' up now, I couldn't look at them eyes no more and I couldn't stop talkin' neither, I would've just broke right there.

"And here we are, all of us, and not a one knows what you're lookin' at, what you're seein'. Oh, you don't have to tell us neither. You don't have to do nothin'. Except eat. Lord child, you gonna slide away, you don't eat. You want them Cheerios yet?" And then I lean close but she just stare up, at me and not at me, fixed.

"You miss your brother? That who you're lookin' for? You miss him? He was a good boy, wasn't he? He always took care of you, too, I knowed that." Then I says but under my breath, "The whole town could see that.

"Oh Lordie child, I love you. You ain't a normal kid. 'Course I never met a normal kid, ain't one of 'em normal. But you . . . you're, you're, you're just . . ."

I brought my face down to hers right next to them cheeks I used to kiss every night 'fore she drift off, after she land into bed, my God, she used to jump from half across the room. "Come on back, honey, just to let Beulah kiss ya again. I'll let you go back, I promise. I'll let you go back wherever you are. I won't stop you. But just come on back for me to kiss you. Just a moment."

I felt her breath right on my cheek, she was breathin' right on my cheek. I turn and give her my breath. Like you do with a little foal. I give her my breath and she give me back another one and I feel 'em both together on my cheek. "That's all I need, honey.

You don't have to do nothin' else. Just breathe. We'll just keep breathin' here together.

"I still got them Cheerios whenever you're ready but I won't rush you. Maybe we're all out here wantin' you to go too fast, and all you want is . . ."

I stopped talkin'. I lifted my face up out of her breath. I laid my hand over her back. Tight as a rock, or no, tighter, like a rock 'bout to explode, like a rock in a fire 'bout to blow. But then I felt she gone steady under my hand. "Easy, girl," I says. "Easy." My hand raised up just a tiny bit, raised up from her breathin', then down slow. "Easy, honey," I says. "Don't blow. I won't talk no more. But I'll stay put here, I got a hour to set here. It ain't all I got but it's all they'll give me. And ain't a thing I'd rather do than sit here and make sure nothin' happens to you. You just keep on lookin', I'll take care of you. Make sure you don't get too cold."

Little waves from a pond, her breathin', waves over her little rock of a body. Then somethin' else come, I felt a teeny shake like she was maybe wakin' but then I thought, *No, it's gone, I was just makin' it up.* But then I felt it again, a small tremble. "Come on, honey, Beulah'll take care of you." But then I seen she was startin' to shiver. I put both my hands on her back.

"Lordie, child, you are cold!" I look around but there ain't no blankets, she's on the only one. I pick her shoulders right up, she's just as tight curled, she don't flop at all, but she's shakin' so hard she's shakin' my hand. I pull the blanket down with my other hand. And then I pull her legs up and they're shakin' just as hard. I gotta yank the blanket to get it farther down, it's tucked in so tight.

I hear the door. I say, "She's cold, I'm gettin' her covered." I look down and she's just a tight shiverin' thing, her whole body shakin' like I never seen.

"Get more blankets," I said. "The girl's cold." I was tryin' to get the blanket out and over her but they come in front of me. They don't got a blanket though, they got a needle.

I say, "The girl's cold," but the doctor, I hear him behind me, he says, "Please, Mrs. Tappen."

They was givin' her the needle. Here I gone and tell her she could go anywhere, that I was there, gonna make sure she don't get cold. I promised her just that little. I see my bag of Cheerios on the floor by the chair and I hear Mike back in my ear, *It isn't that simple, Beulah.*

Her *red rambler rose traveled up the side of the house untrimmed, one green cane crept through the crack between the sash and the frame of the topmost tiny window, one cane growing its way across the rough pine boards. Turning first pale, then white, then bright white, the vine keeps crossing the dark attic floor.*

PART IV

JANUARY 1959

FLORENCE FELT WITH her hand along the edge of the bed to the metal table, past the box of Kleenex, the plastic glass for water they allowed her. Nothing. Nothing. That's right. They took her cigarettes. How come she always forgot? Every morning for weeks now, she forgot they had taken her little darlings first thing. She might burn herself, or someone else, burn up the bed. So many things she could do to inflict harm. They took even her lipstick. What was it? Could she swallow it? Yes, that was it. She could swallow it, they said. She, who cannot even eat the meals they offer could swallow a tube of lipstick. She leaned up on her elbows. She would try to make it to the dayroom. There, she could smoke. One right after another. She longed for a smoke. It had been weeks. There was just the one small problem, getting dressed.

She fell back onto the pillow, pulled the blanket up again. She hated morning, hated its blankness. Night was pain, pain all around seeping in from everywhere, but morning was blank, was the feeling she had to start all over again and she couldn't. She couldn't do it.

She heard Bet greeting the nurses, the orderlies, the patients as she rolled the food cart down the hall. She pulled the sheets up over her nose, she couldn't smell the food now, not now, it made her nauseous. Rubber eggs, toast, grease, she could smell the grease. If only they could just give her the coffee and make that little check in the right box. Florence Buell had eaten breakfast.

"Morning, Miss Buell." Bet with such a round, red face, a kind face. Florence smiled up at her, shook her head, not today, no food today, please.

"Gotta eat, Miss Buell. Stop those shakes."

Florence held her hands together under the sheets, tried to hold her shaking hands still. Like they were alive! A mind of their own, or no, a heart of their own, drumming away. It was almost funny to her, her hands alive and everything else dead. The dead morning.

Bet set the tray down on the table. "Just try, Miss Buell." The smell, it was everywhere. Like night that comes in everywhere, the smell came in, flooded her. Florence sank down farther under the covers, as far away as possible from the smell, from eggs, from morning. Where *he* was. Her David, her *boy*. His large, bright face beamed into her mind. She could smile now. It was her small peace.

Oh, how he moved through his day learning "the ways of the world," he called them, not yet six, his little hand on his hip. "Mom, I want to learn the ways of the world," and then he pointed to the stockings she was washing in the sink. They were just tricks to him, tricks the adults knew, like rinsing his water glass out and turning it upside down onto the drainboard. Then he'd bring his proud face close, whisper to the glass, "Now drain!"

Such a little body, but he forged his trail through the house, ordering thing by thing alive. And she, she didn't even mind the mess. It was a good mess and she was a good mother, everyone said so, and she had proof: he was a good boy, such a good good boy, so good, in fact, that she formed around him, followed him, while he sang her world alive. . . . He was dead. Dead. She couldn't do it. She couldn't make anything live, not one thing, if there was just one thing left living that she could touch . . .

She curled into herself tighter, held herself, her body, her burden to carry into the light, the hard gray light. His face washed through her, over her, colored her. Stop, stop. She couldn't take any more. His little toes. He would not have them piggies, no! Not her boy. They were rats, and each one was named. There was . . . She couldn't remember. What were . . . what were . . . Oh God, she couldn't remember, oh God . . .

"Mrs. Buell! Mrs. Buell, stop! Stop. Calm yourself, Mrs. Buell. Stop." The blankets were being pulled back. They were pulling the blankets and the sheets from her face.

Florence looked out through the blur. It was the orderly, again. He was dead, still dead. Her boy. And all the names gone. Gone. "And I can't ask him. Do you understand that, sir? I can't ask my boy anything."

"Come on, sit up. Sit up now. You must calm down, Mrs. Buell. You have to calm down."

There was the nurse, too, uncovering her arm. Was this her shot? Already? Oh yes, the morning. Take it, the arm, take everything, here . . .

FLORENCE WATCHED THROUGH her one window for the light to change, to begin to dull till it dulled everything, even the far wall and the bathroom door. Then Florence propped her pillows up and got into position. She would stare at the slightly open door into the hall, halfway between the ceiling and the knob. That way she wouldn't miss Michael when he curled his face around with his half-frightened, half-hopeful expression. She had only one chance because as soon as he'd see her eyes, he'd change, he'd become ... She swallowed. Her mouth was dry, stone dry. She took a sip of water. No straw allowed. Another sip. How she wanted her little darlings. Florence laid her head back down on the pillow, perfectly positioned. She had only that second, that moment to catch him because then he would become ... careful. The oh-so-careful Michael, the I-will-take-care-of-you-forever Michael, the Michael that is no longer here because he can no longer look at her, really look. Her husband. She cringed. Oh God, poor thing, husband to what? This shell? This hole her dead son came from? Poor Michael, driving three hours a day to visit, and except for that one moment, that one glance, invisible.

More water. She hated thinking Michael might be talking to him, Mr. Doctor. Michael would believe Him, Mr. Cool Cucumber, Mr. Stare-into-her-eyes, the holes that once were her eyes, Mr. Question, Mr. Test. She heard steps, maybe? No . . . no again, but she had to keep her attention. It was getting quite dark.

Steps, steps, her door, yes! No. The nurse, Mrs. Arner. "Your husband called, Mrs. Buell. He can't come today. He will though tomorrow. He promises. You should have a light on in here."

Florence rolled toward the window, squeezed her eyes shut. Now it was night, everywhere.

MICHAEL! HE SURPRISED her. Florence looked out the window. Still day! He had come during the day! She looked back at him—careful, he was already careful.

"How's my wife?" he asked as he kissed her on the forehead, knowing her lips would be too dry, sticky dry. She licked her lips and then she smiled, reached up to touch his face leaning over her. She had missed him, his one glance. He sat down on the edge of the bed, took her hand. He had gotten so thin, so drawn. "We're both getting older, huh?" Florence said. He smiled. "Yeah."

He twisted around to look through the door into the hall, the door that had to be open now with a visitor. No orderlies. He looked back, not at her, down at her hand. He traced her skin, from her thumbnail down to her wrist and back.

"Florence, I have something to tell you." He had seen Him, Mr. Doctor. She felt it. Thumb, wrist, thumb, wrist. "Eudora's not well, not, doing well."

She sat up. "Not well?" Thumb, wrist. "Look at me, Michael." Her voice stung and Michael looked up, his face transparent, devastated. "Tell me, Michael." Her voice was firm. "Tell me."

He looked back down, kept shaking his head. "She's not doing well," he said again but he was cracking. She was watching him crack. She suddenly understood. He was trying to follow the doctor's instructions but he was cracking. She helped him.

"Where is she?"

"In the hospital."

"Where?"

"Poughkeepsie." And then he leaned toward her, covered his eyes with his hand.

"It's okay, Michael. It's okay." He fell into her and she took him, her husband. "It's okay." Florence held him as he broke apart, his back shaking under her hands.

Michael pulled back, grabbed a Kleenex for his nose. "I'm sorry," he said, "I'm sorry, I just I just . . ."

"It's okay, honey, it's okay." She paused, looked at him. "*I'm* okay." She squeezed his hand tight. "Michael?"

He was blowing his nose again. "Yeah?"

"She's . . . like me, right?"

He looked down, but he nodded. "Worse," he whispered. He looked back out into the hallway for a split second, then whispered very softly, "She doesn't"—he could barely get it out—"respond."

Florence didn't move. There was nothing left of her to hold back what she heard, it washed through her, poured through the silence inside her.

"Doctor Ligget told me not to—"

"I know," and she put her hand up to his mouth. "I know."

Michael looked at her, looked into her eyes, her holes. And they flooded. Her eyes had water, water she hadn't felt in months, years it seemed, water just about to spill.

"Oh, Florence," Michael whispered and squeezed her hand. "I'm so scared."

"I know," she said.

Florence knew this ground, this lowest possible ground. She had nowhere to fall. How could Michael know? She had been among the dead. She could walk now. She could walk for the wounded, touch the wounded. Her little one. Her little, *living* daughter. She was alive!

"She'll be okay, Michael."

He shook his head. "She's not, she's not responding—"

"I know." She looked out the window. Her crow was on the roof, her little friend, then he was gone. "I'm going to go to her."

Michael looked at her, puzzled. "Go to her?"

"See, honey. I . . ." How could she explain? "I live where she is now. See?"

He looked at her full, wet eyes and nodded his big, slow nod.

"THE MAIN THING you have to take into account, Michael"—
Dr. Ligget leaned back on his swivel chair behind his desk—"is
the tremendous risk." Michael always felt a kind of relief here, in
this office where each week he would hear the summation of
Florence's latest reports. For a few minutes, his worry for her, his
fear seemed to float out of his forehead and fill the room, fill each
shelf, each heavy, labeled book on the walls surrounding him. In
a certain way, Michael felt—with this man not much older than
him, though he was fully gray and, God knows, a lot smarter—he
felt safe.

"But then again, it seems it is the only thing we've found that
seems to animate her at *all*." Dr. Ligget leaned forward over the
wide plain of his desk, all the papers, Florence's file Michael
knew was there, her thick file that always made him a bit queasy
when he saw it, as if that stack of prescriptions and reports held a
key that he'd somehow missed, the key to his wife, a key that
when the cards were thrown he never got. But it also revolted
him, that folder, made him shudder, like David's coffin had
done, as if everything he loved in the world could be boiled down
into some rectangular, some lifeless box.

Dr. Ligget faced down as he talked, his eyes looking up over his glasses, his black frames. "One mention of her daughter, one seemingly insignificant question, and her thinking seems to clear right up. She becomes articulate, and even, as I said before, *animated*. Her posture changes, her gestures, everything, she becomes practically like . . . the Florence you knew before."

"It would be just an afternoon, Doctor."

"Well . . ." Dr. Ligget leaned back, his hands behind his head. "We're not talking just an afternoon. We would have to adjust the medication beforehand, see. And we would have to monitor her very closely afterwards. And this is, Michael, in the *best* of circumstances."

Michael nodded.

"That's not even considering the tremendous risk. Especially since"—he leaned forward again and said very seriously—"she seems to have come so far."

"Since she found out about Eudora."

"Yes. It's the only thing that has seemed to elicit a change . . . besides, of course, the treatments. But then there's the concern of their past history." He spoke more slowly now, measuring out each word, his pen in his hand up near his chin. "Florence's reaction when she actually *sees* Eudora, in that condition, might escalate into a real, a real setback." He shook his head and looked sideways as if he were pondering the *magnitude* of what could happen. It always made Michael feel a little dumb. He never seemed to be able to imagine a future, except as just more of today.

"I understand the risk, Doctor."

"We also have to prepare for the fact that Eudora's, that perhaps her probable outcome might trigger intense feelings of helplessness in Florence. She very well might revisit all the panic she experienced around your son. We have to prepare for the worst here, Michael."

Michael just nodded. He was in a foreign country now, being placed in front of a firing squad where he could not speak even a few intelligible words for himself.

"It could trigger a response in Florence that could mean, basically, initiating another set of treatments."

"Shock?"

Dr. Ligget met Michael's eyes and nodded.

"Doctor, I know how important this is for Florence. And I feel Eudora needs . . . her, not just because she's her mother, I don't mean that, I mean *that's* important I know but that's not quite . . . it. They had something different together . . . I mean . . . just the way they, um . . . think alike. They kind of . . . I don't know, before David, they were often in their own world together. They saw the same things, they liked the same things, they laughed at the same things, they shared this world"—Michael flipped his hand back and forth—"this whole way of looking. It seemed different than a, I don't know, a normal mother-daughter relationship." He paused but Dr. Ligget didn't speak. "And Eudora's doctor did say there is no way to predict just how long her condition can last."

Dr. Ligget looked down at Florence's open file. All those papers stacked one on top of the other. "Well, Michael, I know you are a practical man. You've been through a lot. If you are willing to take the risk, I'll sign for it." He looked up over his glasses again.

Michael nodded.

"For . . . how about Monday afternoon? Monday?"

"Yeah, Monday. That's good."

"Because then, you see, we could have the week to monitor her. And I'll have the medication changed gradually so that she won't miss any cycle that could set her back." He put down his pen again. "I do have to repeat that the risk is considerable."

Michael nodded again. His throat was so dry. *Is this how Florence always feels, so thirsty?* "I'll drive her there. I'll be with her the entire time, and then I'll drive her back."

The doctor nodded. "You are a courageous man, Mr. Buell."

No, *just desperate*, Michael thought. The firing squad could take aim any moment. But it made him smile. It made him feel he had a secret he held from this very smart man, and that secret gave him enough strength to stand up, shake Dr. Ligget's hand, and walk out the door with his almighty signature.

FLORENCE CHEWED ON the dry rye bread as she stared out the window at the fields of snow going by, a few patches of bare trees, some bony, some feathery. Winter was so empty, so clean and easy. She couldn't bear summer now, its crush of green closing in. Just the thought could make her claustrophobic. She loved the snow. There could never be too much snow, its layers of forgetfulness covering everything.

If only she could stop her shaking. Or hide her hands. *See those hands? Those are crazy hands, the crazy lady's hands.* More bread, more water. Michael, so thoughtful, remembering to bring a bottle of water. She looked over: Michael, her driver, her anchor. She squeezed her eyes together. *If only, God, we could just get through this one thing.* More bread, more fields of snow. The snow never seemed to cover everything, not the fences in between, the gray lines of stone.

She closed her eyes. The jostle of the car and the quiet, the quiet between her and Michael, moving toward Eudora, *their* daughter. Oh God, she was so far away from those first clear moments! Urging Michael to march in to the doctor. Where was that sureness now? She had been practically cocky, the future like a movie she looked down onto, with Florence, of course, the heroine, the Florence Nightingale, the mother, the good mother. More water, bread. She didn't know anything now. Ahead was just blank. She couldn't see, not even to prepare herself. She could not see in her mind her baby lying lifeless on a bed. Thank God for the snow. She couldn't take even a single flower now. But please, God, give her some line, some road leading into Eudora, her daughter, her *living* daughter. More bread. She was not ready now.

The houses grew thicker, little yards edged with snowbanks, driveways newly shoveled, narrow walks leading to front doors and back doors, a few cars with their white exhaust flying up. Houses with real families, kids that rode buses to school and husbands that drove off to work, mothers that cooked and kept the house clean, and read stories at night in one of the bedrooms under a lamp. There they were, family after family, lined up before her. She turned her head away from the window.

Michael tapped her thigh. "We're getting close, honey. Okay? Doing okay?"

She nodded. "All these houses."

"I know." He kept his hand on her thigh.

"I liked the fields better."

"I know. Only a few minutes more."

Florence leaned her head back onto the seat, kept her eyes closed through the stops and turns, her shaking hands tight together till she could feel inside them the little heart of their own. *Please God, just this one thing.*

The car stopped. Michael turned off the motor. She opened her eyes.

"Well?" he said.

She took a deep breath. "Ready or not."

"It's no problem, honey, if you don't feel you can—"

She shook her head. "I'm ready."

"Sure?"

She nodded toward him, feeling for the door handle with her shaking hand.

"I'll get it."

"Thank you," she said as she leaned back onto the warm seat and stared at the brick wall rising in front of her.

FLORENCE STOOD AT the door of the room, Michael behind her, the doctor behind her. She did not close her eyes. She walked forward to Eudora, looked down at her body curled toward the wall. She leaned over and touched her hair. She was not shaking. She traced Eudora's hair, so newly grown around her ear, touched her forearm. It was warm. Eudora was warm. Florence lay down on the bed alongside her, gently against her, close, closer, she curled her arm around her. There, Florence stopped. She became still, more and more still till she could feel, inside her daughter's taut back, Eudora breathe. She was alive.

Florence knew she could lie still like this a long time. She didn't have to see Eudora's face or her eyes, not yet. Her daughter was alive, and they were together now, alone on the ground they both knew, and beside them, between them was David, her dead son, *her* dead brother.

Florence wrapped her hand around Eudora's fist that was pulled in tight to her chest. She pressed slowly in with her thumb, wiggled her thumb inside. Florence could feel Eudora's fingers closed against her, squeezing her thumb hard.

Florence waited, and as she waited, David slowly lowered, slipped below till he lay beneath them, she could feel his shape fill the ground under them. He held them up.

Florence whispered, "I'm here. Mommy's here."

Michael was behind her. Florence waited. She could wait as long as was needed for Eudora to open her closed fist.

FLORENCE, FINALLY, WAS sleeping. She would not leave. Eudora had, in one seemingly normal moment, relaxed her body and rolled toward her mother, asleep. She could not leave her daughter now. Eudora was sleeping, just sleeping! Behind and around Florence, Michael had made call after call, standing at the phone waiting. He had talked to both doctors twice, sitting and waiting. His wife had finally gotten her shot. She had eaten more bread. He had brought her glasses of water. She had looked, they had looked it seemed for hours at Eudora's face. Florence had closed her eyes, had fallen asleep. Michael had begged the nurse, had argued: The four other beds were all empty, please please turn off the overhead light, the light that had been on for weeks. And now it was dark. His wife and his daughter were asleep on the bed. Michael sat down beside them on the folding metal chair, leaned his head back against the wall and closed his eyes.

He had forgotten how much he loved lying in bed at the end of the day after shutting out all the light, even putting a pillow over his eyes if Florence was reading. He loved the dark before he slept, loved sinking into sleep. He had forgotten everything he loved, everything except his son lying in the coffin, his wife lying strapped on the table, his daughter lying like a stone on the bed. He had stayed alive forgetting everything, driving, working, not working—depending on Susan, on Mark to carry on so he could leave early once again, to answer calls, to arrange the trucks coming in, the men going out, to fix every broken wringer, every broken motor, to learn the new Automatics. But it was peace, his work. Any call not a doctor, not a school official, was peace. Washers, dryers, salesmen, the new pastels, Susan at the desk, Mark and his men doing the calls, that was the life he was good at, that he knew. But how he had loved his home, what used to be his home. And now his family (his family!) lay here asleep.

He reached over and touched Florence's hair, the back of her neck, her bony shoulder blades. Skin and bones. He loved even her bones. He remembered what his mother said when he first brought Florence home: The girl doesn't have enough fat on her. He had smiled then, she was *his* girl. And now she lay there, just bones, no fat to soften the blows. He had tried to protect her. And David. He had tried to protect David, and all of a sudden, one moment, and his head, it was smashed, his head was smashed. Tears poured down Michael's face. His failure was so simple and so large to him, so *thorough*. He had let his son out and he had not protected him. Father Bob had told him, everyone had told him: It wasn't your fault, you could not protect him his whole life, he was not an infant, a toddler. As if that mattered. As if, once you let your son out, you can stop being a father, and what is a father if he does not protect his son? It never stopped or shrunk, his failure stayed pure and large and hard and simple.

He wiped his eyes with his hand. With Eudora, his failure was different, it was slippery. For weeks, months after, he had lived in fear for her, she would ride the bus, ride those horses, jump even, and he would know every minute, every second: *She could hit her head anywhere.*

David had always taken care of her, always *protected* her. He took her to all the basketball games, the football games, taught her how to wrestle, even let her up into his "sanctum," Florence used to call it, to listen to all that awful music.

Michael kept wiping the tears away with his shirt. He had tried, tried to find the right place for her. He had been too frightened to let her stay any longer with the Tappens—Clay with his gun, all the junk around everywhere, the smell, his old father, the poverty—the fears had rained down all over him. He smiled at himself as he cried. He had been so scared for her safety! Her physical safety! But he had never, not once, thought what everyone had always said: She was her mother's daughter, the picture of her mother. Instead, he had seen her head everywhere, her fragile head with those incessantly active eyes. How she *stared* at that casket dropping into the earth, she kept her eyes wide open.

The tears poured down as he listened to Florence and Eudora breathe in their sleep. Something was over now, he could not say exactly what, but it was over. Eudora would have to stay here who knows how long. The doctor's favorite answer: There's no way to tell. Michael had talked to Beulah. The Tappens would take Eudora, of course, whenever she was well, for as long as was needed. They were such good people. And they loved her—Dorrie, as they called her, as she called herself now. He had been so scared. And Florence—oh God, did she *shake* before her shot. She *did* eat though, afterwards, more bread. He would drive Florence back to the hospital, but. . . . Did he know or just pray? No more treatments? Maybe her pills would be enough and she could be at home? What was it that was over? Something he could not name, but he knew it as well as he knew how sleep comes. He had always been able to sleep on a hard chair. Florence used to tease him for it: Her exciting husband, she'd say, sound asleep at the kitchen table. It was coming now, the sleep, the day was over.

FLORENCE WATCHED EUDORA sleep as they lay there, face to face. Each small movement her daughter made—a foot, a leg drawing up, how she tucked both hands under her face—each one seemed like magic to her, as if a mysterious wonder had been let loose in the world. Mysterious and kind. *Kind*, Florence repeated to herself. How she needed that word, drank it in, savored it. Life had loomed up so large and so fierce, she hadn't expected this, this small, forgiving kindness, aimed so directly toward her.

Florence watched Eudora's face open as she woke up, her eyes still shut. "Mommy's here," she whispered, stroking her hair. "I'm here," she said again a little louder, and Eudora, keeping her eyes closed, nodded.

Then tears began to run across Eudora's face and down onto the bed. Florence wiped them away with her hand, with the edge of the pillowcase.

"I love you, Eudora. So much. And your father, too, he . . ." Florence pulled her in close and Eudora pressed her face against her mother's chest. Florence felt, very gently, Eudora's eyes.

"You like the dark, huh? Listening in the dark?" Eudora moved her cheek up and down on Florence's wet blouse.

Florence waited till she felt the tears stop. Then she lifted her daughter's face up. Her eyes were restful, like they were made to be closed, her face so open. "I'm right here." She tapped Eudora's chest. "Right here. Always." Eudora nodded and her tears ran down again. Florence wiped them away. "Always. And you're here." She took Eudora's hand and tapped her own chest, back and forth, chest to chest. Then Florence leaned forward and kissed her face. "My little punkin. But you're so big now, aren't you?"

Eudora nodded again. "Pook," she mouthed silently.

"Snee," Florence said and watched Eudora smile. It was their name together, their little secret. Then she closed her eyes, too, so she could feel the smile wash through her.

Florence said very softly, "David's with you, underneath you." She felt the dark surround each word.

"I know," Eudora whispered.

"Are you scared?"

"No."

Eudora opened her eyes onto her mother's face. Florence opened her eyes, too.

"Not at all?"

Eudora shook her head. "Not at all."

DORRIE WATCHED FLORENCE walk in from the cold, her long coat making her look larger than she was, her face red, her lips red, no lipstick. Florence leaned over and kissed her. "How's my sweet? Dressed?" She smelled of cigarettes and cold. Dorrie shook her head, smiling.

"You're not? Lazybones still in bed!"

Dorrie threw back the sheets, and her mother laughed. "Trickster." Dorrie even had her sneakers on. Today was the day.

Florence raised her eyes, turned to the far bed. A girl, maybe six or seven years old, began to roll over and over, her face shiny, almost cute, then contorted, then gone again into the sheet, the back of her head flat where her straight brown hair had matted. Dorrie watched the pain flood through her mother's face.

"Oh. When did she come?"

"Yesterday," Dorrie said. "She moans a lot."

Dorrie followed her mother over, watched her look down on the twisting body, then reach out to touch the girl's shoulder. The girl flung out her arm, made a loud, frightened noise. *Like an animal*, Dorrie thought. *Like I was.* They waited by her bed till she quieted again.

Dorrie leaned over without touching her, whispered, "Bye now," and turned away. She could feel the tears rise up into her throat, behind her eyes, as she walked toward her suitcase.

Florence couldn't stop looking at the twisted girl. "Let's go," Dorrie said very softly, almost under her breath, but Florence heard and turned.

Dorrie looked back just once from outside the door. She could feel her tears start to sink back down into her belly again. *Where they live now,* she thought.

Dorrie looked at her mother walking with her down the hall. She liked her there, beside her, as they walked toward Beulah and Tappen waiting on the other side of the locked door.

Beulah spotted Dorrie, knelt down on her good knee, and opened her arms. Dorrie dropped her suitcase and ran, pressed her face against her, against the buttons of her coat. Everywhere around her was Beulah. Dorrie stayed for a few moments extra.

Then Dorrie watched her mother's arms lift toward Beulah, watched Beulah take in her thin body. They stayed hugging a long time. Beulah whispered in Florence's ear and Florence nodded, her face resting on Beulah's shoulder, against Beulah's old pink coat. Dorrie understood her mother's face now, she knew it, like she had known her patch of grass. *Just since,* she thought.

Tappen kept his hand on Dorrie's shoulder. He looked strange all dressed up, in a white shirt like her dad wore and brown pants lined with a crease. She had never seen him all clean like this, his hair combed back.

Her dad walked in. Tappen's hand lifted. She watched their hands move toward each other—one short and thick, stained dark with grease, the other long and smooth. She watched each hand held inside the other.

"Today's the day we've been praying for," she heard Beulah say.

Dorrie felt all of them around her, like four posts. They made their own room inside this room inside the hospital. She didn't need to run anywhere. She was all the way inside, her tears safe inside her belly, the floor underneath her, holding her up. *Just since*, she thought again, as she watched all four of them begin to move toward the door.

IT WAS SO cold Dorrie could see each breath of her mother's. They made a trail of small clouds in front of her face that she followed to the car. Florence sat down in the passenger seat, her seat, and closed the door. But then she rolled open the window, and the clouds came back, though they were smaller and quicker to go. She kissed the air, kissed the tips of her gloves, waved her fingers. As Florence waved each kiss toward her, Dorrie watched the new cloud disappear. Her dad was waving, too, even after he started, very slowly, to drive her away, out of the parking lot, back to the hospital. She watched her mother roll up her window, still kissing and waving through the glass.

Beulah stood behind her. Dorrie felt her largeness, her large arm holding the suitcase. She felt Beulah's dress underneath her coat. Dorrie didn't turn yet toward her. She didn't want to see Beulah's breath in the air. But she didn't want her to move. She wanted her to stay blocking the wind. She wasn't scared.

I have never been scared since. But sometimes at school, or in the barn, and always at night in bed, I hear her words, Mommy's here, Mommy's here. *They go on over and over, holding me to her. Like red streamers along the string of a kite. We take turns being the kite. Sometimes it is me in the air and she is far far below me, tiny, like a mouse, an ant, she is crawling, slowly, and sometimes, she is very very far above, silent then, but never still, she is flying then.*

In Dark Water

MERMER BLAKESLEE

A Reader's Guide

A Conversation with Mermer Blakeslee

Q: How did the idea for this novel begin?

MB: One day while I was working in the garden, a new voice came to me—immediate, urgent, delicate. I recognized it right away—it was Eudora, a forty-year-old character in my first novel, now visiting me as a small girl, a ten-year-old. I ran in and started writing. But even though Dorrie's voice was extremely compelling and it obviously had a story it was trying to squeeze out, it was also elusive. Dorrie was hiding, very wary, as if she didn't trust me yet. When I tried to face her voice directly and capture it, it would sneak away.

I had a few "facts" that I knew from my first novel, *Same Blood*—that Dorrie had had trouble with her mother and that she had run away to Beulah's. But I didn't know why. What would have driven such a young babe out of her house? I kept writing "backwards," trying to uncover the layers underneath their mutual pain. With each layer, I got closer to being inside Dorrie's body. Then the image came of Dorrie squeezing her dead brother's toe. That was it, the catalyst. Dorrie's fist. Dorrie's delicate but forceful soul forming itself around her brother's death. Once I knew about David, Florence started to make sense and came into focus. Then I could begin to write "forwards," still into the dark toward what I did not know, but the story could now unfold.

Q: The story takes place between the years 1958 and 1959. Why did you choose this time period?

MB: The time period was purely logistical—one of the givens because Dorrie (Doro) was forty in 1988 in *Same Blood*. But I felt close to that time anyway. And for months, my family had to listen to a lot of radio tapes from the late fifties. All those jingles! And such melodrama in the music—Harvey and The Moonglows, The Platters. It was great to watch anybody who had been a teenager back then listening to those songs—they'd invariably start crooning away.

Q: Throughout the novel, Eudora is intrigued by animals and seeks solace in and identification with them. In what ways do you believe that a child's intuition is similar to that of an animal's? How do you think these instincts change as we become adults?

MB: Let me tell you a story. I knew pretty early on that Dorrie loved snakes. (That's funny, my husband said, when you talk about her voice, it's just like a snake in the grass—here, gone, just a flash.) Still, I was sort of waiting for a snake to come into the book. One day one did, ring-necked with a bright yellow collar. After writing, I walked out the back door and there on the mat in front of me was a baby snake, the smallest thing! And it had a bright yellow collar. It was dead but perfectly intact. I had never actually seen one until then, and there it was. What an offering!

But back to your question. I think part of the reason Dorrie fascinated me was that her vision is very "primitive," instinctual, and therefore close to the animal soul. The world shines for her. It is animated, not inert or lifeless. And it is not separated from her interior life. This way of perceiving would be hard to find in an adult in our predominantly monotheistic, middle-class, white culture with its concept of what is "normal." (Cultures that are closer to the land, to animals, to poverty, or marginalized cultures that have managed to keep their traditions, rituals, and even foods intact, seem to be more in tune with this instinctual way of perceiving.) The predominant culture is part of Dorrie's problem. She blossoms at the Tappens', where her soul is given latitude. But when she is in an environment that has deadened and rationalized the world, she withdraws into herself. In a sense, both Florence and Dorrie suffer from an allergic reaction to our culture, which has little place for grief or the darker shadings of life. Grief gets in the way of its obsessive productivity. In that way Florence and Dorrie, both fully engaged with their troubled, tenacious souls, are very connected.

Q: Despite the misplaced rage in Eudora and Florence's relationship, they seem to be equals at some level—soul mates even. As a parent, what are your feelings about their relationship?

MB: I'm glad you said that. Florence definitely wasn't a great mother. A parent is supposed to take care of her children, feed and clothe them, give them a home, and she was unable, after David died, to do that. But she was something else to Dorrie, and finally, she was needed. They both shared an invisible realm. They both felt David descend. No one else could reach into Dorrie's soul like that. So despite the biology, Beulah was Dorrie's mother, and Florence was, as you say, a soul mate. And in the end, Dorrie says goodbye to Florence *physically* and returns to a life with the Tappens. But after having been initiated, in a sense, by grief, Dorrie carries her mother within her as a permanent internal figure.

And that gets to one more thing. I feel Dorrie's traumatic year is about initiation, not victimhood, and certainly not about abuse or living in a dysfunctional family. It is about a girl who follows each gesture of her soul no matter how low it takes her, as it forms around grief and around the inviolable elements of life: death, love, the loss of innocence. Often, if we are not "normal," we think we need to be cured, fixed. But families are never normal, never rational. They are, thankfully, incurable. The dark streaks that run through every family are often what the soul feeds on. They are what makes us who we are. They bring us nearer to the center of life, where the strong, deep currents run.

Q: **You've been praised by critics for creating such a believable and sincere voice for Eudora. Why do you think you were so successful in narrating via an eleven-year-old girl?**

MB: Just patience. It took me a while to *sink* into her voice. I literally felt I had to descend into her little body. And then I could feel it viscerally. Sometimes my stomach would knot up. When I wrote from her point of view, the world would come in very close and large, and I could never see far into the distance. When Dorrie speaks, she is grappling, trying to survive. Her voice carries with it an urgent necessity. I didn't want any adult retrospect to break the spell of being inside her. But, on the other hand, I did want the reader to see beyond Dorrie, to guess at a larger truth than Dorrie's telling without losing the empathy and identification with her. That was a challenge, especially in the chapter "Procedure," where Dorrie is largely unaware of sexuality.

Q: **Eudora experiences her feelings through her body in a very vis-**

ceral manner. **Do you think that this physical manifestation of emotion is common to children as they deal with grief that is beyond their understanding?**

MB: I think children haven't learned yet to separate their bodies and their souls like adults do. They squirm, wriggle, wag their whole bodies. All emotions, not just grief, can elude our intellectual "understanding," but they can never elude our bodies. Our bodies know much more than we give them credit for. As adults, we often wait until our bodies are screaming at us in pain to pay attention to them—except in rare moments, like in sex or in a risk sport. Then, for a moment, body and soul can merge.

Q: **We witness the sudden, uncontrollable spread of Eudora's "bad" smile throughout the novel. The smile seems almost personified—as if it takes on a life of its own. Can you elaborate on this?**

MB: That's true. And our souls, too, have a life of their own. We don't own them. Beulah sees that same smile and calls it a grin, "Just breakin' across her face." She loves it. And Dorrie only feels the bad smile come back when she starts to lie or when she thinks of her mother. I didn't plan that, but in hindsight I see that the soul's expression can get so twisted when it is not given any welcoming place.

Q: **What was the inspiration behind Dorrie's imagined identity as the cowboy Shane?**

MB: I don't know. I just saw her walk through Beulah's door like that. Then later, I remembered seeing Shane on TV when I was sick. (We never got to watch TV except when we were sick.) I remembered those boots walking down that dusty road.

Q: **How long and in what ways do you live with your characters before they make it to the page?**

MB: Once I hear them, either on the page or in the shower, they move in. My whole family and all my friends have to live with them. I once called up my friend to complain, "That Dorrie is gonna get kicked out of school if she doesn't start behaving. Now what am I gonna do with that girl?" Occasionally, I had to ask my son and his friend to do something Dorrie would do, smash a cup, burn some hair. I made him squirm and wriggle on the floor. I knew exactly what I would feed her every night.

When I was young, maybe ten, I cut a picture out of a magazine of a feisty-looking little girl, barefoot on the dirt in the middle of some chickens, a wild thing. As a kid, I kept the photograph in my journal. For the past fifteen, twenty years, I have had her by my desk. Her face is turned toward the camera like she just got caught.

And Beulah? She teaches me—about raising a child, about handling a horse, about growing plants—to be who they are. She looks at their peculiar convolutions as signs, as messages from their souls, not as problems to cure. I often think to myself, "Now, what would Beulah do?"

Popsy, my grandfather, was the only character taken straight from real life. Born in 1880, he was a potato farmer who could not read or write. I haven't met anyone even remotely like him in our modern world. He lived with us, crippled, mostly incontinent, barely able to see out of his one eye. (Every day before school, it was my job to empty his chamber pot.) We were alone in the house when my parents went on their long vacations. I got him his food, and he told me his stories. His presence made my family life very different from my friends'. I was so excited when he came into the book. He was all *there*, still wild, saying and doing things that surprised me.

Q: **Making Beulah a central narrator added a unique dimension to the story. Why do you think she is such an effective storyteller?**

MB: Ah, she's got the gift of gab, doesn't she? Beulah speaks in the dialect of the rural Catskills—its rhythm, its weight, its swing, its inevitable dive at the end of the sentence back to the land it came from. It's a language that's got *body*, enough substance to hold a lot of metaphor without being flowery. I said before that Dorrie speaks out of an urgency, a need to survive. Beulah, on the other hand, is able to be generous. She tells a story to *you*, for *you*, the reader. She says, "Come on in. Sit down. Let me tell you how it really happened." I grew up with this in the people here. They wrap a story around the ear of their audience. When Dorrie lands at Beulah's door, I wanted the reader to land there, too. Beulah not only takes care of Dorrie, but she also takes care of the reader, too. She lets you in on things. So you can relax for a while.

Q: **The story is told through many different voices, creating a full and layered story. Which voice came most naturally to you, and which presented the greatest challenge? Why?**

MB: Well, I've told you about Dorrie's elusive, secretive nature. I guess Beulah was the easiest; she loves to talk. I wrote only poetry till I was twenty-five, which was always from *my* point of view. When I shattered into many voices, Beulah's was the first to emerge. And I feel so honored that she did.

Florence was a difficult character to get inside of. She wasn't hard to see from the outside. But her internal voice was tough—I really had to let go, because she is so wildly unpredictable. It was like being on a roller coaster. At first, she would just rant and rave and rage in my head. It took a while to get into her body and feel her hand creep across the sheets and reach for the bedside table. And I have to be inside a character's body before the voice becomes clear. Them I am firmly grounded in their place. I can see what they see. Florence lives with so much pain, and to feel that was not easy.

But Michael was the toughest character to discover. I don't think characters get developed as much as discovered.

Q: **I was going to ask you about Michael. How do you personally feel about Michael's decisions regarding Eudora? Do you think he did the best he could given the circumstances?**

MB: Yes, he did the best he could. I loved what Sandra Scofield said about the book—that there is a great deal of pain but no villains. And she used the phrase "the unceasing devotion of the father." Michael, like many fathers in his time, did what he was supposed to do. He worked very hard outside the home. But to the family, he was almost invisible. And Michael was holding so much together on the outside, there was no time or place for letting any of his internal turmoil out. Florence left no room for that. Not till the end. And he had no cultural support for him to be anything else than who he was, somewhat opaque and impermeable. At least in *this* book, because it wasn't *his* story and he was seen mainly through Dorrie's eyes. She loved him, but she couldn't really know him, and she longed for him even in his presence. In a sense, Michael is a hero, albeit a weak, very ordinary one.

Q: **The Tappens' great capacity to love another's child as much as their own is a major part of the novel. In your own life, have you experienced or witnessed this extended notion of family, or does this relationship represent an ideal?**

MB: From the time I was twelve to about sixteen, I lived on a horse farm in the summer with a family I felt part of. Like many teenagers do, I found there my surrogate mom, and then there was her mom, who *everyone* called Grandma. She was Italian and fed us all. The farm was a lot like the Roman notion of "familias" that James Hillman talks about in his "Myths of the Family" lectures. The origin of that word was not based on the idea of kinship but on *the house itself*, the place itself and all belonging to it, the animals, the furniture, the servants. It was not a nuclear family but rather a "psycho-economic organism based on service and participation."

As a single mother for five years, I watched not only my mom and dad but also my closest friends "take on" the effort of raising my child. One of my son's baby-sitters had taken in, for indefinite lengths of time, more than twenty children whose parents were somehow unavailable. Yes, I think the notion of an extended family is still alive. And I think also that biology is overrated.

Q: **Much of the novel's imagery is rooted in nature and landscape. Since you live in the Catskill Mountains, how much of this connection to the earth comes from your own experience?**

MB: All of it. I am married to these mountains and to the place where I live now, an old defunct farm. After college, I tried to live somewhere else, but I felt called back here. It was not a matter of *liking* the Catskills; it was not a choice. They are my kin. I could not leave them. They speak to what is mute inside me, what is underneath all words.

In many English classes, "setting" is talked about as if it is superfluous to a story, a mere backdrop, or else a device to be manipulated for some emotion. But for me, place is primary, a touchstone of sorts. Place governs the tempo and voice of my characters. From within my characters, I can feel *where* they live. I purposely don't use a lot of long descriptions as if looking on from the outside. I want the characters to speak from *within* that place, the details to leak out almost casually, like you would speak about your own home.

Q: **What was the greatest challenge in writing this novel?**

MB: I threw out about one thousand pages. What was the hardest was the break in momentum that comes from my dual life. Over six months of the year, I travel as a member of the National Demonstration Team for the Professional Ski Instructors of America, skiing, lecturing, and training teachers. When I come home from all that, I have to land, literally. It takes a while digging in the dirt, planting, struggling with big rocks, being with my horses on a very basic, wordless level, being with my family, getting quiet again, filling up with questions and letting the answers go. It is never a painless landing. I actually feel a movement of my awareness —from my head down into my belly, my wordless self. Then I can start thinking of writing. I'm empty enough to allow the characters to come in and move about freely.

Q: **What are some of your favorite novels?**

MB: Toni Morrison's *Beloved*; Russell Banks's *Continental Drift*; William Kennedy's *Ironweed*; Louise Erdrich's *Love Medicine*; Gabriel García Marquez's *One Hundred Years of Solitude*, Maxine Hong Kingston's *The Woman Warrior*.

Reading Group Questions and Topics for Discussion

1. The author has stated that ultimately Eudora's story is one of initiation, not victimhood. In what ways do you think Eudora was "initiated"? As human beings, do you think that extreme, often painful, experiences are necessary for putting us in touch with the deeper, more remote places of our psyche?

2. "He, he doesn't ever yell at me. He just takes care of me. He never talks or asks me things like she used to, but he takes care of me," Eudora says about her father after she returns from hiding in the woods. How do you interpret this comment? Is this a statement of acceptance or discontent regarding her father's parenting?

3. Why do you think the author included the scene where Eudora and Pepper are caught naked by Pepper's father? In what ways does this scene contribute to the novel? Do we learn more about certain characters through this disturbing situation?

4. When Popsy gives Eudora a cap to wear to school, he says to her, "Now when you wear this cap, boy, you keep a mind where this bill's headin', hear?" From that time on, Eudora keeps careful track of every direction she takes. What do you think Popsy was trying to say to Eudora? What effect did her constant mental "logging" of her whereabouts have on her?

5. Why do you think Eudora related so well to Popsy? Do you think Popsy was, in some aspect, a reflection of Eudora?

6. Why do you think Eudora became such a vehement target for Florence's rage after the death of her son? Were you ultimately able to forgive Florence for her abusive treatment of Eudora? Do you believe that Florence was redeemed in the end? Why or why not?

7. Following the gynecological exam at her boarding school, Eudora mentally collapses, going into a near catatonic state. Since Eudora's emotional life is so intricately tied to her physicality, do you think it was this frightening physical intrusion that finally put her over the edge? Or do you think that the breakdown was inevitable and not necessarily provoked by this event? Has an intense physical experience ever led you to an emotional awakening or collapse?

8. When Eudora leaves for boarding school, she takes Beulah's unwashed coffee cup along with her. What symbolic significance does this cup contain?

9. Which character did you most closely identify with? Why? Were there any characters that you had difficulty empathizing with? If so, why?

10. The author has said that it was a great challenge to present Eudora's voice in a way that made room for her child-like immediacy without alienating the reader's desire and ability to see beyond her, "to guess at a larger truth than Dorrie's telling." As an adult, what was it like to hear the bulk of a story through the voice of an eleven-year-old child? How did this shape your reading experience?

11. Author Sandra Scofield says that in this novel "there is a great deal of pain, but there are no villains." Do you agree with this? Why or why not?

12. Eudora is unable to control the smile that emerges during emotionally charged situations. What does the smile convey to you? How do Beulah and Florence interpret the smile? Is either more accurate than the other? What do you think the smile means to Eudora?

13. Do you feel that Mary's decision to let Eudora witness the shooting of her horse was appropriate, or was this too violent a scene for a child's eyes? Why or why not? Have you ever had a child express her curiosity about death to you? If so, how did you handle the situation?

14. Regarding Florence's mental deterioration, do you think that she was, to some degree, a victim of an inadequate mental health system? Do you think that the author implies this in any way? How might her condition have been handled differently today?

15. Why do you think Four Eyes' snakes held such intrigue for Eudora? Why do you think it was so important to her to touch the snake's yellow ring?

16. Eudora had a vivid dream one night in her boarding school about a horse being lifted out of the water by a rope: "*They were going to take him out of the water, lift him up. They were going to save him. I knew that if they lifted him into the air going seven thousand miles an hour, all his*

bones would snap. I knew and they didn't. I needed to tell them right away." What was the significance of this dream? Who—or what—do you think the horse represented to Eudora?

17. Why do you think Eudora thrives so wonderfully at the Tappens? Aside from their love for her, are there other aspects of her life on the farm that beckon her frightened soul out of hiding?

18. In your opinion, what is the driving theme of this novel?

NIKKI SPRINKLE is a copywriter at Random House, Inc., and a graduate student in Columbia University's East Asian Languages and Cultures Department. She is also a poet and a freelance writer who enjoys writing about art, Asian culture, and literature. She lives in New York City.

Excerpts from reviews of Mermer Blakeslee's
In Dark Water

"Profoundly moving, this beautifully written novel reflects the often con-
flicted but uniquely special connection between mother and daughter
even under the most trying circumstances."

—*Booklist*

"Dorrie's delicately drawn journey to despair and back is riveting. . . . A
fine novel from the author of *Same Blood*."

—*Library Journal*

"Mermer Blakeslee has written a novel of uncommon grace and soaring
beauty. *In Dark Water* explores a family's deepest grief and a young girl's
amazing journey toward understanding, reconciliation, and redemption.
It is, in short, a triumph of the spirit."

—Connie May Fowler

© Eeo Stubblefield

ABOUT THE AUTHOR

MERMER BLAKESLEE is also the author of the novel *Same Blood*. She is a New York Foundation of the Arts fiction fellowship recipient. Ms. Blakeslee lives with her husband and son in New York's Catskill Mountains.

Don't miss these other acclaimed novels in the Ballantine Reader's Circle program

THE MIRROR
by Lynn Freed

"Freed delivers a tour de force in this diary
of an ambitious, headstrong, sexually
independent . . . woman."
—*Publishers Weekly* (starred review)

SAINTS AND VILLAINS
by Denise Giardina

"High drama . . . Stirring adventure . . . To find a
historical figure like Dietrich Bonhoeffer packaged in
what is essentially a moral thriller is a surprising joy."
—*The Boston Globe*

A WIDOW FOR ONE YEAR
by John Irving

"Compelling . . . Irving's narrative spans 37 years in the
life of Ruth Cole. . . . By turns antic and moving, lusty
and tragic, *A Widow for One Year* is bursting with
memorable moments."
—*San Francisco Examiner-Chronicle*

THE HUNGER MOON
by Suzanne Matson
"Crisp, clean writing . . . Compassionately drawn characters . . . Matson examines the full sweep of women's lives."
—*The New York Times Book Review*

TAFT
by Ann Patchett
"As resonant as a blues song . . . Expect miracles when you read Ann Patchett's fiction."
—*The New York Times Book Review*

THE UMBRELLA COUNTRY
by Bino A. Realuyo
"Realuyo proves that the telling of a novelist's heart and country is contained in the smallest movement of moments. Word upon lyrical word, his novel is beauty that dwells like a beloved's lingering ache, a beloved's familiar voice."
—LOIS ANN YAMANAKA
Winner of the Lannan Award
Author of *Blu's Hanging*

CHILDREN OF GOD
by Mary Doria Russell

"Brilliant . . . Powerful . . . Russell is an outstanding natural storyteller whose remarkable wit, erudition, and dramatic skills keep us turning the pages in excitement and anticipation."
—*San Francisco Chronicle*

THE ALL-TRUE TRAVELS AND ADVENTURES OF LIDIE NEWTON
by Jane Smiley

"Rousing . . . Action-packed . . . A gripping story about love, fortitude, and convictions that are worth fighting for."
—*Los Angeles Times*

A PATCHWORK PLANET
by Anne Tyler

"So wonderfully readable that one swallows it in a single gulp . . . What makes this novel so irresistible is the main character and narrator Barnaby Gaitlin, a 30-year-old misfit, a renegade who is actually a kind-hearted man struggling to find his place in the world."
—*The Philadelphia Inquirer*

Coming Soon

WHAT WE KEEP
by Elizabeth Berg

"Beautifully written . . . *What We Keep* is about ties that are buried but not broken, wounds that are dressed but never heal, and love that changes form but somehow survives."

—*USA Today*

GONE FOR GOOD
by Mark Childress

"Wondrously imaginative . . . Brimming with magic and mystery . . . A modern-day fable with echoes of *Alice in Wonderland, The Little Prince, Peter Pan,* and *The Wizard of Oz.*"

—*The Charlotte Observer*

Published by The Ballantine Publishing Group
www.randomhouse.com/BB

BLACK GLASS
by Karen Joy Fowler

"Highly imaginative . . . In fine-edged and discerning prose, [Fowler] manages to re-create both life's extraordinary and its ordinary magic."
—*The New York Times Book Review*

HANNA'S DAUGHTERS
by Marianne Fredriksson

"Brilliant . . . *Hanna's Daughters* outlines the lives of three generations of women and their complicated relationships with one another."
—*USA Today*

THE EDGE OF HEAVEN
by Marita Golden

"Like *Snow Falling on Cedars,* Marita Golden's powerful new novel is more than a mystery, more than a novel about the effects of a past crime. It's a psychological page-turner."
—LEE SMITH
Author of *News of the Spirit*

Published by The Ballantine Publishing Group
www.randomhouse.com/BB